Grab

Bag

1

FOR LITERARY HEAT

www.barbarianspy.com

WARNING: This book is for sale to **ADULT AUDIENCES ONLY.** Contains graphic gay male sex, reluctance, multiple partners, anal sex, nongraphic violence, and gay love all of which may be considered offensive by some readers.
All sexually active characters in this work are at least 18 years of age.

Published by BarbarianSpy
Jindalee St
Toronto, NSW 2283
AUSTRALIA

Grab Bag

1

by

habu

Table of Contents

Introduction

Grab Bag is a totally unthemed gay male anthology that exhibits the breadth and depth of the sometimes whacky and sometimes touching, but always creative and surprising, writing of that master of gay erotic storytelling, habu. In this "bag" are twenty stories that adhere to no uniformity of theme in time, space, locale, or message and that have never been published as stories before.

As has become the hallmark of habu, this is a collection of tales (and tails) that are guaranteed to excite and stimulate—not just the mind. A true grab bag of surprises and pleasures that are sure to be savored more than once.

Barber Brad

"What's up with this, Nick?" I asked as I entered the barber shop at one end of the college town's most established shopping strip. "Last time I was here you were lamenting that all of your customers were dying out or retiring away and you'd probably have to close." I looked around the seats lining the wall opposite the barber's chairs and saw that there were at least six guys ahead of me—and four of them were young. Probably guys from the college.

"New barber," Nick said, gesturing with the scissors he was using on the hair of one of the town's doctors toward a chair that was currently empty three slots down. I looked up at the nameplate over the mirror behind the chair. It read "Brad."

"Younger guys like him. He's brought in new business. Rejuvenated the place." Nick said this to me, but he wasn't looking at me. He seemed to be avoiding eye contact, which wasn't like him. Nick Parson was an institution in this town. His business, Parson's, had been started here by his father. Everyone who was anyone in the area had gone to this shop for their haircut for decades. Even one governor had insisted on driving the hour over here from the state capitol to have his hair cut.

The trouble was that "everyone who is anyone" was becoming something of the past in this town. Even the younger professors at the college were going to stylists rather than barbershops.

Nick was well into his seventies. I'd assumed he'd somehow ensure the shop lived on after he gave up barbering, but the stylists were putting him out of business. I was just glad that he will have reached a time he can retire before that happened. The same was true of three of his four regular barbers. And the fourth was the one who was keeping the shop going this long. He had the chair in the front window and was more stylist than traditional barber. He'd manage to make the transition. I had expected him to take the shop when Nick retired, but Nick told me Keith wasn't interested in continuing it.

But now they apparently had a new guy. He wasn't there when I walked in and sat down, waiting my turn in the chair, but he came out of the back of the shop soon thereafter and pointed to one of the college-aged guys, who eagerly stood and moved toward the chair under the "Brad" sign. Another of the college guys had sat forward in his seat, in anticipation, but the Brad guy called to him in a deep bass voice, "I'm running behind. It'll be an hour wait. If you want to wait that long."

The young guy looked disappointed, but he sat back in the chair and reached for a magazine. Most be some barber, I thought, for a young college-type guy to be willing to wait an hour for this Brad guy.

Brad himself was a surprise. A big, powerful-looking guy, he was. He was maybe in his late twenties and stood a good six and a half feet tall. I would have taken him more for a professional football player or a hunter more than for a barber. He was heavily muscled, and I thought he must spend all of the time he wasn't in the barber shop in a gym somewhere bulking himself up. He wasn't bad look—in fact he looked pretty good in a rugged sort of way—but he had large hands, meaty fingers, and I wondered why he had chosen barbering. He seemed more like one of the guys in my line of work. I wouldn't be surprised to see him driving a cruiser, maybe even being a state trooper. He seemed to be handling the scissors OK, though.

He and the guy he was working on immediately started talking about bands and the woods and weekend gigs—not sports, which surprised me. The phone in the shop was constantly ringing and most of the time it was for Brad and he either was telling someone when he had openings—which apparently wasn't often—or what was happening at what he called the "Woodsy" this weekend or next. He was citing strange names, some of which I recognized as local rock bands.

But then it was my turn in a chair. I'd drawn the short stick again—I was being beckoned to Nick's own chair. This had been a privileged spot in previous decades, but Nick's hands weren't too steady anymore and he was really too hard of hearing to conduct a conversation with during the haircut. And he was slow as molasses, mostly because people kept coming in off the street and greeting him and jawing for a few minutes. As I'd noted, Nick Parson was an institution in the town, and he was constantly sought out to head or lend his name and photo to a charity drive or to attend some civic banquet somewhere.

I wasn't surprised when I went into his chair that we didn't have much to say to each other. I was more surprised that the conversation from Brad's chair seemed to dry up after Nick had greeted me in a loud voice and asked how "things" were down at the sheriff's office.

Nick was working so slow and was being interrupted so much by people coming off the street that it was a good half hour before I looked up and saw that Brad had finished his haircut and rather than go to the cash register with his young client, was guiding the young man toward the back of the shop and through a door back there. Brad had a hand palmed on the young man's butt as they reached the door, and my antenna shot right up.

An hour appointment for a half hour's haircut—and the next guy willing to wait that long to get into Brad's chair. I was suddenly interested in this. I'd like to say that it was the investigator—the deputy sheriff—in me that was interested. But it wasn't. I was a man's man, and Brad was just the sort of man who turned me on. Just the way he had possessively put his hand on the other guy's butt and the other guy hadn't done anything about that alerted me. And I wanted to check that out.

11

Nick's shop was at the more deserted end of the shopping strip, and I knew that there were windows into his back area at the side and, again, at the back of the building. Immediately beyond the door from the shop was a restroom to the left, against the outer wall, and a break room for the barbers. But there was another room through yet another door beyond that at the back of the building.

After leaving Nick's shop, with Nick being more open and expressive—and making eye contact with me—as I paid him at the cash register, I looked up and down the parking lot. Seeing that no one was noticing me, I slipped around to the side of the building and walked down to where there were two windows near the back. The first one looked into a restroom and was blocked at its bottom half, but by going up on my toes I could see that the room was empty.

The next window was a "Bingo" window. It looked into sort of a supply room at the back of the shop. I could sort of peep in at the side window and see the two of them, their bodies illuminated by light coming in from two windows on the back wall of the shop. The young college-aged guy was only wearing his T-shirt and was bent over a table top, legs spread. Brad, only in his white, short-sleeved shirt, was standing close behind the younger guy, crotch planted to buttocks, and fucking up into the other guy. From the angle I had and the long strokes Brad was taking, I could tell that he had at least seven thick inches. My butt twitched at the sight. His bulging chest and shoulder muscles as he worked impressed me too. He had one hand gripping the younger guy by the throat and arching the guy's torso back to him, the guy's head pushed into Brad's shoulder. The younger guy's hands were moving from trying to spread his own butt cheeks wider to Brad's clinching and flexing buttocks to the back of Brad's head to the table top to maintain himself steady.

Brad's free hand was moving periodically from the table top to the young man's nostrils. Brad's fingers were coated with something white, and I could see a mound of white powder that Brad was dipping them into and then moving to the young man's nose.

The young man was pretty vocal—and was singing Brad's praises. I could hear the words "fuck," "shit," "yes," "deeper" reaching me through the window pane. Only the fan going in the front of the barber shop, I assumed, kept the whole world from knowing what was going on here.

I reluctantly pulled away from the window and went back to my car. I moved the car in the parking lot to where I could get a bead on both the door into Nick's shop and the alley running beside it. About the end of what I gauged was the young man's scheduled hour with Brad, I saw him emerge from the alley, rather than the shop door. He was walking with a lurch, but there was a smile of complete satisfaction on his face.

While I had waited, I had jacked off inside the car, dreaming of that pile driver I'd seen between Brad's thighs.

* * * *

"What's this all about?"

I was walking by the incident room and saw that there were photos pinned up to the cork board and some writing on the chalk board. One of the other deputies, Terry Jones, and a couple of uniformed policemen were standing, looking at the boards, jawing, and drinking coffee.

"A new pusher in town," Terry said. "We're making plans to take him down."

I walked up to the board. A couple of photos of men and a few of some house in the woods, in a fairly large clearing that looked like there had been a big party no one had wanted to clean up after—or that was just in some sort of intermission.

"The pusher?" I said.

"This guy here. His name is Buxton. We were warned to look out for him. Moves into an area and sets up rock gigs in the woods on the weekends. Calls 'em 'Woodsies.' But he serves up more than rock music and booze. Big ugly lug, ain't he?"

I was staring at a photograph of Barber Brad. I had to admit that he did look a lot better, more studly, in person than in this mug shot. Looked dazed and like he'd been beaten up in this photo.

"So, how you going to do it?" I asked, trying to keep my voice on the edge of disinterest.

"Saturday night, two weeks from now. We'll sweep in mid concert and roust them all out for drugs. We've got enough on this Buxton now. But we want to see who else we can catch."

"Good hunting," I said, as I walked off.

I went to my office and called a hair stylist and made an appointment for the next day. Then I called Parson's barber shop and made an appointment there too for the next Monday. I knew Mondays to be Nick's day off. I didn't think any of the other regular barbers would notice me—or say anything to me even if they did.

"But your hair is so nice the way it is, Honey," the stylist said when I sat down in her chair and told her what I wanted. "And you look like you just got it cut."

"And with some blond tipping too, please," I responded. "Want to go a whole new way with it."

When I walked into Parson's barber shop with what was almost a crew cut—with light highlights—any damn fool could see that I didn't have enough hair to need cutting. But what I was counting on—and was successful in it—was that neither Brad nor the other barbers would recognize me for who I was. I figured that when they looked at a man, what they concentrated on was his head of hair, since that was their trade. I also had changed the style of my clothes. No more police uniform or even tailored dress shirt and trousers, with a tie. I was in jeans, a tight red T, and boots today. I must have guessed right. I had changed myself enough to be an entirely different person to them all.

When I was in Brad's chair, he looked at me quizzically in the mirror across from the chairs and said in a low voice, his eyes searching mine, "Doesn't look like you need a haircut, buddy."

"I came for your special," I whispered back. "Heard about it. Want it."

"It'd be a pleasure. You've got a killer body. You know how much that haircut costs, though?" he asked, still keeping his voice down.

"Not sure I remember what I was told," I answered. "But it sounded like I could swing it. I've got cash."

"Seventy-five for the servicing and a hit. Hundred fifty for a doggy bag as well."

"How much without the hit?" I asked.

"Same seventy-five," he answered.

"Let's do it," I muttered back to him.

Fifteen minutes later he gave up on pretending he was doing anything with my hair, made a show of letting me check myself out in the mirror, and gave the back of my neck a razor-cut shave. As he finished that, he pressed on my carotid and up under my chin with his fingertips for a few seconds, sending chills up my spine in anticipation and giving me flash images of him fucking me right there in the chair, with all the other guys floating around and doing their thing and not noticing Brad's cock was churning in my channel.

I got another chill as I felt the palm of his hand on my butt as we moved to the back of the shop.

"Strip, please," he said when we were in the back of the shop and I'd doled out seventy-five dollars to him. "And lean over that table, dick inserted in that cutoff plastic bottle nailed under the table rim."

I gave him a questioning look.

"You're gonna shoot your wad," he said, "and I don't want it goin' all over the place. So, the plastic bottle."

"No, not that," I answered. "I wondered if you meant strip completely down—not just the jeans and the briefs?"

"Naw, take it all off. We got extra time and I wanna see what you got. You look like you're cut fine. I'll get naked too. We can compare. You can keep your boots on."

He gave me a whistle of appreciation when I'd stripped, which I thought was rather nice given all the young college-guy flesh he must have seen. Then I practically swallowed my tongue when I saw him in the altogether. No wonder he was getting good business. I wasn't bad, but in the cut department, Brad had me beat by a mile. I leaned over the table, somewhat painfully pushing my engorging dick into the cut-off plastic milk jug nailed under the edge, and supported the weight of my body on stretched-out arms and the heel of my hands pressed to the

15

surface of the table. I was looking down at little cones of white powder spaced out around the table top. Four mounds and then three places were mounds had recently been.

"Nice, very nice," I heard him say as he ran his hands over my torso from behind. "Not the dicking, yet, I think," Brad muttered. "You're too nice. I'll work us both first. This is too nice to pass up."

He knelt behind me and pulled my cock through my thighs and began paying attention to my cock and balls and hole with his lips and lubed fingers while I moaned softly for him and rolled my hips in slow motion, getting the most of this that I could get.

When he stood, he wrapped an arm around me and palmed my belly while he inserted my dick into the plastic jug with the other hand and then used that hand to help position his sheathed cock at my hole.

Quickly he was entering and plowing up into me and I was groaning and grunting and trying not to cry out. He had thickness and length to die for. And he knew just how to make love to the prostate in passing—and to come back to it and make love to it yet again. My channel walls were spasming, and I felt an electric current surging through my body. When he started to pump, I moved my butt with him, meeting his thrusts with counterthrusts of my own. It was glorious, and he must have thought it was all good too, as he was whispering in my ear how nice my channel was and how good I was. From my perspective *he* was the one who was good.

He moved the hand from my belly to my pecs, where he played for a while and then up to my throat, pulling my head into the hollow of his shoulder.

I saw the fingers of his other hand covered in white powder coming at my face, and I started to writhe under him, trying to pull away from the approaching fingers, but he had me too well in control.

"I didn't—"

"Shush. Just go with it. You'll love it."

And he was right. I did love it. At the first ingestion of the powder, my head seemed to expand in an explosion of color and every fiber of me felt like it had moved to a whole new

16

plane of feeling and pleasure. Images, colors, and shapes were racing through my brain at warp speed, and fireworks were going off snap, snap, snap. His fucking became something I never had felt before. A complete taking. The height of ecstasy. I was floating. No, I was soaring in the clouds, racing across the sky.

I saw his fingers with more of the white powder go beyond my head. He must be ingesting it too. His cock took on the proportions of a baseball bat. His pistoning doubled in intensity, and I could swear that he was reaching up into my stomach with it. But I didn't care. It was all amazing. He was whispering in my ear, speaking with intensity and so fast that I couldn't catch the words other than to know that we were racing across the sky together—welded at the pelvis, tongue-fucking kissing, arms entwined, hands everywhere at once.

We didn't stay bent over the table. He had me on my back on another surface and was fucking me to where I could see the muscles of his chest working hard. I was playing with his nipples and he was nibbling on my nipples and we were kissing—his tongue down my throat, swabbing my tonsils and he was fucking, fucking, fucking. Not far to go, I fantasized, before tip of tongue met piss slit of dick—inside me. And then he was kissing down my chest and belly and was bent over me, swallowing my cock, and taking my ejaculation. He went back to fucking my hole, and I lay back, relaxed and spent and drifted off into some sort of la la land, where I could feel every stroke and each one sent me over the moon. I came again. Exhilaration. It had been years since I could come that close together.

A slap on my buttocks—and not a light one—brought me more or less back into focus.

"Fifteen minutes," a fuzzy face in front of mine was saying. It sounded like it was coming up from a deep well. "Fifteen minutes and you need to be out of here. Use the back door. I'm going back into the shop. Come again soon. Best lay I've had in weeks."

When I was with it enough to sit up and try to locate my clothes in the grimy gloom of the storage room, Brad was gone. I barely had time to clear my head in time to dress and be at the back door when I heard the door to the shop being opened.

I should have been out of here fifteen minutes earlier, I realized. I did manage to get out before Brad entered the room with his next appointment, though. I didn't know how he did it. One an hour. He couldn't have given everyone the service he'd given me. And now that I thought about it, I think he did say a couple of times during the cocking that I was a special one for him.

I stumbled down the alley and to my car and just sat there, waiting for the world to come into focus. Still in the glow of the memory of it, I fished out my cock and slowly jacked off again. I had enough of a buzz on to enjoy it immensely. I sort of could see why these guys got into drugs. The combination of Brad's cock and the drug were enough to pull me back to him for more of the same. If it didn't scare me shitless, of course.

I wondered what it was he'd put up my nose—and whether there were any long-term effects. He'd taken me by surprise on that. I thought I'd made clear I didn't want the hit with it. But I knew now that I shouldn't have been surprised. He was a pusher, after all. Everything else was done to get the young college students hooked and coming back for more. I wondered if that was totally true with me, though. He kept telling me he enjoyed the fucking. I had to believe that his body wasn't lying about that.

I became more alert, but I dared not leave yet. It would be the end of me to be pulled over by one of my own patrolmen and found to be high. I ejaculated but was still hard—still in lust. I began stroking myself again. I wondered if this—the ability to keep it up, keep it spouting—was a function of the drug or of Brad. Most likely the combination of the two. Whatever, I'd never felt so high on it and able to shoot again and again. I was on top of the world.

So, I sat and waited—for nearly two hours—for my mind to come completely back, for my body to stop craving the working of my cock, the miraculously close-timed ejaculations. And as I waited, I fantasized. He'd be taken in just over a week now, unless he moved on before that. I could tell him, of course. But I wouldn't do that. The sex was OK, but the drugs weren't. He needed to be stopped on that.

That raised the question of Nick Parsons. He surely knew what Brad Buxton was doing in the back of his barber shop. He must be getting a kickback that was helping him keep the shop open. But Nick was an institution in this town. And he was an old man who surely was going to retire soon. The arrangement couldn't have been going on for more than a month. No, I'd do nothing about that. If the police found the connection with what they were targeting out in the woods, so be it. But I wouldn't report anything. I'd just let nature take its course on that.

But back to Buxton. I wanted him again. Even after just having been with him, I already wanted him again. He'd be held in the county jail for a while, before being moved someplace else. I was pretty sure about that. My mind started to work on how difficult it would be for me to arrange that he be put in an isolated private cell. It might be tricky. I'd have to make sure that I maintained my distance. Couldn't have any of the guys thinking I'd had a piece of this guy myself.

I was sure, though, that there should be some sort of favoritism I could come up with while he was in our jail that he'd want to trade for . . . while he was all alone in an isolated private cell.

Can't Get No

Scott felt him going soft. He'd been straddling Tyler's hips and riding him. He'd felt Tyler jerk and sigh, knowing that he'd come, but Scott hadn't come. He'd ridden on. But he looked down now and tried to look into Tyler's face. It was too dark in their bedroom. But Tyler began to snore, so there really was no question.

Scott gave up and climbed off Tyler and stretched alongside him, on top of the sheets. The ceiling fan was going whoop, whoop, whoop overhead and Scott was sweating from the exertion, but he ran his hands over Tyler's chest and belly and down onto his thighs and found Tyler's skin cool to the touch.

Tyler was achingly beautiful, his facial features blond and ruggedly handsome, his muscles with the perfect definition that only long hours in the gym brought, curly down on his chest descending to trimmed and shaped pubes and a nicely plump cock and balls. Scott was lucky to have him. Tyler was probably the most popular guy at the small "jock's" prep school they attended, using their first two years of college to improve their grades enough to enter a university with academic qualifications to meet their athletic prowess. Scott was a swimmer. Tyler was tops at any sport he wanted to be. He was working lacrosse and tennis now. He said, only half jokingly, that he didn't want to mess up his face with sports not protecting it better lest his commercial worth was diminished when he went pro.

Any other guy saying something like that would draw a derisive laugh, but when Tyler said it, everyone took him seriously. All of the guys who wanted guys wanted Tyler.

But Scott had him.

Sort of.

Scott lay there, awake, most of the night, fretting and frustrated. They'd been together for a year, a year tomorrow—or today, he thought, as he turned and looked at the luminous dial of his nightstand clock.

As the fingers of light stole through the broken slats of the blinds on the bedroom window, Scott turned toward Tyler again. The young blond god's privates were captured in a shaft of light, and Scott couldn't resist sitting up and leaning over and sinking his lips over the shaft. He allowed his hands to wander, one to Tyler's day-old whiskered chin, down along his pecs and belly, and the other between Tyler's legs, cupping his balls and fondling them.

Tyler moaned, half awake. And as he slowly came awake, he hardened and his hands went to the back of Scott's head, holding Scott's lips over his skewering cock, and his hips began to roll.

Scott gagged as Tyler increased in size and his hands trapped Scott's head in place, not giving him release—not letting him disengage until Tyler had come, giving no warning, and shooting his load down Scott's throat. As Scott pulled away and coughed and fought to clear his passage, Tyler bounced out of the bed and bounded into the bathroom and closed the door behind him.

While Scott was fixing breakfast, Tyler came into the dinette and sat up on a stool at the counter. He'd spent most of an hour in the bathroom. Scott was familiar with Tyler's morning ritual. Tyler had to have everything "just so." He was very particular about his appearance—even when he only was going to the gym. Which appeared to be what he intended to do this morning, what he'd dressed for.

"It's Saturday, Ty . . . and a special day. I thought after breakfast we might—"

"Can't today. Goin' to the gym and to the hair stylist after. Then tennis. We're going to Sean's tonight, remember. Thought you'd make that dip that went over so well a couple of weeks ago."

"Ty."

"I think I'll wear the red T tonight. It's dirty, though. Maybe you could run a wash."

Scott didn't make another effort. Tyler was already gone—and he hadn't asked why this was a special day.

That night, at Sean's, Tyler was the center of attention, as always. Scott sat in the corner, watching him, and wishing and hoping. Maybe tonight. Tyler had a buzz on and sometimes when he was half high, he was playful.

"He's quite something, isn't he?" Jackson had plopped down beside Scott on the arm of his chair and wrapped his arm around Scott's head and tilted it up so he could look down at him with pouty eyes. Jackson was a bit too flamboyant and obvious for Scott. And, beside's, Jackson, who was also a swimmer—a diver really and probably better at that than Scott was at swimming, Scott thought, really wanted the same thing that Scott wanted.

And Jackson had tried with Tyler—all of the guys wanting to be topped had tried with Tyler. But Tyler contemptuously called Jackson a girl. Jackson took it, though, because when all else was said, he still wanted Tyler.

Scott was thinking just then that most of the guys who pined for Tyler were ones who hadn't had him yet. Still, just looking at him made Scott melt—and wanting something, something he'd yet to have. Not just with Tyler, but with anyone. Scott had long ago decided maybe it was his fault. Maybe he wanted too much. Maybe what he wanted wasn't to be had.

Jackson had left him while he was still thinking about this, flouncing off with a "You're no fun," which Scott might have felt sorry about—but that was Jackson. There weren't any hard feelings over it. Jackson knew Scott didn't have what he

23

wanted—just as much as Scott knew Jackson couldn't bring satisfaction.

While Scott watched Jackson shimmy away from him, his eyes stopped at a quiet guy who was sitting across the room and looking at him. Now that Scott thought about it, he realized that the guy—Dixon, who was in one of his classes—seemed to have been looking his way before. But Scott didn't keep his eyes on Dixon very long—they just slid off him and he was looking around for where Ty had gone off too. Dixon was on the wrestling squad, and he'd had an elbow catch him in the nose one too many times, it looked like. A good body, as far as Scott could see, but a pretty messed up face. And he seemed a little creepy in class. Mostly sitting there and looking intensely around. But that was because he didn't seem to want to wear his glasses, and his eyesight appeared to be for shit without them. He had them on now—old four eyes—and was staring Scott down.

After checking out that Dixon was watching him again, Scott moved his eyes to the corner of the room, which was dark—and occupied by a couple of guys moving beyond the definition of "making out." He felt a jog at the arm of the chair and Cody was there now. Cody was quiet—except when he was on the football field, when he was a lion. Cody was almost as good looking at Tyler was, but Cody couldn't give Scott satisfaction any more than Jackson could. All three of them were looking for the same thing. But Cody seemed comfortable with himself. Scott and Tyler had discussed Cody before.

"He's gettin' it from somewhere, I'm sure," Tyler had said. "He walks with a strut and hums. He's gettin' it from somewhere. And I don't think it's from anyone at the prep. I think I would have heard, if he was."

Scott had asked then if Tyler wanted to do Cody himself, but Tyler had unexpectedly gotten angry about that. It was only later than Scott decided that Tyler saw Cody more as competition than conquest. Cody was almost as hunky as he was. It wasn't a sex thing. Scott was beginning to think that none of it was a sex thing with Tyler, really—unless Tyler could have sex with himself.

"Frustrated?" Cody asked when he sat down beside Scott.

Scott looked at him in surprise. "No, of course not. Do I look frustrated?"

"Yes, a bit," Cody said and then he gave a low laugh. "You don't have to be frustrated, though. Let me give you a tip."

"A tip? That's something I don't think I need, is a fuckin' tip," Scott said.

"Yeah, you do. See that guy, Dixon, over there. He's got a monster and can go all night. Eight, maybe closer to nine juicy inches. And I think he's got the hots for you. He'd treat you right."

"Him? Give me a break. I've got Ty. Ty's a god against that guy over there. What would I need with him when I've got Ty?"

"You'd be surprised," Cody said. And then he laughed. "Well, I got another tip for you if you don't like that one."

"Full of good tips, are you?"

Cody didn't take offense. "I've been watching you. I think maybe you do. Remember this in case you want to try it out: Thursday, late afternoon, the truck stop out on 81. Look for a dark blue Volvo semi and ask for Elmer."

"Elmer?" Scott exclaimed, almost spitting out the beer he was drinking. "You putting me on?"

"Nope."

The noise in the room had changed, and both Scott and Cody look up. Tyler had moved toward the door out of the apartment and he had Alphonse, the hunky half-back of the football team, who Tyler had been going with before he and Scott had gotten together.

Scott watched as the two of them left the apartment together—without Tyler so much as looking back at Scott. On this, their one-year anniversary.

"What was that second tip again?" Scott asked as he turned back to Cody.

* * * *

Scott was standing in the truck lot behind the 81 rest stop. He'd parked his car in the auto lot in front and sat there for

25

a good twenty minutes before getting up the courage to walk past the restrooms and to the back of the lot.

There were picnic tables in a grove of trees between the back of the restroom block and the asphalt of the truck parking lot. There were several rigs parked back there. A couple of them were dark blue, but Scott had no idea whether any of them was a Volvo. Three guys were sitting at one of the tables, drinking Cokes in cans and shooting the bull.

One of the guys was old and flabby, but the other two were younger and in pretty good shape, especially a red head with a florid complexion who had tattoos running down his arms from the armless T he was wearing.

They all noticed Scott walking up at the same time, and they all gave him sort of a knowing leer—enough so that he almost turned and walked away. But he didn't do that. He wanted satisfaction, and he wanted to know if that was possible. Cody had told him it was. But he didn't know whether to believe Cody or whether satisfaction for Cody would be much different than for him.

"You Elmer?" he asked hopefully, looking straight at the red-haired guy.

"Nope. You want Elmer do you?"

"Yes. Is he here?"

"His rig's here. And there he is climbing out of it," the fat guy said. He was looking out toward the trucks and Scott followed his gaze, and he felt the disappointment surging through his body.

Elmer was no spring chicken—or hunk for that matter. He was tall and rangy, wearing jeans, cowboy boots, a cowboy shirt, and a Stetson hat. In fact everything about him from this distance cried out of old, weather-beaten cowpoke loser.

"So, what'er you lookin' for, sonny?" the third guy asked. "Maybe the three of us—"

But Scott was already on the move, walking out onto the asphalt, toward Elmer's truck. That's the name Cody had given him. What he actually felt like was bolting altogether, but he'd come too far down this road not to give it a try.

The closer Scott got to Elmer, the uglier Elmer looked—all angles and stringiness. His face was long and thin and looked

26

like he'd been hit with a shovel earlier in his life. He did look like he had all his teeth, though, which was a plus. As Scott approached, he lifted his hat up off the front of his face and his leg up on the running board of the sleeper cab—a pretty big one—behind the truck cabin.

He was staring Scott down real hard, like it was him deciding if Scott was good enough rather than the other way around.

When he got close enough, Scott stopped and drew a breath and said, "I'm told you'll give satisfaction for $50."

"How old are you, son?" The accent was sheer Texas. Scott looked at the man's hands. They were big, his fingers long and thin. Calluses on his palms attested to the hard life he led. His arms were randomly covered in tattoos and he was so rangy and hard-bodied that his veins stood out in blue, competing with the design of the tattoos.

"Twenty. Twenty and a half."

"You got ID? You comin' from the jock's prep school on the other side of town?"

"Yes to both." Scott took out his wallet and flashed his ID. He started to take bills out of it as well.

"Put that away for now. I guarantee satisfaction. You sure you want this?"

Scott hesitated a nanosecond, but then he gulped and said, "Yes."

"You gotta be sure at the start. You'll be tied. I won't stop once I start."

"Tied?" Scott asked, the concern showing in his voice.

"Yep. You don't want that, you don't want it bad enough." He reached for the handle to his sleeper cabin then and opened the door and stepped up on the running board and turned away from Scott.

Scott didn't know if he was being dismissed or being told to follow Elmer into the truck.

"I can go $75," he blurted out. "And however you want to do it," he added in desperation.

"Well, come on up in here, then. It ain't gonna get done out here on the tarmac."

The cabin was surprisingly commodious, although the single bed along the back wall took up much of the space. There was a shelf over the bed, so the headroom wasn't all that great. What gave Scott a pause, though, when he looked at that bed was seeing wrist restraints hanging down from the top of the side wall at the head of the bed.

"You can fold your clothes and put them up on the shelf over the bed."

As Scott was doing this, Elmer came up behind him and wrapped strong, sinewy arms around him. Elmer had already stripped—and Scott could feel he was ready for powerful action.

"Umm, I don't know. I—"

But that's as far as Scott got before he was fully under Elmer's spell. Elmer turned and gently pushed him down on the bunk spanning the back of the cab, holding him in strong arms. When Scott was seated, Elmer just continued on down on his knees between Scott's spread legs, and for the first time in as long as Scott could remember, someone was giving his cock and balls—and eventually the rim to his ass channel when Elmer rolled Scott's hips on up on the bed—total attention and loving.

Scott closed his eyes, not looking at the man making love to his cock—not seeing an old, wiry, weather-beaten cowboy. Just enjoying what that man could do with his lips, tongue, teeth, and hands.

Scott was moaning and moving his hips in an involuntary waving motion and gritting his teeth and groaning when he finally couldn't take any more and blurted out, "God, I'm gonna come, I'm gonna come."

"Why yes, son, yes you are. If got it in you, I'm gonna get it out. Let it go."

And Scott did let it go, jerking and flopping around and coming for all his might, while Elmer took it, humming, and telling him how good his flow was.

Already exhausted, Scott was flopped back on the bed, his head on the pillows, but pushed into the back corner, as Elmer stood up in the cabin. And when he did, Scott gasped and moaned at the size of the man's erect cock.

He whimpered softly and made hesitant moves to leave the bed, which was prevented immediately by Elmer, who reached over and took Scott's wrists in his strong hands, pushed them over his head, and trapped them in the wrist restraints.

Elmer moved his hands to Scott's hips and lifted Scott's pelvis from the surface of the bed to where the head of his club of a dick was kissing Scott's well-prepared entrance.

What happened after that was the fuck of Scott's life—and not just once, but twice, with Elmer riding him hard and deep, raising Scott on waves and waves of ecstasy at how well Elmer anticipated where the edge of the next plateau to heaven was. He'd linger there until Scott was begging for more, and then he'd have Scott burst through to a new level of satisfaction.

When he was finally done, having made Scott the center of all sensual sensation for nearly an hour, he reached up and released Scott's wrists. Scott couldn't move, he was so used and exhausted—and he didn't know what else.

"If you're satisfied, leave the fifty on the countertop right over there. You're a good fuck. If you're not satisfied, sorry I can't be a help to you."

Satisfied. That was it; that was the word Scott was striving for. It was what Tyler wasn't giving him. But now he knew it could be had.

Elmer was dressed and gone out of the cabin before Scott could even regain regular breathing. He dressed—rather painfully, but with a sense of awe—and left the $50 on the counter at the side of the bed. He would have been happy to have left more, but he was pretty sure that Elmer would take that as an affront to his pride and a put down to his class status. When he stepped gingerly down from the cabin of the semi, Scott looked over to the picnic area and saw that Elmer had joined the other drivers there and was jawing with them. None of them overtly seemed to be watching him as he stumbled to his car, but Scott got the feeling of three sets of eyes boring into the back of his head. But not Elmer's, he didn't think. He thought that Elmer probably was fully confident in the worth of himself—and of his fucking mastery—and Scott would not have argued with him.

He'd have to ask Cody if it was acceptable to have a return visit.

* * * *

The encounter with Elmer had been three days previously, and Tyler hadn't seemed to notice that anything was different. What he most didn't notice was that Scott wasn't asking him for sex—and wasn't coming for it, and didn't make any moves when they were in bed.

Tyler didn't make the moves either. And this gave Scott pause to think back. He couldn't remember the last time Tyler had made the moves on him.

What was the use of a beautiful body if the guy was going to be no better than a mannequin. Elmer had been old and ugly as a fence post. But he'd had a cock and a technique that sent Scott over the moon. What's in a face and toned body then?

Satisfaction. What constituted getting sexual satisfaction?

When Cody called with an invitation to a party at his place, Scott said he'd be there. But he said Tyler couldn't make it. He had no idea, of course, whether Tyler could have made it or not—or whether he'd even want to go. He wasn't going to give Tyler that option. He didn't need or want Tyler at the party.

"By the way, Cody, thanks for that tip . . . the one about the Volvo semi."

"Glad you decided you'd give the tip a chance," Cody answered.

There was a pause, in which Scott didn't say anything but neither one of them clicked off.

"Umm, Cody, about the other tip—"

"Those two tips went together, Scott. The biggest difference is that with Dixon you don't have to pay the $50."

"Well, umm. Is . . . ?"

"Yes, Dixon's already said he's coming. I can certainly tell him you'll be there too. You want me to put a reserved sign on my bedroom door?"

"Yes, please."

Capitol Takes

Gordy was a pushover. From the moment that Bryan Albertson entered the Wilson apparel and gear tent at the Legg Mason tennis tournament in Washington, D.C., the tennis star knew the cute young twink who was modeling tennis apparel and helping at the ball serve exhibit was his for the asking.

This wasn't the first time today that Bryan had seen Gordy. The first time was out in the players' and staff parking lot, where Bryan was standing at the players' booth and picking up his credentials. A BMW convertible driven by an older guy of about forty or so had motored into the lot and over near the staff tent, and this really great-looking younger guy had unfolded himself from the passenger side and leaned over and given the older guy a big sloppy kiss.

Bryan had then recognized that the older guy was a TV anchorman for one of the news programs based in Washington. Wally Haimer, Bryan thought. He'd heard rumors about Haimer. It looked like the rumors were true. In any case, he'd gotten himself some really nice tail in this young guy. He was a tall blond with blue eyes and a good build. He had a sunny smile and an "oh my gosh" aura to him. Bryan doubted he was more than nineteen or twenty, and he looked fresh, barely broken in. Surely an old guy like Haimer couldn't have given him the ride he deserved.

Bryan had hung around just beyond the gate and followed the young guy to the Wilson Sports retail tent and looked in there from afar long enough to see that this was probably where the young guy was working. Bryan didn't want to stay out in the open like this for long, because tennis fans were beginning to recognize him and a few had already asked him to sign their programs or tennis balls. So, he turned and retreated to the locker rooms under the stands.

He wasn't playing until the next morning, being one of three players who had gotten a bye in the first round. But he'd wanted to get in some practice today. His coach wasn't coming in until the next morning, though, so he'd have to try to pick up one of the other players. Maybe one of the Ergon brothers—a Turkish men's doubles team. He'd been in a tournament with them in Munich a couple of months previously. They had a good fuck session there with one of the eighteen year olds that tournament used for ball boys. That young guy certainly could yowl. Of course it had been the three of them at him, and the ball boy fucked like it was his first time. Bryan had hoped to get it on with the two Turks again here—they'd been a lot of fun and had nice, big cocks. And maybe this young guy in the Wilson tent would be just the ticket. It was a tennis fetish of Albertson's. He had to have a good fuck the night before a match to do well.

Nobody he knew was in the locker room. In fact, the place was almost deserted. There were players out on the court, but it was pretty early in the day and in the tournament, and momentum hadn't started to roll here at Washington's Carter Barron tennis complex yet. Bryan went back out onto the concourse and walked over to the Wilson tent. All of the players had agreed to float around to the vendor tents for a few hours during the tournament anyway, and he decided he might get some of that out of the way sooner than later.

He wandered around and stopped and posed for photos and signed autographs here and there, but he found himself zeroing in on the Wilson tent. He really wanted to get up close to that young blond he'd seen. When he entered the tent, the blond guy looked up from the serving cage that had been set off to one side as a come-on to get people into the tent to buy apparel and tennis gear. There was a camera at the end of the cage and a big bull's eye on the back wall, and whoever was serving was told to try to hit a certain mark on the bull's eye and the camera would record the speed of the serve. There wasn't any prize—just bragging rights if those standing around saw you give a good, fast serve.

Bryan walked to the spotlighted circle where the players were to stand to give autographs. Some children began to form around him for autographs, but he could see immediately that he'd also caught the attention of the young blond guy from the parking lot, who flashed him a warm smile. When Bryan had worked his way over to the serving cage, he found the blond guy busy demonstrating how the exhibit worked to a couple of Hispanic dudes.

"Hey, not bad," he said when the blond guy had hit the perfect spot on the bull's eye at a 98 mph speed.

"Uh, thank you," the blond guy said as he looked up and then did a double take when seeing that it was one of the top seeds in the tournament who had delivered the compliment. "We, of course, can't get the higher speeds here. The conditions aren't really comparable to being on the court. You're Bryan Albertson, aren't you?" He asked the question as if he couldn't believe Bryan Albertson would be on the same planet with him, let alone standing next to him.

"I was when I woke up this morning. And you are . . . ?"

"Uh, sorry. I'm Gordy. Gordy Martin."

Bryan put his hand out, and Gordy awkwardly took it in his hand. Bryan could feel that Gordy was trembling at the touch.

The Hispanic dudes lost interest in trying the serve at least long enough for Bryan to sign the sleeves of their T-shirts. As he did so, he continued to look at Gordy and converse directly with him.

"Do you play well on the real court?"

"I hold my own pretty well," Gordy answered.

"I need someone to hit balls with me for a half hour or so. My practice court time is coming up and I can't find anyone in the locker room to hit with me. If I asked your manager real nice if he could spare you for an hour or so and I stood you for a cool one before that, would you like to hit with me?"

"Uh, yeah. Of course," was Gordy's response—although it came out a little tongue tied. He was completely star struck.

"This is gonna be a piece of cake," Bryan thought, quite satisfied with himself, as Gordy preceded him to the back of the tent where the manager's desk was set up. As they walked, Bryan put a palm on Gordy's butt. And although he felt the young blond shudder, Gordy didn't make any move to separate Bryan's hand and his butt.

"You from Washington?" Bryan asked, as they sat in front of the Singha concession at a high-top table and sipped beer. Every couple of minutes a tennis fan recognized Bryan and stopped by for an autograph and a "best wishes" for Bryan's chances at taking the tournament. Bryan could tell that Gordy was duly impressed at the attention.

"Naw, I'm a California coast guy," Gordy answered. "Play a lot of tennis and got a chance at modeling for Wilson, though, and I thought I'd take a look see at this side of the world."

"So, modeling is your gig?"

"At least until my goal of being a movie maker takes off."

"Which is why you're living in California?"

"Yeah, but I like to travel like this; it gives me ideas for movies. And how about you? Do you call anyplace home?"

"Just the tennis court, and . . ." at this he looked Gordy in the eye and laid a hand on his knee under the surface of the table ". . . and in the bedroom."

Gordy blushed, but, again, he didn't brush the hand away. "So, you're not a home-based kind of guy?"

"No. Pretty much a hit and runner, always going to the next tournament. When I'm not playing, I'm working out at Bollittieri's setup in Florida. I usually find someone to bunk with when I'm there. Whoever I bunk with, he never complains."

Gordy said nothing. He didn't really have an opportunity at that point, because another fan had seen Bryan and sauntered over for an autograph.

When the fan had drifted off, Bryan turned to Gordy and said, "I won't beat around the bush. I need to get laid today. It always helps my game, and if not you, I'll need to hook up with someone else soon. Do you take cock or do you give it?"

"Excuse me?" Gordy was suddenly coy—and his face blushing virginally.

"I don't think I guessed wrong," Bryan continued, still cocky, "I saw you smooching up that TV commentator out in the parking lot before you came in. Top or bottom? Give good head, do you?"

"Umm, I don't really do much . . ."

"Top or bottom?"

"Uh . . . bottom . . . I guess. But I don't often . . ."

"Here, feel this. You want it, it's yours." Bryan had taken one of Gordy's hands and placed it on his basket. "You don't think you can take it, tell me now. Isn't a dream of yours to get laid by a hung tennis champion?"

Gordy was trembling, but he didn't take his hand away from the basket—at least until he noticed another fan zeroing in on Bryan. And he didn't say no, either.

After the fan had left the table, Bryan downed his beer and stood up. "It's time for that practice session. It's hot as hell in Washington in August. So, let's play skins. It will give the spectators a thrill, and I want to see you move half naked—and I want you to see me move as well. Afterward, we'll hit the showers here and I'll fuck your lights out. I like that, I'll take you home with me tonight. Problems with any of that?"

Gordy was speechless, but he stood up from the table and, evidently cowed by Bryan's directness and assured arrogance, the young blond meekly followed Bryan to the practice courts. And he didn't do badly in hitting with Bryan during the practice, which was a miracle considering how keyed up Bryan had made him. Seeing Bryan shirtless and moving around the court, magnificence in motion, made him pant, though—along with a two-deep crowd of young women—and not a few men—clinging to the wire fence around the periphery of the court.

* * * *

"Oh, god . . . I don't know if I can . . ."

"You can. Just watch the teeth; unhinge your jaw; keep 'em out of the way. There like that. Ahhhh, yes. Oh, fuck, yes. Open to me!"

Gordy gagged and pulled off Bryan's cock, but after a couple of coughs, he opened to Bryan again, who slid inside Gordy's mouth, the access much easier now—and deeper—and, holding Gordy's head to his crotch under the cascading water of the shower cubicle under the tennis stadium stands with his hands, he began a slow pump.

"There, that's good. For never doing this before, you're doing just fine. Ahhhh, yes."

Gordy had a wild-eyed look about him as Bryan pulled him erect with hands on his waist and then turned him and gave the command, "Bend over. Grab your ankles."

Bryan was loving this. He'd rarely taken a guy—certainly not a guy this hot—who seemed so new to it. Bryan was feeling like he was the first with this blond hottie, and his cock was all the harder for the sensation.

"Oh shit . . . . oh fuck!" Gordy cried out as Bryan slowly plowed up into him. Gordy initially almost collapsed, his knees going to rubber, but Bryan held him up with hands clutching the young blond's waist. Gordy reached up, though, and grabbed the towel bars on the wall with his fists and arched his back and whimpered and moaned as Bryan continued driving his cock up inside him.

When Bryan started to slow pump, Gordy arched his back up to Bryan's chest and wrapped his wrists behind Bryan's neck. He turned his face toward Bryan's and, as the two kissed deeply, a charge of electricity ran up through Bryan's body from his cock up to the top of his head. Gordy was moving his hips, back and forth, on Bryan's skewering cock. Fucking him now. And now Bryan's moans and sighs were merging with Gordy's. It was as if Gordy was a pro at this. Bryan knew now that he'd be taking Gordy back to the hotel for the night. This was the prematch fuck he'd been looking for; he could almost guarantee victory in his second-round match now.

Bryan was also thinking that Gordy was too good to be keeping to himself, as his thoughts went to his last really great fuck—in Munich. He'd won that tournament—which was what had given him the great seeding in this one. The Turkish brothers had won the men's doubles too.

* * * *

"God, I don't know," Gordy said as they were dressing in the tennis stadium locker room. "It's all a little overwhelming. I'm so sore. I've hardly ever—"

"That TV guy, Wally Haimer, fucked you last night, didn't he?"

Gordy didn't answer. His eyes were downcast in evident embarrassment.

"Was that your first time?"

"Uhh." That and nothing more from Gordy, his eyes still downcast.

Bryan reached over and put his arms around Gordy and lifted his chin so that he could take Gordy's lips with his. It was a sweet kiss.

"Is he picking you up here this evening?"

"No. No, certainly not. It was an accident, really. I didn't intend . . . he just . . ."

"Was so seductive?"

"Yes."

"And did he fuck you better than I did? His cock possess you deep inside as well as I did?"

"Please . . . I don't want to talk—"

"Did he?" Bryan had grabbed one of Gordy's hands and placed it on his basket. Gordy was trembling, but he didn't take his hand away.

"No." The answer, when it came, was almost a whimper.

"I'll pay you $100 if you'll come back to the hotel and sleep with me tonight."

"I . . . I don't . . . know."

"Yes you do. You know, don't you? You want to. You want me again."

"Yes." It was a whisper.

* * * *

Bryan was in the hotel room bathroom showering again. Gordy would be next. Bryan had suggested they shower together again, but Gordy said he knew that would lead to sex and he wanted Bryan in bed. He had blushed and pointed out that there was a mirror beside the bed and he wanted to watch this time. Bryan had just laughed and muttered something about Gordy being on the fast track in learning to be a slut and had sauntered off to the bathroom, bare buttocks undulating and a towel flipped over his shoulder. If someone was being described as the cock of the walk, that would be Bryan walking to the bathroom.

While Bryan showered, Gordy moved around the room nervously, looking at this and that on the wall and behind the drapes at the window. He stopped in front of the wall opposite the one with the mirror on it—on the other side of the bed— and examined the painting on the wall. It was quite a colorful and "busy" one. Lots of abstract circles in different sizes. Gordy smiled, lifted the painting off the wall, and reached into his pocket for his pocketknife.

Later, when it was Gordy's turn to come out of the bathroom, after his shower, naked and toweling his hair, he did a double take and almost fell backward into the bathroom again.

"Relax, Gordy," Bryan said. He had been standing close by the bathroom door and moved behind Gordy and encircled his chest with his arms, pinning Gordy's arms to his sides. "These are friends of mine. Surely you recognize them. Doubles partners. Mehmet and Mahfouz Ergon. They play with me. They want to play with you too. You'll enjoy them. I know they'll enjoy you."

All three of the men Gordy encountered in the room were naked—all already crowned with condoms, so Gordy was left with no doubt what the three intended.

"No . . . please, Bryan," Gordy whimpered. "I told you that I . . . oh, god, oh shit!"

"It'll be a fast $300, Gordy. I wouldn't ask you to do it for what I said I'd pay just for me."

"Oh, god," Gordy whimpered.

"We'll take that as I yes, shall we?" Bryan said, with a big smile. "Good. 'Cause you comin' out of the bathroom looking that good, I think it would happen anyway."

One of the Ergons was kneeling in front of Gordy and had taken the blond youth's cock in his mouth and was expertly going down on it. Gordy struggled a bit, but when Bryan took possession of his lips in a deep kiss, Gordy settled down.

He was writhing again, though, as, with Bryan still holding his arms and torso prisoner, the Turkish tennis player stood and lifted and spread Gordy's legs and began working his cock inside Gordy's passage. The second Turk came over and stood beside Gordy and worked the young blond's cock with his hand while his brother fucked him and Bryan held him close and worked his mouth. Neither of the Turks were as long as Bryan, but they both were thicker—and were more brutal and pistoning in their taking.

When the first Turk—Mahfouz, Gordy caught the name correctly—was finished, they carried Gordy to the bed and pushed him down on his back, his butt at the foot of the bed. Bryan crouched between Gordy's legs and fucked him second, while the other Turk—Mehmet—straddled Gordy's chest and fed his cock into Gordy's mouth.

Gordy whimpered and pleaded, but the three kept at him, laughing and joking among themselves and commenting on what a nice, young, fresh piece of ass they had to work this time.

When Bryan was finished between his legs, Mehmet pulled Gordy off the bed and pushed the blond youth onto the floor on all fours and mounted him and fucked him like a dog.

The Turks took him in another round on the bed, with Gordy having reached the stage where he just flopped back and moaned and gave no opposition or help at all. The Turks offered Gordy to Bryan at the start of the second round, but Bryan just laughed and said he had Gordy for the rest of the night and for them to each have another fucking before showering and leaving.

As the Turkish brothers showered—together—Bryan laid stretched against Gordy's panting and whimpering body and held him close and whispered in his ear what they'd do together when they were alone. Gordy, in obvious exhaustion, merely murmured unintelligible words back at Bryan and drifted off into a state of semiconsciousness. Bryan found him so luscious in that state that he went up on his knees, lifted one of Gordy's legs and side split him in a quick fuck. Gordy remained comatose.

When Gordy started to become aware of his surroundings again, Bryan and the Turks were at the hotel room door, joking and talking tennis and of their coming matches and their prospects for victory. The Turks were dressed and Bryan had a towel wrapped around his waist. When the Turks had gone, Bryan went into the bathroom and closed the door.

Gordy waited for the shower to start pumping water and then he sprang off the bed—seemingly rejuvenated. He was smiling and not moving at all like a newly initiated guy who had just been gangbanged for a couple of hours by three virile and demanding cocks.

He strode over to the painting beside the bed, pulled it off the wall, and extracted the miniature, wide-angled video camera he'd attached to the back of the painting with its lens against the hole he'd cut into the busy-design painting with his pocketknife.

Bryan was still under the shower stream and singing happily to himself when Gordy finished dressing, swept the $300 Bryan had promised him off the dresser, quietly exited the hotel room, and clicked the door shut behind him.

"Not bad for less than a week," he was thinking. "First that pitcher with the Washington Nationals baseball team, and then that TV anchorman. Three pro tennis players was a bonus here. And I've already got a hookup arranged with that Republican congressman tomorrow night. A couple of more days of video editing and splicing and my *Capitol Takes* movie is gonna be ready to go viral in the gay movie houses."

Cold Stone Tomb

I was fighting to come up from a great depth, swimming hard against the current, trying to force my eyes open.

"I want to live," I moaned, although whether internally, to myself only, or out loud, I did not know. "But I want this too. Deeper, thicker. Stretch me, possess me. Wrap your dick around my heart and squeeze me. Harder, deeper. Moooaaan. I want to melt into you, ride your dick forever."

I fought up into consciousness. Belly against the cold stone of the mossy tomb surface. The monster of a cock deep inside my ass, growing, thickening, pulsing, rhythmically fucking me as I've never been fucked before.

A heavily muscled, pulsating body covering my back, with a powerful arm around my chest, forcing my arms above my head, holding me powerless with the strength of a lion, far greater strength than I had. And my strength ebbing. Sharp nails at my buttocks, skewering me to the surface of the cold stone tomb. Lips at my stretched neck. No, more than lips. Teeth at my neck, incised into my flesh. Blood trickling down my neck, but not all, not most. Most being sucked up into his mouth with a pulsing, gurgling noise. A rhythm matching my quickened heartbeat.

Blood dribbling down my side from the fingernails dug in my buttocks. Blood dripping on the surface of the tomb from the slashes on my chest, from when, spent with running, already under him, being fucked, I turned on him and he slashed my shirt off me with broad, violent sweeps of his sharp fingernails.

I can feel my life ebbing. And I want to live. "I want to live," I cry out. But I want the glorious fuck too. Never like this before. The ultimate. I want it to go on forever and ever.

Naked on the stone, both of us naked. But covered, covered by his black satin cape. Rhythmic rise and fall of the bodies, in unison, under the billowing cloak. Undulating up and down to the rhythm of my heartbeat, to the rhythm of the sucking at my neck, to the rhythm of the fuck. Sighing, groaning, moaning.

I want to live. Fighting now, writhing under him, feeling my life ebb, my limbs going numb. The probing cock growing and growing, filling me to splitting. Wanting to live but wanting the fuck to go on.

I had dressed for the fuck. I had walked into the French Quarter for the fuck. I had entered the Club Fantastic for the fuck. I had even looked at him from across the room, conveying "fuck me" to him. He returned a level, knowing stare that sent shivers up my spine. And a wicked smile that had me turning and walking quickly out of the club and out of the quarter, and up Promenade, my pace quickening, my panic growing.

I was at a jog, afraid he was behind me—afraid and hoping he was behind me—almost like I could feel him loping along in my wake, easily covering the ground at my own pace even though I was panting and my lungs were beginning to burn. I was in shape; I was in terrific shape. But I was running scared. Yes, running now, because at a corner, with a black sedan sweeping by, not offering any help, any sanctuary, I turned my head and saw him back there—pacing me. His cloak held tightly to his chest but billowing out at the side.

At the entrance of a cemetery, I stopped, dead in my tracks, my mind suddenly telling me that this was what I had come for. Over the weeks, days, months, I had sought continuously more arousing encounters, bigger cocks, more-public fuckings, the erotically exotic. I had heard that Club

Fantastic had it—something special, something not of this world. Whispered rumors, secret looks, nodding heads. Normal sex was boring me. I wanted the exotic. I wanted a jolt.

I was panting in fear, but also in arousal and excitement. Turning, I saw that he had stopped too. He was grinning at me. What had been handsome and dark and alluring was morphing into a skull, a grinning scull. His mouth opened and he laughed. He raised his arms up and out, flinging the cape wide. Underneath he was stark naked. His body was magnificent, a Zeus of men, and his cock was the most monstrous I'd ever seen, in full, upward curved erection.

I turned and walked, slowly now, into the cemetery. Down a narrow asphalt trail to the older section of the cemetery, where the tombs were big stone boxes, raised off the ground. I chose one half obscured by the weeping branches of an ancient oak—tomb moss covered, tree draped in Spanish moss.

I turned when I reached the tomb, deliberately, and he stopped twenty yards from me, on the asphalt path, and gave me a sardonic look, cupping his cock in his hand, waiting for me, although I had no idea what he was waiting for—other than that I somehow knew that if I made any move to leave—to escape— at this point, the effort would be fruitless. I knew I already was under his power. I shivered, in delicious fear.

I unzipped my jeans and peeled them off my legs. Then I stripped off my bikini briefs and slipped off my loafers. I wasn't wearing socks. I started to unbutton my shirt.

He was on me in a flash, making guttural animalist noises. He lifted me by my arms in a superhuman grip and slammed the small of my back down on the tomb surface, moving his hands to my thighs, and splitting them apart in the same swift movement that he split my ass with a massive up thrust of his huge cock. I howled in pain, panic, shock, and glorious satisfaction. We were both howling to the wind, in harmony, each getting instant satisfaction. This! This was what I came out to find tonight.

He pistoned me hard and fast and deep, as I writhed under him, never having had anything like this in all of my years of seeking. I was well used and slack, but I was quickly filled and stretched and near to splitting to limits I'd never known before. I spilled my seed quickly and then lay back and moaned as he worked me like a jackhammer on its way to the center of the earth.

He leaned over me and sought my mouth with his and brutally kissed me. I bit his lip and laughed, reveling in the rough sex. But he reared up and scowled at me, his eyes going yellow as a dribble of blood laced down to his chin. And suddenly he notched up his wild man performance. He lashed out at my chest with his fingernails, shredding my shirt and then slashing my chest. He lowered his head on my chest, and I heard the sounds of slurping and felt the heat of his tongue and the sting of the slashings—until I cried out and arched my back as his teeth sliced into the rim of one of my nipples and he began to feed in more earnest. I couldn't get away if I'd wanted to; his cock was deep inside me, pinning me to the cold stone of the tomb lid.

The pumping of his cock matched the rhythm of his sucking of my nipple, and I found myself moving with the rhythm and feeling more pleasure than pain in the sucking.

He lifted his head and pulled his cock out of my channel, and I turned and scrambled farther up on the surface of the tomb, ready to break this unearthly encounter and flee now that I had ejaculated, had satisfied myself—titillated by the experience, but enough was enough.

This was the direction he wanted me to go in, though, and he scrambled up onto the tomb with me, covering me from behind, one of his arms wrapped around my chest and pinning my arms above my head, sinking fingernails into my buttocks, and thrusting his cock inside me once more.

I whimpered and pled with him. He laughed and I felt his lips at the side of my neck and then I cried out as his teeth sliced into flesh and he found a vein.

"I want to live," I murmured. "I want to live."

I felt myself going, my eyes closing, a great sigh floating over me.

A blinding light jerked me out of my reverie. It did more than that to my assailant. He was off me in an instant and crouching at the dark side of the tomb, covered with his cape and whining in a high-pitched tone.

A vehicle was going through the cemetery, pointing a strong floodlight here and there. It's light had swept across us, but nothing else was happening, so whoever was driving it wasn't alarmed.

With a groan I lay back, full length, on the top of the tomb, unable to move, trying to collect my wits and my strength. The light rolled across me again, at which point I must have looked like I was just part of the tomb.

As I gathered myself, a great, heavy sensation of disappointment and want descended on me. It wasn't anything I could have even begun to describe. But it was a feeling of loss, a feeling that I had now experienced it all—that there was no "up" from here, no chance of greater fulfillment, of deeper satisfaction.

I lowered an arm over the side of the tomb, on the dark side. Reaching for it—for him—for whatever. It wasn't something I wanted to do. It scared me witless. It wasn't something I should seek, should have anything to do with, I knew. I should be ecstatic that I had had this brush with the overpowering and had escaped it. But had I? Was it already too late? What was there after this?

My lowered hand felt . . . nothing. I rolled over and looked down. Nothing. No one. Had it even happened? Yes, certainly. My body was ravished, both externally and internally.

I lay there, bringing my breath back to normal—or as close as I could in the circumstances. I tried to pull up gratefulness, relief, adrenalin from a tragedy avoided. Nothing. I felt nothing of that. What I felt was loss.

When I felt that I could walk, I struggled down off the surface of the tomb, leaned down—and almost falling over as I did so—retrieved my jeans and briefs. I was too exhausted, too weak to put them on. Then I walked, struggling to stay erect as I moved—disoriented. I wasn't walking toward the cemetery entrance; I was walking farther into the cemetery, into the older part, into the section where an asphalt path had never been blazed through.

He was stretched out on another tomb, much like the first one. Just laying there, his head propped up on his elbow and the heel of his hand. Watching me with a steady, sardonic look on his face. He was still in magnificent erection.

I walked slowly to the tomb. I was too weak to climb up on it, but he reached down and helped me up, and stretched me out along his body, my back cuddled into his front. He lifted my thigh with one of his hands, and I felt the long, strong, slide inside me of his monster cock. And then he started again inside me. This time different. Just as magnificent and satisfying, but slow, deep, with long strokes that had me gulping each time his bulbous glans kissed the rim of my ass and then gasping as it slid deep inside my intestines. Gulp, gasp. Gulp, gasp.

His other hand cupped my chin and stretched out my neck to his slicing teeth. He fucked me in rhythm to the sucking at my neck to the rhythm of my beating heart to the ebbing away of my very being.

I came, not once but twice—to a passionate cry first, and then to a quiet, weak sigh, as his cock plumbed my depths and his mouth lapped up my life.

I never wanted this to stop. The never-ending fuck, into eternity. Deep, filling, glorious.

"I want to . . ." I murmured, but I couldn't remember what I wanted—beyond the never-ending fuck.

I felt the beating of my heart thumping louder and louder in my ears, the sound rolling over me in waves. So cold; I was so cold. I had been so hot, but now I was cold. I felt his body tense, ready to explode—and then an earth-shattering ejaculation. Again and again and again. I was being flooded inside by his boiling cum, burbling up his still-thrusting cock, out of my hole and onto my thighs. I felt . . .

Condolences

"I'm sorry, Evan, I probably shouldn't have come."

"Please, please, Ben, I'm glad you did. Eleanor would have been pleased that you were here. She always thought so highly of you. Look, she's wearing the diamond stick pin you've always admired so. Well, she's wearing it for the moment, of course."

"It was so sudden."

"Yes, yes. Eleanor was always going on about the great differences in our ages, but she was always so fun loving and I thought of her as ageless. It just won't seem the same with her gone."

"Will you be able to keep the house? Here, let me help you back to your seat."

"Thanks, Ben. I do feel a little wobbly. It all just came a little unexpectedly." Benjamin Barkley, Evan's tennis partner, and the tennis pro, down at the Westview Country Club, encircled Evan in his arms and helped him move away from the casket in the center of the viewing room and back to a chair, where he helped his friend sit down and then stood, ready to move away. Other mourners were circling, nervously, in the room, wanting to offer their condolences to the bereaved

47

widower and then be on their way to whatever they really wanted to be doing on this day.

"The house?" Evan sat, tugging at Ben's sleeve and responding as if he only now had heard the question. "Well, I assume the house will go to Teddy. He was Eleanor's oldest. And the house has been in the family for generations."

"Oh," Ben said, revealing a bit of disappointment.

"There was a prenup, of course," Evan continued. "But Eleanor was quite generous. I don't think I'll be wanting for anything."

"Oh," Ben said again, but this time with distinctly more cheer.

"And here is Teddy now. Teddy, Teddy, did you come directly from the airport?"

"Yes, but, if you don't mind, I'll stop by the house a bit later. I believe now is as good a time as any for us . . . to take up that business in New Orleans from last spring."

There was a pause before Evan spoke. "Ah, yes, I quite agree," Evan then said. But even as he said it, his eyes were shifting toward a young member of the funeral parlor's staff, who had caught his eye and appeared to want a word with him. The young man had been quite helpful over the past four days. Evan had become quite reliant on him for helping with all of the arrangements.

"Excuse me, Teddy, Ben," Evan said, as he rose and went over to the side door and conversed with the funeral parlor aide in low tones. Teddy turned and moved over to his mother's coffin and took on what he assumed was an acceptable face of bereavement. He leaned over, folding his hands in prayer over the open casket. He'd heard what Evan said about the diamond broach, but he was sure he could slip the ruby ring off his mother's hand from this position without anyone being the wiser.

Ginger Miller, sitting a bit away with Ann Wilson—both Tuesday morning bridge partners with Eleanor Henderson for these past three decades—leaned over and whispered in Ann's ear, "Meeting at the house later, they said. Her son probably wants to count the silverware, and that boy toy husband of hers probably has already hocked it."

48

Ann Wilson looked scandalized, but she had to fight hard to suppress a bout of giggles that Ginger would set off if she made one more crack. It already had been the hardest thing for her to do not to laugh out loud at the comment Ginger had made about the tennis pro who manhandled Evan back to his chair. That had been absolutely scandalous—but she couldn't wait to repeat it when she reported back to the other girls about the outing to Eleanor's farewell.

"Again, my condolences." The voice of the funeral parlor aide could now be heard clearly in the otherwise-hushed room.

"Thank you, Matthew," Evan replied. "It will take time to adjust. A time for grieving. It was all so unexpected and sudden."

"The final accounting should be ready this afternoon. I could—"

"Yes, please do bring it by. You know the address, I think."

"Yes, you gave us your card."

Evan turned away from Matthew to return to his seat, and his eyes were sweeping the room, looking for who would be the next to step forward to give him support, He stumbled a bit as he returned to his chair and maintained his face set in just the perfect, studied aspect for the occasion.

Ginger, who had leaned over to whisper something else in Ann's ear, snorted, and Ann looked shocked, pulled away from Ginger, and looked her straight in the eye. "Do you really think so? This soon. Well, I'll be."

* * * *

"OK, I'm coming. Just a minute, please."

The door opened, and there stood Evan—in a short, shimmering silver silk robe and probably nothing else.

"Matthew," he said, a bit stunned.

"Uh, you did say to come on by this afternoon, Mr. Henderson."

"Please, it's Evan. You make me sound so old. And I'll bet I'm not more than four or five years older than you."

"Uh, sorry . . . Evan. I can come back or, if I misinterpreted, we can do this at the office."

"You didn't misinterpret, Matt. Not at all, not at all. Yes, please do come in."

Evan reached through the open door and took hold of Matthew's sleeve. The young man hadn't changed from the suit he was wearing in the funeral parlor, but he had dressed down considerably. The suit coat was gone and the tie, and the white shirt was open down a couple of buttons. Evan had already been able to see in the funeral parlor that Matthew didn't have an undershirt underneath it—he was nicely tanned and very nicely muscled, and he had a downy patch of dark hair running from underneath his pecs down his six pack. Now, though, with the tie and coat gone, Evan could see that Matthew had a gold necklace with a small medallion around his neck, with the medallion resting in curly hair at the center of his chest—and, even more inviting—he had gold rings in both of his nipples. He now also had a little gold loop earring he hadn't had at the funeral parlor.

Evan hadn't guessed wrong in his interaction with Matthew these last four days.

"Here, let's sit over here on this couch. Would you like something to drink?"

"A beer would be nice. I'm really sorry about bringing the paperwork out here, I—"

"No, no, I wanted you to," Evan called from the kitchen. He continued the conversation, as he walked back into the room. While he'd been gone, the sash on his robe had somehow become loose, and the lapels had spread wide, showing a good bit of the chest that Evan put a lot of effort into toning, not to mention his well-muscled calves and thighs—and just a hint of something else there, peeking out below the sash. Well, perhaps more than a hint—and becoming more pronounced as Evan watched Matthew's reaction to his progress across the cavernous living room.

"Well, again my condolences," Matthew said in a tight little voice, his eyes following Evan's approach very closely.

"You have been wonderful about that—and I sensed that you got to know her so well in our talks about what she needed in these past four days that you are mourning her too. I think you might need comforting too. Perhaps we can comfort each other."

For a moment when he sat down close beside Matthew, Evan placed a hand on the young funeral parlor aide's knee and looked tenderly into his face. But that lasted only a moment, as what Evan saw in Matthew's face assured him that when he then sank to the floor and moved between Matthew's spread thighs and started pulling down the zipper to his trouser, Matthew would very much appreciate some comforting as well.

* * * *

"Oh, god, yes. Fuck me hard. Oh, yes, yes. Oh, shit!"

Evan was laying on the bed on his back, his knees drawn up and spread, his lower back propped up by a pillow. Matthew, as naked now as Evan was, was kneeling between Evan's thighs and, hand encasing the base of his cock, moving his tool in circular patterns inside Evan's channel. He was working at a shallow depth, his cock head rubbing against Evan's prostate.

Evan had been delighted to find that there was more metal to Matthew than the nipple rings and earring. He also had a big, heavy ring through the glans of his cock. Evan had been so delighted in finding this when he unzipped Matthew and pulled his cock out, that the insistent attentions of his mouth had almost made Matthew come right there in the living room. As it was, they only made it into the bedroom hall before Matthew pushed Evan down on the floor and took him from behind in a doggie fuck.

They had lain there on the floor of the hall, panting and recovering their lusts until Evan raised his head to Matthew's chest and gave a ringed nipple a love bite and then, as Matthew gasped and reared back, broke free and scampered to the end of the hallway. Matthew had caught him at the foot of the bed in the master bedroom and pushed him down underneath him, as Evan grabbed for and positioned the pillow. Evan arched his back and cried out, as Matthew strongly entered him again, and then, while they both gathered themselves and Matthew had acquired the rhythm of the deep fuck, Evan put his lips to

Matthew's ear and made the request that made Matthew laugh a deep, guttural laugh.

At Evan's request Matthew pulled his cock out to where the gold ring in its head dragged over Evan's prostate again and again and again, as Evan moaned and groaned his pleasure.

The two became aware they weren't the only ones grunting and groaning. The sound was coming from across the room, and both men swiveled their heads in that direction.

"Really. Just how long do you intend for me to stand in this closet, Evan? It's as cold as a witch's tit in here, and I can certainly see that Eleanor was no housekeeper. The dustballs have dustballs."

"Oh, sorry, condolences, Ben." Evan called out. "I'd like to say I didn't forget you, but this cock ring of Matthew's here captured my mind. You're welcome to join in, of course."

The pique didn't last long of Evan's tennis pro friend at being forgotten in the closet, where he'd retreated when Evan had gone to answer the door, after he'd joined Matthew and Evan on the bed and found that Evan very much wanted to give him a blow job while Matthew was fucking him.

"Here I am, all ready to take up from where we left off in New . . . Christ almighty, Evan, don't you have any respect? Mother's not under the ground more than three hours and—"

Teddy stopped at that moment, seeing in the expression on the faces of the three men on the bed how ridiculous his complaint was. Eleanor's son had let himself in with his own keys to the house, but by the time he'd reached the bedroom, the keys, dangling from his fist, were the only thing he was wearing.

"I needed comfort," was the only explanation Evan gave, talking to his step-son—who was only a year younger than he was—through the legs of his tennis partner, while the funeral parlor's aide turned back to plowing his channel.

"Apparently you do, yes," Teddy answer. "I could use some comfort too," he added.

"By all means pile on. More the . . . what's that?" Evan said.

Three heads swiveled toward the French door out to the garden, where a quite delicious-looking young man, just in skimpy shorts, had tapped on the window of the door, and was trying to peer into the bedroom.

"Ah, I forgot it was the day the pool boy came," Evan said. "And on the day's he comes, he likes to come, if you know what I mean. He was quite fond of Eleanor. Teddy, go open the door for Miguel. I'd like to pass on my condolences, and I'm sure he will be mourning Eleanor and would like some comfort from the rest of us too."

Desserts

It had been a grueling six-hour drive from their last stop on Sheila Worthington's nostalgic sweep around the region in which she had grown up before leaving for New York, a chorus line, and then a succession of well-heeled husbands, all of whom heeled over themselves during the past parade of decades.

As Dominic maneuvered the Jaguar around the last hairpin turn and turned into the long upward-incline drive up to the resort hotel that wound around the peak of the mountain overlooking a large lake and several lakeshore communities, Sheila sighed and said, "Let's go ahead and eat at the hotel restaurant right after checking in. When I get to the room, I want to sleep the sleep of the dead."

"Sounds good to me," Dominic said, forming a charming smile on his pouting-lipped chiseled face and tossing a black curl out of his eye. And indeed it did sound good to him. He'd felt like he'd been on a tight leash for several days of the trip now. Sheila was OK, and she paid him well to drive her on this trip—and for other driving services—but, boy could the old babe talk. She'd yakked incoherently for the last two hundred miles about people he barely knew—and felt little loss at not knowing well—at the tennis club where she'd picked him up, dazzled him with an overstuffed pocketbook, bedded him, and planted him in her pool house.

When they approached the hostess desk at the restaurant, the host gave them a well-trained gaze and assessed them as money and boy toy hunk. He could see that the woman was nearly spent. She was tall and thin and had been quite a looker twenty years earlier, but now her high-fashion clothes looked a bit rumpled, her heavily applied makeup was beginning to droop, and not every starched hair on her head was behaving. And the hunk, a steamy Latin who looked every bit the nicely muscled tennis pro he really was, looked tight as a stretched rubber band and ready to spring in some direction or other in frustration. He'd also given the host an up-and-down look of speculation that the host had long ago identified as possible sexual interest.

Dominic's eyes met those of the host, while Sheila rattled off somewhat catty—but quite accurate—comments on the over-the-top Western style décor of the restaurant perched high over the lake below, the vistas provided being the establishment's best feature—and the host gave Dominic a knowing look that permitted Dominic the slight escape valve of being able to roll his eyes in a "women, what can you do with them?" fashion.

With a thought not only to the preferences of his fellow workers but also, he thought, to the preferences and needs of this Latin stud standing before him, the host picked up two menus and a wine list and said, "Come with me, please, I have just the table for you."

It was a very nice table by the window overlooking the vista—which Dominic latched his attention on while Sheila talked about the impossibly spoiled frou-frou dog her friend, Maurine, had just acquired. "You'd think that anyone with white rugs and white furniture—all white décor—would think twice about getting a high-strung Pomeranian that . . ." Dominic didn't so much see the mountainside tumbling charmingly below him to the edge of the lake as that, looking out of the window, he didn't see Sheila with her mouth flapping as she devoured a hunk of pita bread like a cougar having its last meal. And this, of course, was why he was gazing so intently out of the window.

"Wine, beer, or me?"

"Excuse me?" Dominic said, as he turned. There was his waiter standing beside his chair, talking down just to him and smiling. Sheila was lost in her rambling of all of the cleaning supplies Maurine had tried thus far without success.

For the first time Dominic noticed their waiter, who he now remembered as the young man who showed up after the host had said, "Sandy will be your waiter. He'll take good care of you," and then had smiled and wafted off.

Sandy. Yes, Dominic could see where the lad had gotten that name. He was a redhead, although it took Dominic a minute for the "he" to register. The voice had been male, if a bit squeaky, but looking closely at his waiter now, Dominic could see that the rest of it was some sort of question mark. He was small of body and wore black tailored trousers and a tuxedo shirt with a ruffle. And he was standing there, hands on hips and slightly bent at the side that Dominic thought of as a "Bette Davis" stance. All he needed was a long cigarette holder in one hand and he'd slip all the way over into the Tallulah Bankhead pose. His face was made up. It was subtle, but he unmistakably was wearing red lipstick. His hair wasn't long on top, but it was slicked back in an obviously carefully considered "do," and there where long curls over his ears at each side. He was looking at Dominic with an "I just could eat you up" expression in his eyes.

Dominic looked over to Sheila, but she had moved on to rambling about the mistake her friend Dorothy had made in the choice of a tennis outfit or her latest husband. Dominic couldn't gather which it was, and his noncommittal mutterings of ascent seemed to satisfy her and keep her motor running.

Throughout the service, Dominic could tell that the waiter, Sandy, could hardly keep his hands off him and, indeed, he did brush by awfully closely from time to time.

But it wasn't just the waiter, Sandy. Quite frequently, far more frequently than even a famished camel would require, another waiter came by their table, water pitcher in hand, offering to fill Dominic's full glass, with a broad smile or taking away plates one by one when he could have managed all in one trip. This young man was more substantial and a good bit less swishy than Sandy was. He was a tall, well-built black guy, probably a couple of years older than Sandy—and not more than five years younger than Dominic himself.

He was wearing one earring, and his moves were those of a dancer—not nearly as pronounced and given to a fling of the hips as Sandy's were, but in a manner that Dominic knew well—and that he found arousing, having frequented a certain gay club often in relief from the duty his pocketbook required of servicing middle-aged women—and men—at the tennis club.

Dominic could tell just by the way that the young black waiter looked at him, that he was interested as well.

And keyed up as Dominic was—all this time on the road with Sheila and no opportunity to pursue the variety of sex he was addicted to—made Dominic go hard and begin to fantasize what he'd like to do with one of these waiters—or both.

At the end of the meal, both Sandy and the black waiter's assistant were standing there, by the table, while Sheila was taking time out from her monologue of society in the town she'd said she wanted to escape for a while, to mull the desserts, finally deciding on the crème brlé e.

Sandy turned to Dominic with a smile. "And you, sir? What would strike your fancy? We have a special on strawberry shortcake and also on chocolate cake."

"I'm not sure I can decide," Dominic said, with a winning smile of his own. "They both sound so enticing." Both amused and aroused, Dominic had caught on to the double entendres the waiter named Sandy had been dropping. The black waiter's assistant hadn't said anything during the meal, but Dominic was all the more intrigued by him because of that.

"Oooo, I love your accent," Sandy gushed. "And such a rich, deep, masculine tone. Are you from Mount Olympus?"

"No. I'm Spanish," Dominic answered with a laugh. "We don't have a Mount Olympus. Our people are earthy, not heavenly." He could double entendre too, Dominic mused.

"Oooo, that makes me tingle; it just takes my breath away." Sandy preened, fanning his face with a dessert menu. "Well, if you can't decide, then by all means have both, sir. And after dinner may I recommend our side rooftop terrace for an after-dinner delight drink and gazing at the stairs in our clear sky here. It's really quite private."

"I'm much too tired for anything after dinner," Sheila said.

All three men turned and stared at her. There had been no warning that Sheila had cut off her monologue and was now paying any level of attention to what they were saying. She had made her statement with a completely innocent face, though, and hadn't followed up with anything but her own preference for sleep rather than any after-dinner activities, so the two waiters dropped back a step and went invisible, leaving it to Dominic to pick up the conversation with her.

"Well, we'll just get you settled in the room then, and I'll bring my laptop back to the library they have here and check my e-mails and do some catching up," Dominic answered with a concerned voice. "You get your rest, Sheila. We have another 250 miles to drive tomorrow afternoon."

Less than twenty minutes later, Chocolate Cake knelt between Dominic's thighs on the rooftop terrace and gave Dominic's nicely proportioned cock expert suck, while Dominic held Strawberry Shortcake at his side, a hand on Sandy's buttocks with fingers snaking into his channel and his other hand stroking Sandy's pert little cock.

Sandy was making little high-pitched babbling sounds, which Dominic stopped by taking the little waiter's lips in his, forcing them open with his tongue, and swabbing Sandy's tonsils.

Strawberry Shortcake panted and whimpered as Chocolate Cake reached over and pulled his trousers and briefs off his legs and then held Dominic's cock erect and steady as Dominic lifted Strawberry Shortcake up and turned him around and swung his leg over Dominic's lap. Together, Dominic and Chocolate Cake settled Strawberry Shortcake on Dominic's cock as Sandy writhed and babbled a range of contradictory short, breathy statements: "slow, slow, slow, hurry, all of you. Oh god, god, oh god. You'll kill me. Yes, yes, yes."

Together, Dominic and Chocolate Cake, with Dominic palming and spreading Strawberry Shortcake's butt cheeks and Chocolate Cake holding Sandy at his waist, lifted and lowered him on the full length of Dominic's cock until he stopped writhing and started to moan and beg for the fuck.

Dominic stood then and walked slowly around the terrace, raising and lowering Strawberry Shortcake on his cock, while the young redhead clung to his midsection and groaned and gasped—and, in short order, fountained his ejaculation.

Then Dominic gently lowered the red head to the deck of the terrace and turned, strongly erect still, not himself in flow, not yet satisfied, opting now for chocolate cake for dessert.

Chocolate Cake stood and turned fully toward Dominic, smiled, leaned his rump back on a terrace table, and started to unbuckle his belt.

Dominic strode deliberately toward Chocolate, giving him time to drop his trousers. And, that done, he moved faster, grabbed Chocolate roughly—as Chocolate laughed a hearty laugh—turned him belly down on the top of the table, used one hand to establish purchase of his cock head inside Chocolate's gaping hole and used the other hand to lock one of Chocolate's arms behind his back.

"Yes, yes, Fuck me hard!" Chocolate cried out in a rich baritone—the first thing Dominic had heard him say all evening—as Dominic slammed his cock up inside Chocolate's wide channel. This was the tension reliever Dominic wanted. This was what would unwind him from all those miles on the winding mountain roads today "yes maming" and "no maming" Sheila's inane conversation.

And Chocolate Cake, well muscled and sturdy and robust, cried out that he wanted him rough and deep—and with pneumatic force. Dominic leaned his torso down over Chocolate's back, CC threw his free hand back and laced it around Dominic's neck, and they turned their faces to each other in a deep kiss as Dominic pumped, pumped, pumped.

Strawberry Shortcake moved behind Dominic and grabbed and squeezed his butt cheeks and helped maintain the rhythm of the fuck. Chocolate Cake also was helping, essentially fucking himself on Dominic's cock with long backward thrusts of his hips.

All three cried out as Dominic came. He backed up and plopped down in a chair, while Chocolate Cake turned and lifted Strawberry Shortcake up, laid him down on his back on the table top, slapped the little red head's legs aside, thrust his own hard cock inside the channel Dominic had so recently reamed for him, and started to fuck him with a frenzy that had the little red head sliding back and forth on the surface of the table. After a short breather, Dominic approached Chocolate from the rear again and Dominic fucked Chocolate Cake while fucked Strawberry Shortcake, bringing on a triple ejaculation.

Sheila was already asleep when Dominic came into the hotel room and climbed into bed that night. But half way through the night she was rested enough to nudge Dominic onto his back and fondle his cock and balls enough for him to attain an erection in a half-awake state, and then she mounted him. Exhausted, Dominic let Sheila drive.

The next morning, a now-fully alert Sheila, a sleepy and nearly hobbling Dominic in tow, arrived all cheery smiles and gushing accolades in the hotel dining room for breakfast.

Once again a more-than-eager Sandy was their waiter, backed up by a big-smiling black assistant waiter.

As their breakfast was coming to an end and Sheila was babbling about how she wanted to change the curtains in her living room, Sandy leaned down and said sotto voce to Dominic, "Would you have time after breakfast for some dessert, sir? The roof terrace is a great place for dessert and coffee in the morning." Chocolate Cake was standing behind him, looking ever so hopeful.

Dominic raised his eyes, a response on his lips that no doubt would be a classic, but that has been lost to history.

Sheila suddenly stopped running at the mouth, and in a clear, steady, not unfriendly tone, said. "I wouldn't suggest two desserts this morning, dear heart. If you must, I'd suggest just the chocolate cake. It looks more substantial. I was rather hoping we'd indulge in our own dessert of fine old port and cheddar cheese when we returned to the room—and what I was served last night was a little limp from too many sweets."

Five-Day Liberty

"Man, how did you score five days of shore leave?" Navy E-2 Tex Collins muttered, faking a hurt.

"Aced the last three inspections and built up my days," E-1 Randy Harrison answered. He was standing at the mirror just a couple of steps from their upper-lower bunk on the destroyer, the USS *Deringer*, parked just outside of the inner harbor at Manama, Bahrain.

"You're gonna' miss me," Collins said, making his voice into a pout.

"Yeah, I know," Harrison answered. He came over and sat on the bottom bunk next to the legs of his bunkmate. Harrison was in the midst of decking himself out in his sparkling enlisted dress whites, having put on the tight trousers. The white undershirt and the pullover tunic and blue tie still were draped on the hanger hanging from the corner post of the bunk.

Harrison was young—not yet nineteen—and on his first naval cruise. He was straight off the farm, strong of arm and chest and narrow of waist. He worked himself hard and looked good. His sandy-colored hair and pretty-boy face had attracted plenty of attention on their other berthings on the *Deringer's*

Mideast cruise, and Randy was pretty sure he could score well here.

Collins, older and wiser, had only managed to pull down two evenings of shore leave, and he didn't want to waste them yet. The *Deringer* would be in port at Bahrain's capital city in the Persian Gulf for a week.

The day was hot, and Collins was stripped down to athletic shorts, but still his dark, hair-matted chest was beaded in sweat.

"I know what you're gonna miss most," Harrison said, and then he gave a low laugh and worked a hand up Collins's thigh under the hem of the athletic shorts and brought it to rest on Collins's cock, which answered the call.

"You bet," Collins muttered. "How are you gonna keep out of trouble in Manama for four nights?"

"I'm not, I hope," Harrison said. He was encasing Collins's cock with his hand and had his thumb on Collins's piss slit. Collins shuddered and gave him a dreamy look. "Some of the guys have been here before and gave me some spots to hit in Bahrain. They say it's the playground of Arabia, and I mean to see just how playful it is."

"You've come a long way, Randy." Collins said it in a low growl of a voice, his hips starting to roll, his well-muscled body tightening up. He raised a hand and ran it along the well-sculpted, smooth-skinned pecs of his young protégé.

"Thanks to you," Harrison whispered. He withdrew his hand from the leg hole of Collins's shorts, but only long enough to move it to the older man's waistband and to pull that down to below Collins's balls. The senior enlisted man's cock was at full staff, and Harrison began stroking it with his fist.

What Randy Harrison acknowledged was correct. He'd gotten and given head before he joined the Navy, but it had been Tex Collins who, on dark, lonely nights tossing on the high seas, had taught Randy that he wanted cock and how to take cock.

"You gonna come back here for the nights?" Collins whispered.

"Not if I get lucky," Harrison answered. Then he leaned over and took Collins's cock in his mouth and started to give him slow, languid head.

"Gonna miss you those four nights, son," Collins whispered. "Oh, yes, Goddd . . . just like that. Softest mouth on the ship."

* * * *

Even with the address and the directions, Randy had a hard time finding the club. It was tucked away in a walk-down staircase from a parking deck under one of the new skyscrapers that had been thrown up almost overnight, mostly by Sudanese construction workers, in the cash-rich Gulf island state. Although there were cars in the garage, many of them stretch limousines with smoked windows, there didn't seem to be too many, and there wasn't anyone around—or there didn't seem to be anyone around.

Randy did sense that he was being watched as he moved across the concrete-encased cavern, but he didn't mind. He was here to be seen. He was decked out in his sparkling navy whites, and he knew he looked good in them. He moved into a strut, heading for the back corner of the garage, where he saw the innocuous sign with the words "Club Emile" on it, above a staircase leading down into the darkness.

On the half level below the staircase, Randy found a guy lounging against the rail who straightened up as he approached and gave him the once over. Liking what he saw, he smiled and beckoned Randy to continue down the stairs.

At the bottom of the stairway was a red door with another bouncer standing in front of it. He smiled as well and opened the door for Randy.

Beyond the door, Randy was standing on a landing yet another level above the floor of a whole other world than the one he had left. The smoke-filled room below was teeming with men. There was a lighted center area with a four-sided bar as its axis. Four silver poles ran up at the corners of the bar to the ceiling two stories up, and nearly naked young men were dancing the poles. Randy could hardly see the floor itself for the number

65

of men swirling around, dancing to the music here—and engaged in close conversations there.

Some of the men were in jeans and T-shirts, but probably more than half wore the traditional *galabiya*, the long, white tunic of the Arabic Peninsula. The staircase Randy stood on was flat against one wall. The other three sides of the room each supported a two-story gallery supported on Moorish arches. These galleries were deep and in the shadows. There were banquette booths with tables along the back walls of these galleries on both levels, and Randy saw that many of them were occupied by men as well.

The liquor and tobacco—and recreational drugs as well—were openly in evidence, which, in itself would be enough to elicit a raid by the authorities—if Bahrain wasn't the region's wink-wink playground, and if the Bahrain authorities weren't very much cognizant and heavily invested in tucked-away clubs like this. The decibel level, when the conversation babble and the music the pole dancers were swaying to were taken into account, probably could be heard across the gulf in Iran.

The *Deringer* had just reached port today, and most of the sailors were husbanding the little shore leave they had, so Randy was the first spiffy U.S. naval sailor to reach this club during this port call. Many of the heads snapped around to take his striking figure in as he stood at the top of the stairs getting his bearings, and there was little doubt that Randy would not have to be buying his own drinks this evening.

Randy descended the stairs and walked over to the bar. A path opened for him as other men turned to give him an assessing stare—many wondering what his preferences were and what their chances were of being able to fulfill them.

Randy found an empty stool, perched on it, and signaled to the barman. But the time the barman had reached him, there was a middle-aged Arab in a galabiya at his side offering to pay for his first drink in salute to the U.S. Navy, and Randy thanked him without enthusiasm or encouragement, but nonetheless took the free beer offered.

He watched the young men on the poles—two Arabs, an African, and what was probably a Russian, for a few minutes while he got his bearings. Then he turned and surveyed the crowd. He was looking for something in particular, although he didn't want it this early in the evening. This was the first few hours of the first night of his liberty. He wanted to just feel free of the confining ship for a few hours—and to revel in the looks he was getting. He was probably the youngest man in the club, and he knew he looked good. He knew that two-thirds of these men wanted to fuck him—and he knew that two-thirds of them would also be happy to have him fuck them.

Most of them were Arabs, though. Randy hadn't come here to hook up with an Arab. He knew that's mostly what he'd find here in Bahrain, but he hadn't picked the port call. He would have been happier to be cruising in Scandinavian waters. He wanted a big man. A big muscled man with a big dick—like Tex was. But he also wanted a rich guy. He didn't really want to go back to the ship on the nights. And he didn't want to sleep in a flea-bag hotel, either, although from his walk in from the docks, he wondered if there were any hotel rooms in this town that went for less than $500 a night. He wanted a good-looking, preferably older guy—in his thirties, maybe—who oozed of money. And a European or an American.

He realized that most of these guys were Arabs—but he set himself to look right through them in search of the face and figure and style of the guy he was looking forward to sharing a free bed with tonight. But later. Not right away.

It wasn't long before Randy saw him. An elegantly dressed, distinguished-looking European who was perhaps in his early forties—graying at the temples, but filling out his suit like his body was pampered and well worked. He was sitting at a table inside the center area by the north gallery. He was with two other men, both Arabs, one in a Western-cut suit and the other in a galabiya. But all of them looked rich. Obviously a business meeting set to end with young men in their beds.

Randy had noticed the man, because he had already noticed Randy first. He was carrying on a conversation with his colleagues, but his eyes were on Randy. And Randy could see from the way the man's eyes were slitted and the flare of his patrician nostrils that he was interested.

It was too soon, but if, in an hour or so, the man had made an overture, Randy thought he was possibly the one to take him home.

Randy turned back to the bar to find a thuggish muscle man in black suit and black skin standing beside his stool.

"The shaykh would like to invite you to his table," the man said in heavily accented English. Randy couldn't determine the origin of his accent. Randy was from the Midwest; he had no interest in, or understanding of, foreign accents.

"Oh, he would, would he? I'm sort of still just looking around thank . . ." Randy stopped, because the thug had moved the lapel of his black suit to show the handle of what was causing the bulge at his left armpit. Randy got the subtle message.

"The shaykh would like to invite you to his table," the man repeated in a monotone.

As Randy was led toward the gallery at the western wall, he saw that only one of the banquettes in the section they were approaching was occupied. The surrounding tables were empty, which was rather a surprise in a room this crowded. Randy got the message that not only did this shaykh guy have muscle, but he also had clout.

Unfortunately, the guy sitting at the banquette who appeared to be the shaykh not only was Arab, but he was wearing a white galabiya. He wasn't alone. There was a young guy in jeans, his T-shirt off, the Arab's hands on his chest and belly, sitting with him as Randy and the black-suited black man approached, but the guy in the galabiya waved to one of his goons from the group gathered at otherwise empty tables nearby, and the guy took the young man by the arm and pulled him out of the scene.

Randy stood in front of the table, giving the guy in the galabiya a look see. He was maybe in his early thirties. On the thin side, but he had dark good looks, and he was groomed well. He also had an air of assurance that indicated he always got what he wanted.

"Are you from the U.S. naval ship that came into port today?" The man spoke good English—probably English English. Randy didn't know his accents, but he'd watched a few episodes of Masterpiece Theater. He thought he could tell real English when he heard it.

"Yes," Randy answered. "The USS *Deringer.* Good-will call in Mideast ports."

"And your name is, young man?"

"Randy. You can call me Randy."

"Well, Randy, you are a very handsome young man. Would you like to sit with me for a few minutes and share a drink?"

"Well . . . sure, for a few minutes."

"I'm drinking Scotch. Would you like that—or should we have another beer brought over?"

"Scotch is fine," Randy said as he lowered himself into the banquette next to the Arab guy and behind the round table. He figured if someone was going to pay for a Scotch, that would be just fine with him.

The Arab turned his face to Randy and gave him a little smile. His face was all right with Randy, but Randy still wasn't looking for an Arab to score with.

"Do you know what sort of establishment this is, Randy? Do you know that this is a men's bar—what I gather they refer to in the States as a gay bar?"

"Yes. That's what I came for," Randy said. The Scotches arrived and Randy took perhaps a bit too big of a slug of his and coughed. It burned like hell. It was probably the most expensive Scotch they served here.

The Arab gave a little laugh and said. "You can take your time with that. We can have as many as you want."

"Well, I'm only sort of just looking around at this . . ."

"Do you like men, Randy? Is that why you've come to this club tonight?"

"Well, yeah," Randy answered. "I know what kind of bar this is."

"And do you go with men, Randy?"

"Yeah, sure. That's what I like."

"You look quite smart in that uniform, Randy. Would you let me feel you . . ." he paused to watch Randy's reaction, and having done so and seen nothing that dissuaded him, continued, "for, say, $25?"

"Uh . . I don't . . . well, OK, for $25. Here at the table. Where it isn't too obvious."

No one spoke for the next several minutes, as the young shaykh turned to Randy in the banquette and, first, ran his hand up under the hem of Randy's naval tunic and undershirt and felt his hard stomach and chest muscles and lingered momentarily at his nipples. Randy worked at keeping his breath steady. Then the hand undid his belt and unzipped his tight trousers and palmed his cock.

"Yes, very nice. As nice as it promised to be," the shaykh murmured as he withdrew his hand. "Robert, $25, please, for this young man."

One of the thugs stepped forward with a wallet and doled out $25 in U.S. currency and laid it on the table in front of Randy.

"Would you like to feel me, Randy?" the shaykh asked.

"Well . . . I don't . . ."

"For another $25?"

Randy didn't say no, so the shaykh took Randy's hand in one of his and lifted up the hem of his galabiya with the other hand. Randy was a little surprised to feel naked flesh when his hand was put on the Arab's thigh, and he didn't encounter any undergarments on his way to the cock and balls. The shaykh held Randy's hand on his cock with his own hand.

"Is it satisfactory? You see it already is hard. Would you suck me for $100?"

"Here? Now?"

"You do give blow jobs, don't you?"

"Well, sure. But here, now? I'm sorry, but the evening's just begun. Maybe later, if I'm still around. No offence. It's a very nice cock. But the evening's still young."

"A hand job then. $50 for a hand job—on top of the $50 you're already getting. That's $100 for a fast trick. Very quick, then I'll let you go do your cruising, if that's what you want to do. And the offer would still be open if you didn't find something else you wanted. $300. I'll pay $300 if you let me fuck you."

Randy didn't answer, but he half turned toward the Arab and he started stroking the man's cock underneath his galabiya.

The shaykh took his own hand away and leaned his head back into the padding of the banquette. He sighed and then moaned and groaned as Randy brought his cock to and then over the edge of ejaculation.

As Randy took his hand away and wiped it on the edge of the tablecloth, the shaykh opened his eyes and sat up.

"Thank you. You have a very nice touch. And you are a beautiful young man. Robert, please. $75 more for our young American sailor. And, Randy, I like you very much. I'll pay you $500 if you let me fuck you."

"I . . . I . . . really just got here. I'm just looking around at this point. But maybe later. Yes, maybe later." Randy stood and scooped up the rest of the money and stuffed it in his pocket after he had zipped his fly and buckled his belt again. Then he took a tentative step away from the banquette, looking from one thug to the other to gauge whether they were going to let him go.

But the shaykh signaled them away, and they all stepped back. Randy walked out into the center area and to the bar, without looking back into the alcove where the young shaykh was sitting.

He perched on a stool and ordered a beer and, seeing a pole dancer he thought was really cute, he watched him for several minutes. When he thought of doing so, he looked around for the European-type guy he'd picked out before, but he was gone and the table was now occupied by three queen types in ratty T-shirts, jeans, and heavily applied makeup.

Disappointed, Randy turned his eye on the alcove where the shaykh had been, but he was gone too.

This was just one of five bars Randy had been told about, and he was getting bored with this one, so he downed his beer, which he didn't have to pay for thanks to another unsuccessfully hopeful patron, and climbed the stairs.

He'd barely made it to the top of the stairs into the underground garage, when the lights of a nearby limousine flickered on and its engine roared and two thugs grabbed him from either side. The back door of the limousine opened as they reached it and Randy was literally thrown into the vehicle and the thugs came in behind him. The door slammed shut, and the limousine burned rubber toward the garage's exit.

* * * *

Randy was slung across the wide back seat of the Limo with his back hitting the corner where the top of the back seat met the window. He had the sensation that a crowd was milling around in that back seat, although the two thugs who had tossed him in the door and followed him were pretty much the bulk of what there was. Randy did see, though, that they'd propelled him past the seated figure of the shaykh he'd so recently given a hand job to.

The shaykh sat calmly in the middle of the back seat while one thug handcuffed Randy's arms over his head to a grab handle near the back edge of the ceiling, and the other thug was unzipping his navy white trousers and tugging them and his bikini briefs off his legs. One of the thugs was the black-suited black guy with the pistol at his arm pit. The other was an Arab. The money dispenser, Robert, was sitting in a jump seat across the wide expanse of flooring toward the front of the limo. He was just sitting there and enjoying the view.

"You have annoyed me," the shaykh said in a low voice. "We waited for you for too long."

"I didn't know you were waiting," Randy shot back. "No need for this."

He was grunting, though, because the black-suited black guy was fingering his hole with lube—and none too delicately. The shaykh snapped his fingers and pulled his galabiya over his head. Hearing the snap, Robert produced a condom packet from his trouser's pocket, slit it open, extracted the condom, and handed it to the shaykh.

Randy had the presence of mind to wonder if Robert was also going to roll it on the shaykh's rather normal-sized cock too, but it seemed royalty was able to do that sort of thing for themselves.

"You don't have to do this this way," Randy said again. "$500 is fine. I'll take cock and give you a good time. These handcuffs aren't necessary."

72

"You made me wait," the shaykh said. "I don't like that. And the $500 is no longer on the table now. Now I own you—if I like you. Otherwise . . ."

Randy started to object, but now he had two thugs at him, one on each leg, as they wishboned his legs and tilted his pelvis up. The shaykh came up between his spread thighs with his knees buried in the cushy seat.

Randy let out a gasp and a yell as he was skewered fast and deep and the shaykh started to pump him in quick strokes.

"You make too much noise." It was the first time Randy had heard Robert speak. Randy turned his head to find a cock being waved in his face as Robert hunched over him.

"Here. Suck this and be quiet. And be good," Robert commanded.

Randy did as he was told, and he started to let his hips roll with the fucking the shaykh was giving him. This was what he'd come out this evening to get. And this was kind of neat and arousing. Four guys all to himself. Him sucking one, the royal one cocking him, the black-suited black guy stroking Randy's cock, and the Arab thug playing with his balls.

The limo had come to a stop before the shaykh had ejaculated and Robert had covered Randy's chin and the front of his navy white tunic with his cum.

The four guys sat up and adjusted themselves. The black-suited black guy helped the shaykh put his galabiya over his head, and Robert was already exiting the car.

Randy took the moment when no one was paying attention to him to look out of the windows and reconnoiter. They were dockside in Manama harbor. Much of his view was blocked by a mammoth white yacht taking up a good third of the harbor and docked beside the limo, but Randy could see beyond it out into the outer harbor, where the USS *Deringer* rocked in the waves. So near and yet a world away.

"You may have him now, if you like, Tego," the shaykh said, as his two thugs helped him out of the back of the limo. Another one, probably the limo driver, an Arab wearing a galabiya, was standing outside the limo, holding the door open. "And if there's anything left of him when you are done, bring him to the ship. He still owes me a blow job—and Mustafa might be amused by him as well."

Randy eyed the black-suited black guy as he stripped his clothes off, folded them neatly, and laid them on one of the jump seats. He handed his pistol to the driver, who took it and closed the door of the limo with an ominous click, leaving Randy and the black thug inside. The thug was a muscle-bound mountain of a man. And he had a big black cock, now in arousal, that put what the shaykh had to shame.

Despite the tenuous situation, Randy melted at the sight of the hunk. This was every bit as good as he had come out for today. There were only a few guys on the ship who cocked him who came anywhere close to what this black thug had.

The thug reached up and released Randy from his handcuffs.

"The shaykh likes it this way, but I like it a little different," he growled. "You make it to the door and out, past me, and I'll let you live. You don't even try, and you're a dead man."

Randy tried. But he didn't make it anywhere close to the door. Randy put up a good fight, just as he knew the black thug wanted him to do, but he lost, just as was OK with Randy. The limo rocked wildly, as the thug picked Randy up and threw him, butt first, into the center of the back seat—and holding his arms out with fists gripping Randy's wrists—forced Randy's thighs apart with his knees and skewered the young sailor's pelvis to the back of the seat with his cock. And he thrust and thrust and thrust, as Randy yodeled to the plush ceiling of the car. Then the limo moved like a wave on the ocean, as the black thug threw Randy to the floor of the vehicle on his belly, held the young navy man's arms pinned to the floor with his fists, and his pelvis pinned to the floor with his cock, and went up on his toes and proved he could do 500 deep-thrust pushups over Randy's body and slam down to the root inside Randy's hole with each downward thrust.

Randy didn't want to reveal it, but he enjoyed every thrust.

Then the thug let Randy put his now-rumpled navy whites back on for the short stroll to the yacht.

74

"You are good," the thug said. "We'll do this again later, maybe."

"What if I had not pleased you—or the shaykh?" Randy asked.

"You would not be walking to the yacht then," the thug answered simply.

* * * *

The shaykh's yacht motored out of the harbor and within hailing distance of the USS *Deringer* on its way southeast down the Trucial coast of Saudi Arabia toward the postage stamp-sized emirate that the shaykh could call his own—and where his command was law. Randy didn't see his home ship, however, because he was busy in the shaykh's stateroom, the shaykh on his back in the center of his bed and Randy, his hands tied together at the wrists behind his back, crouched between the shaykh's legs and giving him the slow head that the shaykh had asked for in the Club Emile and not gotten. After that, Randy straddled the shaykh's hips and took a long ride on his cock.

The shaykh had had a boy of his own lounging in the stateroom when the club party had returned, and this lad was none too happy to see the shaykh return with competing entertainment. So, after this one session and to silence the screeching of the jealous catamite, Randy was locked in one of the other cabins, where, through the night, he was visited by, first, Robert, who fucked him in traditional style, and then by the Arab bodyguard, Mustafa, who belabored him cruelly with a riding crop and positions Randy had never even imagined before. Later the black Tego joined them, and Randy was double-teamed the night away.

It had been the night that Randy had dreamed of having, this first night of his five-night shore leave. He hadn't been required to spring for a room—the appointments of the yacht were luxurious beyond his wildest dreams—he'd been well-fed with both food and cock, and he'd been taken in expert and imaginative ways throughout the night.

There were only a few wrinkles. He wasn't his own man at the moment, wasn't even in the country he was supposed to be in anymore. And he was steaming toward a country where the shaykh's word was unfettered law. These were pretty difficult wrinkles, to be sure, but he had three more nights of shore leave to get them ironed out. Randy was the optimistic kind. And he'd led a pretty lucky life until now.

Besides it was nearly dawn and he was still busy. Tego was sitting on his chest and feeding him with his cock, and Mustafa was busy trying to get both his dick and a dildo into Randy's ass.

And Randy was having too good a time to think much about tomorrow.

* * * *

The harem chambers Randy were escorted to after only a couple of hours of sleep were straight out of an Arabian nights' fairy tale and had an excellent view of the shaykh's yacht—and another one that arrived in the late afternoon—riding at anchor in the Persian Gulf, from a belvedere, a covered porch, the only disadvantage of which was the iron latticework designed to keep the harem in and lusty marauders out.

There were only three other guys in residence in the harem, two young Arabs who chattered to each other in Arabic incessantly, and a morose European, who wouldn't even look at Randy, let alone talk to him. Randy had no idea whether he could either speak or understand English, and Randy certainly couldn't speak another language; he'd never seen a reason to try to before now. All three treated Randy like he was temporary, and it pleased Randy to think he was too. He only had three days and two nights left on his leave pass. It would be murder for him if he didn't make it back to the ship on time.

Randy figured there was a women's harem here too, and from what he'd heard about Arabs, it stood to reason that they'd see the importance of producing sons even if their pleasures went in another direction.

He decided he was right, because they could hear the cat fighting from where he was and when he went out into the belvedere, he found there was another one right next to theirs and he could actually get a glimpse of women flitting around in

76

the chamber that led from the belvedere. There seemed to be more in there than in the men's harem.

Randy thought they were being quite neighborly here, because the guards of the male harem included Tego and Mustafa, and Randy didn't have to get anyone else up to speed on entertaining him. Tego and Mustafa weren't shy about asserting their access rights to Randy.

He thought it was really good that the weather was so warm here, because they hadn't let him keep his navy whites. He was virtually naked in just diaphanous harem pants that hid nothing, a skimpy embroidered vest, and thick gold bands on his upper arms, wrists, and ankles.

That evening they came for him. He was taken to a covered pavilion overlooking the water, where a small band was playing weird tunes softly in the background and near-naked boys were passing trays to the shaykh and an older guest—a gray-haired Arabic man, not unattractive of face, who was burly but not exactly fat.

"Dance for them," Tego leaned over and hissed in Randy's ear when they had arrived before where the two men were reclining in a pile of cushions.

"I don't dance," Randy whispered back.

"You will dance tonight, or you won't see the dawn," Tego hissed back.

Randy was in a quandary. Three days from now he had to be climbing back up into the USS *Deringer* from a tender—or he'd be in a heap of trouble.

So he danced for them. He figured all they wanted to see was him move his body and swing his cock, anyway—and he seemed to be right; the two men seemed to enjoy him a lot, and they talked animatedly between themselves. To Randy's ears, it sounded like they were haggling about something and that the older man was frustrated and getting a little worked up. By the time both Randy's vest and harem pants had been tossed aside, though, the older man was all smiles.

Tego only had time enough to let Randy know he'd been sold to the older man before Randy was being bundled out of the pavilion by a new set of thugs.

The old man's stateroom in his yacht was more utilitarian than the shaykh's was, and the bed was in a corner rather than in the center of the room. There was a mat on the floor in the center of the room and a mean-looking hook in the middle of the ceiling with chains hanging down from it. And Randy soon found out that there were slots in his wrist bands that hooked quite conveniently in the ends of the chains and that, when he was hung from the ceiling, his feet barely touched the floor.

The older Arab had an amazing number of different toys to use on Randy through the night, and his cock was thicker and longer than the shaykh's too, so Randy's second night was just another version of how he had planned to spend the nights of his shore leave—and once again he didn't have to worry about room and board.

Randy thought this second night was great. The older Arab had made him come three times, and the hanging part was interesting and arousing—it was something he'd be unlikely ever to experience on board the ship. So, it was all good—maybe not every night, but as a new experience, it was just fine.

Randy was a seasoned seaman by the time his first cruise reached the Middle East, so he had no trouble, using his powers of observation and the "feel" of the float of the yacht, to determine that they were motoring northwest, back up the Trucial coast toward Bahrain, where they had started from.

* * * *

Bahrain, that playground of the Arab world, had a special beach, called the Shaykh's Beach, where the well connected could swim just like they do on the Riviera. In most places in the Middle East, an Arab man or woman who wanted to go into the ocean was covered nearly from head to foot, for modesty purposes and to keep the local Muslim clerics from separating their heads from their bodies.

If you could get permission to use Shaykh's Beach, though—and it wasn't guarded by anything more than common sense and the desire not to lose one's head—the women could go topless just like they did in Nice—and anyone could go bottomless too, if that was your desire. You could do just about anything you wanted there, actually.

Midafternoon of Randy's third day of shore leave found him lying on a beach towel on Shaykh's Beach, a Speedo at his side, his thighs spread open, and the thugs of the older Arab man who had bought him selling his ass to passing interested men by the minute.

Randy had to admire the way his new owner made his investments work for him.

The arrangement worked pretty well for Randy too. He was learning all sorts of new positions. He'd have Tex experimenting all the way back across the Atlantic.

The trip to the beach worked out well for Randy. There were lots of toys at the beach, and some Arabs who could afford them but had no fucking idea how to operate them.

When the two thugs and the guy who had been working between Randy's thighs had their attention arrested by the collision of two parasailers high in the air and over the water just off the beach, Randy merely struggled up from the towel and walked through what was a pretty crowded day on the beach and up onto the road into Manama. At the edge of the road, he stopped to put the Speedo on that he'd brought with him. He looked back to where he'd been holding court on the beach, and he saw his guards racing around and looking for him, but the numbskulls didn't seem bright enough to figure he'd head straight for the road.

Randy didn't know if Arabs knew anything about thumbing a ride, but he gave it a shot. A van stopped for him, and he saw too late as he approached it that the two guys in the front seat looked entirely too interested in the expanse of body his Speedo didn't cover.

There proved to be two guys in the back too, and they rolled the side door open, pulled Randy into the back of the van, and the four randy Sudanese construction workers worked over Randy's body in succession as the van drove slowly back into Manama.

* * * *

79

The third night of Randy's "liberty," although he wasn't thinking that word fit too well just now, found Randy in a small room at the back of a club in Manama, flat on his back on the bed, which took up most of the space in the room, and opening his legs to men who paid to get at him. The Sudanese in the van had sold him once again. Randy was amused to think that he was flipping over more transactions on the same piece of goods than a dollar bill moving around in a McDonald's.

Randy didn't mind it all that much. Three nights in a row now, and he was fulfilling dreams and fantasies that he'd conjured up all the way across the Atlantic and around the Horn of Africa. And he'd yet to spend any money on room and board. Of course he no longer had either his navy whites or the money he'd come with—but he still remembered his ATM number, and all he had to do was get to a banking machine and he'd have plenty of money to draw on. He'd have to think about those navy whites, though. He could hardly return to ship in what little or nothing he'd had to wear during the first half of his leave.

The guys who fucked him—mostly Arabs, of course—all had different techniques and fetishes, and he found the experience kind of interesting. Variety was the spice of life, he kept telling himself.

He didn't think too much about how he was going to get from here to the ship at the end of his leave, but he decided not to worry about that. He'd already been taken out of the country and returned the next day, all without him having to do anything or to even worry about it. So, he had faith it would work out.

And early in the night it began, miraculously, to start working out for him.

The first evidence of this was when he looked up and found that his next customer was the European-style guy he'd seen that first night in the Club Emile and had decided he'd maybe like to have ball him.

And here he was, willing to pay to do just that. And he'd paid for an hour and a half of Randy's time, because he said he'd remembered seeing Randy and wanting to have him, and he liked to fuck real slow.

And that's how they did it. Randy gave him slow head to start with, bringing him all the way to ejaculation. And then, while the European guy was reloading and getting into the mood again, he massaged Randy's body and tongued him, all the way down to Randy's asshole, where he worked inside Randy's entrance and stroked his cock until Randy had come as well.

Early in the foreplay, the European let Randy know they were in the back rooms of the Club Emile, and Randy laughed at the irony that not only was he back in Bahrain but also back at the club from which he'd first been kidnapped.

Forty-five minutes into the session, when the European had just started fucking him, yet another fortuitous occurrence walked into Randy's lucky life.

He heard a voice out in the corridor that he recognized. The cocksmen on the USS *Deringer* liked to cruise ports in a pack. Chuck, an E-2, was the most forward of that lot. He was the first to head for the back rooms of a club to get a fuck. Randy heard him in the hall and knew this meant that other guys he'd fucked with on the ship, including his own bunk and fuckmate, Tex Collins, were probably in the club.

"Do you have some place we can really fuck?" he whispered to the European. "Some place less depressing than this? You could fuck me tonight and tomorrow night too—for free, for nothing more than a roof over my head and some food and beer if you have some place and will take me there now."

"I have a flat, yes. Just me. And I'd be delighted. But I know how it works here. We can't just walk out. You are money to these people."

"If I'm right, we can walk out, yes," Randy said. "And we should be able to get at least to the club floor easily. They think you're in here for another half hour. They won't be looking for you—or both of us—to be walking out."

The backroom guards did see Randy and the European leaving when they got close to the beaded curtain separating the back rooms from the club floor, but the two were out on the floor well before the guards got to the beaded curtain.

And Randy was living under a lucky star, because five of his burly USS *Deringer* shipmates were at the bar, in a group, and had already established a "don't fuck with us" zone.

"Hey, Tex," Randy called from across the floor. "Look what I got."

"The Frenchie looks good on ya," Tex yelled back, "but what is it with the Arabic nightshirt?"

"Long story, and I doubt you'd believe it if I told you," Randy answered as he and the European he had in tow reached the perimeter the sailors had set at the bar. "And long story short," he continued as he turned and saw the backroom goons approaching, "See those thugs walkin' on us? Me and this guy here need to get out of the club and away from them. Need your help."

"Sure thing," Tex responded. He had the other sailors formed into a wedge, with Randy and his friend in the center, in no time, and they had no trouble getting out of the club and past all forms of security.

In the covered parking garage, standing beside the European's Mercedes, Tex said he and the guys had to go back in the club. "Chuck's in there, and if he likes what he sees in back, the rest of us are going to dip too. We only got this one more night of shore leave, and we're gonna make the most of it. You goin' back to the ship now?"

"Nope. I got a date," Randy answered and he gave Tex a wink. "One thing you can do for me, though."

"Sure thing," said Tex.

"What's your address, stud?" Randy turned and addressed the European lounging against his Mercedes' fender. "Can you write it down for my friend here? And, Tex, I need a new set of navy whites to return to the ship in—no, don't ask; if you're good to me on ship, I'll tell you about it—could you bring a set of mine to this guy's apartment?"

"Sure. In the morning?"

"Yeah, if you can't be away from the ship longer—but I'll be there tomorrow night too—if I don't fuck up the hospitality."

"Boy, you know how to get the most out of a five-day liberty pass, don't cha?" Tex said, and he laughed. "Nice stud you got there. He should give you a good ride. And it only took you four days to land him."

"Piece of cake," Randy answered. "You have no idea what a ride these four days have been."

82

Gaycruise Daddy

"It's a great way to throw your money away; that's what it is."

"Well, let's see, Pete. How much have you spent on the site's hookup service, and how many guys have you actually hooked up with?"

"I've had some real hot conversations and cybersex with some of them," Pete sniffed.

"Purely in cyberspace, right? At, what, a dollar a word?" John answered, with a snort. "And I'll bet the photos they showed weren't any more of them than yours are of you."

"But three K at a single throw?" Pete retorted. "Just to go out in the ocean and back and watch young men fuck? And there won't be any hiding behind a fake photo for you, either. You'll have to be in a Speedo, or you'll stick out like a beached whale."

"The boat's going to Bermuda. We'll get off in Bermuda. I've never been to Bermuda. And, besides, I've got a good enough body," John answered indignantly.

Pete wheeled his office chair from beside John, where both had been staring into John's computer screen, and made a big deal of pushing his glasses down on his nose and giving John a sarcastic stare. That tableau held for about ten seconds.

"Well, I do for a man my age. Certainly better than yours."

"OK, I'll grant you both of those."

"And I bet I'm hanging lower and thicker than most of the young guys who will be on the cruise too."

"I'll grant you that too. But there's no chance any of the guys on the boat are even going to get an opportunity to see your—"

At that point Pete broke off because he saw one of the cashiers, Julie, standing in the door to the grocery store manager's office and looking pained. John noticed the change in Pete's demeanor, and his face swiveled toward the doorway.

"Yes, Julie, what is it?" John's fingers went instinctively to his keyword and toggled the screen from the homepage of the Gaycruiser gay male dating site to the chart of last month's inventory statistics at his Baltimore branch of Krogers.

"A display got knocked over at the end of aisle three and there's pickle juice running on the floor and it doesn't look like Eddie's gonna get it cleaned up any too fast. He's already slid and fallen in it twice."

John took a deep breath and let it out in a sigh. "Thanks, Julie. Pete, could you—?"

"Hey, don't look at me, I'm management," Pete interjected. But he was already struggling to his feet.

"Yeah, but you're lower management and I'm upper management."

"Middle management," Pete muttered as he followed Julie's retreating figure through the floor and down the corridor to the main store floor.

What John was muttering at the same time as Pete walked away was, "Bermuda's gotta be better than this—and watching young guys fuck on a cruise ship will be a whole lot better than on a computer screen anyway."

* * * *

John was riddled with mixed emotions—nerves, arousal, a bit of dismay—as he stood in line waiting to register with the clipboard-laden, Speedo-clad tour director at the bottom of the gangplank up to the sleek, small *Poseidon's Spear*, the cruise ship that was to take him two days out and two days back to Bermuda from Baltimore at the top of the Chesapeake Bay.

It was true, as he had actually hoped, that he was the only fifty-something man standing around waiting to get on the ship. The up side, though, was that the other men there were almost universally young hunks he would love to sink his dick into.

The cruise was one of the ones offered by the Gaycruiser Web site on a quarterly basis that augmented their on-line dating service. The fees were stiff, but the Web site no doubt thought that charging sixty men cruising for hookups on their site for the added hookup chance of four days out on the ocean on a sleek yacht where clothing was optional and fucking like bunnies was actually encouraged helped their paid membership statistics. Especially as extra money could be made from selling videos of the cruises on sex sites.

The cruise was going to be extra expensive for John. He had something of a plan—and there wasn't much of anything else in his life to spend money on. So, he'd reserved, and paid a high premium for, one of the suites on the ship. And before arriving, he spent weeks in the gym. His muscle tone was fine—for his age—but he had needed to get a little less thickish around the middle, and he'd at least partially succeeded at that. As he approached the cruise ship from the stern, he'd done a mental comparison of his torso with that of the Poseidon depicted on the fantail, and he didn't think he came off that badly. A man in his fifties had to be expected not to have a willowy figure. He'd had his gray hair styled and highlighted in a shimmery silver that caught the light and the loose hairs plucked from all of the unattractive places so that what was left on his chest was a pleasing—at least to him—patch that trailed intriguingly down his belly to his pubes, which he'd also had trimmed and shaped. He'd left curled tuffs in his arm pits, enough so that they wouldn't give the impression they'd been purposely shaved. And he'd spent enough time in a tanning both for a sort of all-over tan so that he wouldn't look like the office worker that he was when he got to the ship's pool.

And he'd bought some spiffier, expensive-looking clothes at the Tanger Outlet near the Chesapeake Bay Bridge. He'd been lucky to find a Speedo with sort of a bull's eye design on it that would help emphasize his best feature—his thick, eight-inch cock.

When he got up to the tour director, a well-built hunk with blond-highlighted curly hair with a chiseled face and a practiced smile, he opened up his gambit.

"Ah, and you are?" the young man asked dubiously, looking down at his clipboard after a quick look up and down John and a slight sniff of his nose.

"Jonathan Pender. From Baltimore. Although, I'm not sure what home base was given you when the reservation was made. It could have been the Hamptons or Aspen too, I suppose."

The cruise director's slight supercilious smile had already started to turn more respectful as he found John's name on his clipboard, but, hearing what John said, he looked up with a far more welcoming—and interested—look on his face. John was also pleased to note that the men immediately behind him in line had stopped whispering to each other and were more attentive now too. At least they had stopped snickering.

"Yes, well it does say Baltimore, and I see that you are booked into the Neptune suite." This latter discovery had been the reason the tour director's attitude had already changed. "May I be the first to give you a hearty welcome aboard. My name is Tony and don't hesitate to ask if there's anything—absolutely anything—I can do to make riding . . . riding the waves a greater pleasure for you."

The young man fluttered his eyelashes and held out his hand for a handshake that held for several seconds longer than fully necessary and felt, John thought at the time, a little strange, because the young man had folded a finger inside the traditional grip and rubbed it across John's palm.

For a moment John wondered if this was some sort of signaling in the world of men who liked men—and he supposed that he should have spent more time researching on the Internet.

"It notes this is your first cruise with us, but I certainly hope it won't be your last."

"Yes, well," John answered, with a sigh. "The Hamptons usually are the best place at this time of year. But with the house refurbishing . . . well, I thought I'd try something a bit different."

"We can certainly offer you something different here, sir," Tony answered in a coquettish voice. "If you don't mind, I'll seat you at the captain's table for dinner tonight."

"That would be fine," John answered in a tone he hoped would convey that it was no more than what he would have expected anyway.

On his way up the gangplank, John was congratulating himself. He thought that was an auspicious beginning. And he hadn't even lied about anything. There always could have been a mix-up in listing his home in the reservation, the Hamptons no doubt *were* delightful at this time of year, and surely *some* house there was being renovated.

He gave a little chuckle, looking forward to pleasures to come, if he was lucky and clever. As he entered the ship, the first thing that caught his eye was an etching of Poseidon rising from the sea, with his trident a thick column rising between two meaty balls and ending in three hard-phallus points. He chuckled at this too.

He didn't do much chuckling that afternoon as the ship was steaming south down the center of the Chesapeake Bay and then turning southwest out to sea. As he had expected, all life gathered around the pool on the top deck in the center of the ship and most of the cruisers were starting their festivities early with drinking, cavorting in the pool, and sucking and fucking on the lounges. There were very few inhibitions to be seen and many an arousing distraction to watch. The young men were almost uniformly gorgeous, and the rewards for a voyeur were high.

As much as John liked watching, it was obvious that the young men weren't flocking to him. He had donned the bull's-eye Speedo and taken a prominently displayed lounger and laid a towel over his less-pleasing bits, but no one—with the occasional exception of someone doing a double take when seeing the line of his curled-around cock inside the Speedo—was paying much attention to him.

This changed a bit at dinner. He had to admit to himself when he looked in the mirror that he looked quite distinguished in his rented tuxedo. There was something about a tuxedo that brought out the best in a gray-haired, mature man, and John said a little prayer of thanks to the hair stylist he'd gone to rather than his regular barber earlier in the week.

The captain might not even have known that John was at the table that evening. The cruise director obviously was under strict orders to seat the most meltingly beautiful submissive young man on the cruise beside the captain on the first night, and they had not even made it to desert before they all had to rise when the captain did so as he escorted his entertainment for the evening from the table and to his cabin.

The cruise director obviously had similar plans for John. John had been conveniently seated next to Tony, and during their dinner conversation, Tony pumped John for background information, and John ran the thin line between being from a famous family of retailers and being the manager of a Kroger grocery store branch. John must have done it successfully and Tony must have heard what he wanted to hear, as, while those left at the table were being served coffee, Tony laid his hand in John's lap under the table—and, John was pleased to hear, gave a little gasp—and asked John if he could come to the Neptune suite later in the evening.

It was at this point that John knew that his scheme and the money he had invested in this cruise were going to pan out. When the cruise had come up on offer and while Pete and he discussed what young men seemed to be looking for when they played the hookup game on the Gaycruiser Web site, John reasoned that there were three reasons a young man would fuck a stranger. One, the stranger was a young hunk. This left John out, he readily acknowledged. But there were two other, more hopeful reasons. One was that they were looking for a good fucking and the last—the biggest reason by far, John thought after researching the traffic on the dating site—was that they were looking for a sugar daddy who would take care of them in the manner in which they would like to be accustomed.

Of the three, John saw his greatest hope as being the good fuck, because he had been magnificently endowed and had had decades of practice before his opportunities began to thin out as he aged, dwindling to nothing but memories soon after he pushed by fifty. Unfortunately, as John grew older, fewer and fewer young men who he fancied had stuck with him long enough to enjoy what he could give them down deep. And then John thought about the sugar daddy angle. He reasoned that if he got into it before others discovered the opportunities it accorded, he just might be able to play the sugar daddy card long enough to get his dick inside a couple of these studs and subdue them to begging for him. At that point, John thought, the good fucking might become as important to them as the sugar daddy aspect.

And, eureka, before *Poseidon's Spear* cleared Hampton Roads and was sailing out into the Atlantic, John's research assured him that he was the only one on this cruise who looked and acted the part of a sugar daddy—apart from the forties-something captain, who had his own entirely different avenue for dipping his wick as he pleased.

John left nothing to chance that evening. When he answered the knock on the cabin door and determined by look through the keyhole that it was Tony, as expected, John had the lights out, music with a jungle beat going softly and subliminally in the background, and all he was wearing was a silver silk robe, open in a swath at the front that followed the line of his sculpted chest hair down to his sucked-in belly and then on down to where his proudly displayed penis and balls reached for the floor. The only light was what was coming from the corridor with the door open and a filtering of moonlight through the gauze draperies at the balcony door.

When the cabin door was closed and Tony was kneeling between John's knees as the grocery store manager sat on the edge of the bed, there was little light, and all Tony could concentrate on with astonishment and lust was John's engorging dick and the glorious difficulty—for both of them—with which he was soldiering to get it all in his mouth.

And the night had grown even darker when John laid back, stretched full length, on the bed and let Tony ride a cock that he had to work hard, with great groans and grunts and cries of passion, to accommodate. John showed him too, now that the atmospherics had been equalized and the rhythm of the beat of the music in the background was becoming more intense, that John's hands were not too old to massage Tony's cock in quite pleasant ways while he rode John's master phallus. This was something that many years of experience enhanced. A man of John's age and experience knew how to please another man—at least in the dark and with a thick, eight-inch cock. And a man of John's opportunities was far more attentive than a younger man would be to his partner's needs.

After working Tony's cock up, John moved his hands to the young cruise director's waist and tilted him slightly toward John's chest. At the same time John raised his knees between Tony's thighs, spreading Tony's thighs, and rolled his own pelvis forward. The head of his cock moved down to the pleasure spot inside Tony's channel that a seasoned expert like John knew was there. Tony cried out in never-before-felt pleasure as John's cock head rubbed across Tony's prostate once, twice, three times and then, as Tony gasped, plunged deep inside him, only to drag slowly back up his channel walls. Tony fisted his own cock and beat it to the increased intensity of the specially selected jungle music in the background. Rub, rub, rub, plunge, drag; rub, rub, rub, plunge, drag. And Tony soared over the moon and came in profusions of cum such as he'd never experienced before with a younger man. And then when Tony thought it was over, rub, rub, rub, plunge, drag. John had had years to perfect being able to hold off and to prolong.

Hearing Tony's moans was all John needed to know that a man with real experience was good to have on a fuck cruise.

When he left the cabin slightly before dawn, Tony seemed quite pleased with the two hundred-dollar notes John pressed into his hand after patting the sweet, tight buttocks he had had the pleasure of splitting a second time after Tony had recovered from his first hour-long ride on John's cock.

The young cruise director must have spoken of the highlights of the experience the next morning, as John hoped he would, because when he came out to the pool and settled on a prominently placed lounge, he wasn't alone for long. Several young men gathered around him, asking about life in the Hamptons and Aspen and seeking advice on stocks and bonds and then, standing and posing for John and asking whether this or that muscle needed more definition or whether their tan lines showed too prominently. John laughed when one asked if he could dispel the rumors and see John's most important muscle, but John didn't give out easily. He teased them along while taking the opportunities as they came to cop a good feel here and there.

And they were ever so grateful when John was willing to rub the suntan lotion on them, particularly the young man wearing nothing who thought perhaps his cock might also burn if it was left uncovered and who lay there on John's lounge chair, John sitting at his waist, and smiled and arched his back and slitted his eyes and moaned as John expertly, forefinger pressing into piss slit, brought up the young man's own white fluid to spread on top of the tanning lotion on his cock.

When the saucy young drinks waiter brought back John's tequila sunrise, he asked the older man if there was anything else he needed in such a nice way and with his fingers tracing John's cock through the bull's-eye Speedo that John, at last, let him bring his phallus out into the air—which was especially good for John, as now all eyes were on that and he could stop sucking in his stomach and stretching to tighten up his pec muscles. As the young man lowered his mouth over the bulb of John's cock and started flicking John's piss slit with his tongue, John sighed in satisfaction and reached for the proffered cock of a deliciously divine chocolate young man sitting close to him on the neighboring lounger.

"I would very much like to take this lovely cock elsewhere," the waiter murmured to John after John had come and he was still slowly stroking John's cock. "May I come to your room tonight, Mr. Pender?"

"Alas, Emilio," John said, trying to feign a face of deep regret but saying the words with the greatest of pleasure, "I have three engagements already this evening. And there are limits to what I can do. I do have an opening or two on the return trip from Bermuda, though."

John knew he was on top of the world, though, when, as he was departing the pool area—and right out there at midday, under the sun, rather than in a dark cabin—the delicious young man the captain had no doubt fucked the previous night came up and begged to ride John's cock—right there and then. John picked the sweet young thing up and settled his butt down on the flight of stairs going up to the bridge—where he could see the captain watching them. The young man licked his lips and spread his legs and hooked his heels over the railing at each side, as other young men gathered around, their eyes locked on the weapon John was wielding between his legs. All sighed—not just the beautiful young man—as John slowly fed his cock inside him and changed the angle so that his bulb was planted on the young man's prostate. Rub, rub rub, plunge, drag; rub, rub, rub, plunge, drag. The young man cried out in ecstasy and writhed under John's masterful attentions, and all of the other young men around murmured and fisted their own cocks.

John went on forever—rub, rub, rub, plunge, drag—and the gorgeous young man whimpered and weakened and started to babble and his legs went to rubber and other young men had to lean in to hold them up and out as they gazed down at the root of the thick cock moving in and out of the puckered hole— shallow, shallow, shallow, deep, draaaagg back to the sound of a weak moan. The young man came but John didn't stop. He was tired, but this was lesson time, his time to make his point. Rub, rub, rub, plunge, drag. Rub, rub, rub, plunge, back, plunge, back, plungebackplunge, and the young man cried out as he came again with John. Moans all around as one by one, all the other young men came too.

After that, there was no question that whenever John could get it up during the cruise, he would have a fresh conquest moaning for what he could give them. No one on the cruise cared after that that he had gray hair and a thickish waist and age spots and a few wrinkles and sagged a bit here and there and couldn't play pool volleyball or drink the younger guys under the table. What mattered was what he could do between their legs on top of the table. No one even subtly quizzed him on how much he was worth in dollars anymore. He had a monster, talented cock, and he could give a guy the master fuck of his life.

It was so heartening, John thought, that the youth of the day could see what was important in life once they'd tasted it.

* * * *

"You look worn out," Pete said.

"I feel that way too." John fought hard to keep the smile out of his voice. He sighed heavily, for effect.

"Found you were too old for a cruise like that, didn't you?"

"It about did me in, yes."

"Didn't I tell you it would be a waste of money?"

"You sure did," John said as he turned away from Pete and toward his computer screen. He couldn't hold back the grin any longer. Of course, on a basis of pure cost-efficiency analysis, it probably was pretty pricey. He figured he'd wound up spending $4,400 in all. He tried to compute it in his head. Was it twenty-eight or twenty-nine lays? Uh, no, he wasn't counting those three times on the beach on Bermuda. And not the blow jobs either. Must have been over a hundred dollars an ejaculation. But then the food was good and plentiful and fully covered too. And the drinks. Maybe he should have drunk more booze—but where would he have found the time? He had an apartment here, so he really couldn't discount on the use of the suite.

"You look like you haven't slept in a week."

"Nope. Didn't get much sleep out there on the ocean."

"Just a ridin' those waves, right?"

"Yep, just riding away. Riding, riding, riding." Expensive rides, yes. But they came with the feel of young flesh, and the sound of another man's moans and begging for him. The feeling of being young again himself, wanted—by young hunks, ones he could feel in real life. Pete's way of using the Gaycruiser Web site services meant he rode alone.

"Well, I told you so."

"Yep, you sure did." John tilted the computer screen away from Pete's adjacent desk. This was his good thing. He didn't want Pete getting ideas and horning in. And most of all right now he didn't want Pete seeing that he was signing up for

93

the fall cruise to the Bahamas on the *Poseidon's Spear*. It wouldn't be as expensive next time. Gaycruiser was offering him a professional discount.

And look, his profile on the Web site was lighting up like a Christmas tree. Requests for hookups—right here in Baltimore. So, maybe the cruise was going to be cost-effective after all.

Hidden Flute

It took three concerts for him to notice me. Luckily it was getting progressively warmer in Munich's spring. I had every reason to believe I'd have to attend the full season of the free outdoor concerts in the Hofgarten park before I could meet him. If I'd settled on this flutist in the fall instead, each time I had to come back would have been progressively worse.

It would have helped if I initially enjoyed flute music. I'd certainly had my fill of young men playing the flute professionally in Bavaria. I was fairly certain, though, that this was the young man for me.

He had an air of melancholy about him that I found alluring when matched with the mournful sound of his instrument, which, in his hand, was nothing like the flute music I'd heard before. I could see the attraction of him. He was probably in his mid twenties. He was small and willowy and had an angelic face. His eyes were a watery blue, his skin the glowing alabaster of the serious scholar, and he had a northern European blondness about him that was belied by jet black, curly hair on his head. It was this mystery about him that had attracted me to him in the first place—an incongruity in his appearance. This was accentuated the second concert I attended, where he managed quite well reading his music without the eyeglasses he wore for the first and third concerts.

Could it be, I wondered, that he was really a blond?

He seemed a young man hiding from something. At first I thought maybe it was from life itself he seemed so withdrawn into himself as he played his flute in concert. But then I thought it perhaps was something more earthborn, something that spoke to me in my quest. And thus I stopped attending on other orchestra performers and concentrated on this one.

He did notice me in the third concert—as I wanted him to. I sat as close to him as I could—in the seat next to the one I had occupied for the second concert. I would have sat in the very same seat if it had been available when I arrived for the concert. And I wore the same clothes for both concerts.

I watched him intently throughout the entire performance, and when he finally looked at me, with a startled look of recognition of someone there was no reason he should recognize, I smiled at him.

After the concert was over, I remained in my seat as those in the audience as well as those in the orchestra on the bandstand gathered their belongings and moved to depart.

The young man was slow to pack up his flute. I had noticed this in the first two concerts also. He moved slowly, deliberately, and I could see that he winced from time to time. He seemed to be suffering from some sort of malady that caused pain in the movement of his extremities. He was far too young to be arthritic, I thought. But I also thought that this added an attraction of vulnerability and mystery to the young man.

I wanted him. I wanted to take him in my arms and gently make love to him. But that was only a surface want. I wanted to crush and possess him—to bring passion to those eyes. He played his flute with deep passion; even I could tell that. But his face, as beautiful as it was, seemed dead even while he was playing. I wanted to bring passion to that face to match his music. And I wanted to do it by possessing his body and making him beg to have me inside him. I could see how he would have this effect on other men. I increasingly was sure he was the one I sought.

"You play beautifully."

"*Danke*," he said.

Ah, I thought. Not really Suddeutch—southern German—a northern dialect. More Nordic, as I thought.

He had thanked me, but he hadn't looked up from putting his flute away in its case. And he spoke in a soft, shy voice.

"I like it so much that I've come to all of your concerts in the park this season."

"I noticed." There was a blush on his cheeks, and he looked up at me and smiled. It wasn't making me want him any less.

"Would you . . . would you care to have a coffee with me in a café nearby?" I asked. "I would like to discuss your music further. I know of a quintet a banker has play on salon evenings that needs a good flutist. Perhaps—"

"Sorry, I have a commitment . . . a class . . . to attend. Sorry."

"Ah, you are a university student then? Studying music perhaps?"

"Yes. Yes, of course."

"Ah. I am a professor myself. But not music. My university has a very good music department, though. Perhaps—"

"I'm sorry. I'm late now. Maybe another time."

"Maybe no time, are you saying? Can you look at me, please?"

He looked up then, and I could see that I wasn't unattractive to him.

"You looked so sad," I continued. "I thought you might like to have a little company. Someone to talk to. You don't have many friends here, do you? You're not from here, are you?"

"I'm Dutch. And I do prefer staying to myself, yes. I don't mean to be rude, but—"

"I believe you would enjoy having a friend. I won't press. But I will come to all of your concerts until you decide you might like to join me for that coffee."

After the fifth concert he followed me to the Café Wein, where other musicians gathered and that specialized in playing Mozart in the background. It had threatened rain at the park as he was putting his flute away, and the elements gave him very little time to hedge when I offered him the coffee again.

"Your accent doesn't sound quite Dutch to me," I inserted into otherwise innocuous chitchat, which had included passing conversations with a couple of men I had paid to address me as "professor" and make remarks on my brilliance in musical critique.

"I've only really been to the Netherlands on holidays. I was born and raised in Central Africa. My family . . . ."

But he stopped there, his voice having choked up on the word family, and he turned his head from me. He didn't do so, though, quick enough for me not to see the tearing up in his eyes.

I moved deftly into another topic—on where he had traveled in the world. I might have asked him why he'd left Africa and come to be here in southern Germany. But I increasingly thought I knew, and it might not have gone well for me to pursue that point. I was sure I knew, but I was not positive. I needed to be positive.

"Have you given any thought to the quintet I mentioned? The banker pays well, and they are quite good—I've heard them several times."

"Yes, I might be interested, thanks."

Here was the crux. "I have the information in my rooms, which aren't far from here—in fact between here and the direction of your university. You could stop in and pick the contact number up."

"Or you could bring the information to the next concert," he countered.

"Alas I'm sure they will have filled the chair by then. There is another salon night soon, and they have little time."

When we reached the apartment I had let by the week, having arrived here from Africa myself not more than a month earlier, I sat him at my small dining table with a bottle of cold beer and retreated to my bedchamber. When I reemerged, I had changed into a short cotton robe and held a slip of paper with a number that would connect to one of the men I'd hired—who would tell him "So, sorry, we have found a flutist" on the off chance the young man would have an opportunity to call. And in the other hand was a bottle of excellent Scotch whiskey. Although the young flutist looked a bit shocked—and like a deer in the headlights of an automobile—he didn't rise from the table.

I set the paper and bottle down on the table and lifted his chin with my cupped hand so that his face was staring into mine. And I took a chance and took his lips in mine.

His mouth was dead at first, but slowly, hungrily he yielded to me. I had gambled that underneath that shell he was frustrated and wanted to lie with me. The kiss confirmed this.

He was paralyzed by the situation, though. He was trembling and tearing up and seemed not to be able to stand on his own when I pulled him up from the chair. He didn't resist, but he gave nothing of himself either.

I took him in my arms and carried him into the bedchamber and laid him on my bed. I stood over him and let the cotton robe I was wearing fall to the floor. He whimpered at the sight of my nakedness, which I knew was not displeasing to a man wanting to be fucked by another man. I could see a spark in his eyes now, but his lips were murmuring "No, please not . . ."

"Shush," I whispered. "Just relax. And let me comfort you. I know there is something. Something wrong. I don't think it is that you don't want me. Let me comfort you."

I lay down beside him on the bed and took him in my embrace. He didn't fight me, but, again, he made no move of acceptance either. Only detached acquiescence. I would not be defeated, though. I hummed to him and rocked him in my arms.

"When you can speak of it. Tell me. Tell me what is a barrier to us making love. I know you want to." I had moved my hand under the waistband of his trousers and briefs and had found assurance that he wanted me. "This tells me that you want me. You have lain with another man before, haven't you?"

"Yes." It sounded bitter, almost defiant.

"And men have made love to you, haven't they?"

"No." Even harder, more bitter.

"You have never had a man's cock inside you?"

"I didn't say that."

"Ah, you have been taken by force then. Is that it?"

"Yes."

99

"In Africa?"

"Yes."

I had opened his trousers and unbuttoned his shirt by now, and I was gently fondling him with my hands—the hand of the arm I was embracing him with was stroking a nipple and the other hand was gliding along his belly and down to his cock and balls. He was relaxing a bit and was softly moaning—although I'm not sure he even realized I was already preparing him. Or that he was letting me do it.

"Perhaps if you give voice to it, let the demons out, it would be the start of healing. I am not forcing you, am I?"

"No."

"And it is giving you pleasure, isn't it? Pleasure you haven't had in some time. Pleasure you need."

He didn't answer, but I didn't give him much time or opportunity to do so. I had moved my lips to his again, and he was opening to me, letting me possess him. And then, for the first time reciprocating in the kiss, hungrily sucking on my tongue and groaning. I could feel the melting of the iceberg that had been him in the engorging of his cock in my hand.

"Tell me," I whispered when I released his lips. I had to know for sure. "Tell me of this sadness and bitterness inside you."

He lay there for several minutes, not saying anything, but his eyes held mine and his hips were beginning to roll with my slow pumping of his cock with my fist.

I was going to fuck him. I knew that. And now he knew that as well—and he was resolved to it.

"Have you heard of William Jason? Major William Jason?" the young man suddenly asked.

"Yes, I believe so. Central Africa."

"Yes, when he and his regiment mutinied and took over the government, they paid special attention to the Dutch-descendent farmers."

"You? Your family?"

"Yes." It was a whisper.

"You don't have to tell me. You can just let me make love to you and make the memory of it go away," I murmured. And indeed, he didn't have to tell me. Now I knew for sure.

But having started, he let it out as if a mighty river had burst the damning of his soul. "As they lay in wait to attack our farm, they must have heard me practicing my flute. Otherwise I would have been dead too. Who would have known that the butcher, William Jason, was a classical music lover?"

He laughed an ugly, bitter laugh, and I took his lips in mine again to keep from losing him. I had retrieved a tube of lube from my nightstand that I had left there open and I was lubricating his channel with my fingers. And he was letting me do it.

When I released his lips, though, he continued with the story. "When I was the last one, cowering in a corner, the major pushed his way through the semicircle of soldiers backing me into the wall. He is a monster of a man, you know. Gigantic in every way. He fucked me for the first time then—brutally. Not caring that I had never done it before. Then he informed me that I played the flute divinely. He used that word. 'Divinely.' It was shocking to hear from the lips of such a monster. He said he was taking me back to the palace with him, and that I would play for him. And not just the flute."

"Shush. Enough. I want to make love to you now."

"He had a special chamber—more than one—that he'd set up in the basement of the palace. Of course, as far as I knew his predecessor had had the chambers too. I was strung up every which way over the next months—and taken in every way he could think of. He laughed once, telling me that all I needed to play the flute for him were my lips and my fingers. He broke everything else in my body in his rough sex torture. You may not have noticed, but I move slowly and deliberately. I am in nearly constant pain. That is what he gave me."

"I will be gentle. Here, this will be comfortable enough, won't it?" I had moved between his thighs with my knees. His legs were bent and I placed pillows under the small of his back to raise his hips to me. I presented the bulb of my cock at his now-loosened and lubricated hole and gently pressed in. He groaned for me, but he gripped the sides of my torso as I was hovered over him. And he moved his pelvis, drawing me inside him himself.

He sucked in his breath and moaned deeply as my cock head disappeared inside him. I held there. "Am I hurting you?"

"Yes. No. Please. Oh, god. Ohhh, ohhhh, ahhhh."

I was inside him and he was opening to me as I slowly sank deeper and deeper.

"I escaped," he said in a low, breathy voice. "Those who helped me, paid for it. My freedom was their death. Yet another guilt I must bear. But I was alive. I ran and ran. And I hid. I dyed my hair, changed my appearance as much as I could. Came to Europe to forge a new life."

"Relax. Go with me. I'll love all of those memories into the back of your mind."

I began to slow pump him.

"Oh, god, oh god, ahhhh."

Later I sat there in a chair, looking at the bed, as the young man slept the sleep of the fully satisfied, exhausted by a master cocking.

I almost regretted it, but there was nothing to be done about it now.

"What? I can't! Why?" he muttered as he slowly came to. "Why am I bound?"

His wrists were handcuffed through the strong slats of my headboard and his ankles were handcuffed as well.

"I'm sorry about that," I answered in a voice that I hoped conveyed as much regret as I felt. "I'm really sorry. But the Major sent me to find you. He wants you back."

* * * *

Later, as I sat alone in my rented room and finished off the bottle of Scotch, I made the decision that I needed to find another way to earn my money. I had become too hard, too uncaring. But now I had gone too soft to be of use to the clients who sought me out. I would, of course, tell the Major that I had scoured Munich for his flutist without luck—that he must have been given bad information, or that the young man had already moved on. I would tell him that I certainly was willing to follow up any other lead he might have, but that it probably wasn't worth the money he was paying.

Of all my regrets, the deepest one was not asking the young flutist where he would flee to next—so that there was always a chance I might meet, and have, him again. But if I knew the Major as well as I thought I did, it was probably best I really didn't know—in the likely event that the Major didn't believe me.

Luck of Henri

"Monsieur Arnaud, is that you back in the stall beyond Cleo? My, but you gave me a fright."

"Come closer, Henri. I have something to show you."

"It is so dark back here, sir. This is just where we keep the feed for the . . . Oh, Monsieur. What?"

"Come sit by me on this hay bale, Henri. Oh, don't . . . now I have you. No, don't struggle. Sit here beside me."

"Oh, Monsieur. We mustn't."

"I know you have wanted it, Henri. I can see the looks you give me. See how big it grows. Feel it. Here, don't resist. That is what you do to me. No, don't struggle. You are such a beautiful young man. It wants you. Neither of us can fight it anymore."

The stable lad was trembling in the overpowering embrace of his master's second son. But when next he started to speak, Arnaud Van Briand covered his mouth with his own, and while holding the younger man in thrall in the embrace of one arm, his other hand started unbuttoning and opening, gliding, searching flesh on increasingly yielding and revealing flesh. And encircling and slow-pumping to sounds of gasps and moans and shuddering as Henri, not so unwillingly now, gave up his seed.

"And now me," Arnaud whispered in the young man's ear.

"Oh, Monsieur, I don't think I could."

"Oh, I'm sure you can, Henri. But not like that. Me inside you."

"Oh, ohhhhh," Henri whimpered. "OHHHH!"

Arnaud had pushed the stable lad belly over on the hay bale and was crouched behind him now, his mouth plastered to the young man's virginal ass.

"Ohhhh," Henri gasped as he writhed under the older man's attention. He panted and groaned, but his hands went back to cup the back of Arnaud's bobbing head in acquiescence.

He shuddered and began to babble incoherently as Arnaud rose and pushed his chest into the young man's back.

Arnaud's lips were next to Henri's ear. "I'm going to give you now what you have been showing you wanted for weeks."

"Pleaaasse," Henri moaned.

"Please what, Henri?"

But Henri was at a loss for words. He didn't himself know what he wanted to happen now—or was too frightened and shocked to speak the truth.

So Arnaud spoke it for him.

"You want me, don't you, Henri? I saw you watching me do it to Didier. You want what I give to Didier, don't you?"

"Please, Monsieur."

"Say it, Henri. Or better yet, say that you don't want it. Now, in your next breath."

A pause, and then, "Oh, Monsieur, plea—. Oh, god, ohhhh, gooodd!"

And then Henri could do no more than cry out and pant and groan and moan as Arnaud's cock bulb made purchase and then pushed in, in, in, followed by a thick and deep journey that took Henri's breath away and reduced him to tears and babbling again.

And then, when Henri's channel was completely open to Arnaud's invasion, the gasps and moans began to change texture and tone, and soon Henri was working with Arnaud and turning his head and returning kiss for kiss.

"There. That's what you wanted, Henri. Admit it. You only needed to be freed of your burden," Arnaud whispered in the stable boy's ear when he had taken what he wanted. "You wanted it. Admit it."

"Yes," Henri whispered, full of shame, but somehow buoyant from the release of the mooning about he'd done these weeks. Curious and envious of Didier.

"And you are mine now?"

"Yes, Monsieur. Oh, yes."

"And you will remain loyal and faithful to me as your family has to mine for centuries?"

"Yes, Monsieur. Oh, yes."

"Do you feel me rising again?"

"Yes, Monsieur."

"And do you want it again?"

"Yes, Monsieur."

* * * *

Arnaud Van Briand most likely would have been pushing on to new endeavors and climes anyway. A second son in a rich, clever, and ruthless French merchant family in which the father never intended to die and the robust first son inhaled every bit of responsibility and privilege he could—and both keeping the second son in their sights and at a distance—had few prospects in the family business.

For that reason Arnaud had been trained in electrical engineering. And he had just finished his involvement in a project that electrical engineers dreamed of. It was 1889, and the Eiffel Tower, the centerpiece of the Paris Exposition Universelle, had just been dedicated. It almost missed its dedication date, though, a near-fatal delay that was put to Arnaud's debit. So, whereas such a project should have made his career, it actually choked it off in the bud.

No one in French society at the Van Briands' level cared two figs that Arnaud liked to debauch young men, so that wasn't what put him on the ship to Africa. And at that level, they certainly didn't care when he decided to dabble in the lower classes—and even very close to his family's own chateau.

But, despite the many generations of service of the family of Henri, the young man who served the Van Briands as a stable boy, to the Van Briand family who lived in the chateau a half day's ride from Paris, Henri's father, a florid man with a deep sense of pride and justice, decided that neither Arnaud nor Henri should live for what they were found doing. The Van Briands barely noticed any hint of scandal—indeed, it wasn't any form of scandalous behavior at the heights at which they lived. But they did notice the murderous looks and brandishing of knives Henri's father was putting on display.

So, just because it was easy for them, they simply booked Arnaud passage to Central Africa and quietly saw to it that Henri's father suffered a fatal accident in the field several weeks after Arnaud was gone.

Arnaud took Henri with him—in service as both a body servant and a body to service.

If Arnaud had not been a slightly superstitious man, his whole life may have taken a different casting.

Although he was fond of Henri and Henri was a convenient bed companion when Arnaud was unable to debauch another young man along his path, Arnaud didn't think that his father and elder brother had been as generous as they might have been in the monetary support they had given for his journey and his setting up a new life in Central Africa. So, having heard there was a lucrative trade in young, well-formed European men, Arnaud's plan had been to sell Henri in the slave markets of Dakar in the French West African colony of Senegal to which Arnaud was sailing.

However, there was a gnarled old gypsy woman on the ship who accosted Arnaud and insisted that he must have his fortune told—or he would be cursed. Arnaud believed just enough to think it inconvenient to be cursed for not taking a half hour's entertainment on a ship moving ever so slowly down the African coast.

"You do not travel alone," the old crone said after examining Arnaud's hand for moments—moments that he found considerably dismaying as the woman did not appear to have washed in the previous decade.

Her statement, however, took Arnaud aback. He had not allowed Henri on deck, and the gypsy woman would not have been permitted in the cabin area where Henri was being kept either. Arnaud had only encountered her because he was searching below decks—slumming, as it were—in search of the wine room other passengers had purported the ships officers were keeping to themselves.

"No, but what does my lady have to do concerning my fortune?" he asked.

"Mistress it may be, but I see no lady," the old woman muttered. And then she cackled. "But mistress you must keep beside you—always. This one is your luck. It will be folly to part with this one."

"Why would I—?"

"It is what you plan, is it not?" And then, before Arnaud could react, the old crone snapped up the coin he had laid down but had had no intention of actually giving her, and had disappeared into the shadows of the below decks.

Arnaud did not believe the old woman, but the small sliver of superstition that lived within him made him decide that Henri would be much more valuable to him working in the diamond mines that Arnaud had the notion to explore in Central Africa than to be some tribal chieftain's catamite. Besides, Arnaud had just remembered that he never had developed the knack of dressing himself.

* * * *

Two years hence, Arnaud was to congratulate himself for keeping Henri with him—by that time having convinced himself that neither an old gypsy crone nor his own slight superstition had a jot to do with his decision. While Arnaud lolled on the veranda of the Gentlemen's Club in Dakar, Henri had found and brought back an amazingly large cache of uncut rough diamonds.

Arnaud's own efforts, however, had not been totally absent. For one, he had managed to woo, bed, and acquire another young man, by the name of Bertie, who had been left adrift at the Gentleman's Club by an inconsiderate titled British ne'er-do-well, who had, through no effort of his own, outlived his hardnosed father and been begged to return to the side of his indulgent mother in a cold castle near the Scottish border.

Arnaud took Bertie for a young man abandoned, innocent, and vulnerable, which is the way Arnaud liked to take young men. In this particular case, it was also just how Bertie wanted to be taken.

When Bertie's titled momma's boy was saying his good-byes and his somewhat shallow regrets to Bertie at the coach entrance of the club, Bertie made sure all saw the plight he was in by morosely climbing the steps, entering the bar, and collapsing at a table in suppressed sobs.

Although Arnaud wasn't the only one who was quite willing to give Bertie succor, he was the first one to the table. He sat down by the young man and put a reassuring palm on his shoulder. "There, there, are you all right, young man? Have you lost someone? Nothing is worth those tears on such a handsome face. Anything I can do to help? May I stand you a drink at least?"

"You're too kind, Monsieur," Bertie responded in a weak little voice. He placed a hand on Arnaud's knee. "Yes, if you wouldn't mind. Maybe a small sherry—or a beer. So that I can think about what is to become of me."

Arnaud signaled to the bartender, who didn't need to be told what Bertie liked to drink. He took only the best Scotch, and he took it neat.

Arnaud was running his fingers through the thick, blond curls of Bertie's head. He'd wanted to do this for weeks, ever since the young man and his self-possessed sponsor had arrived.

"My . . . friend has been called home—back to England. He is in grief over his father's death. And when he was in that condition, I couldn't possibly tell him that my own funds haven't arrived as scheduled. Oh, I don't know what I'm to do."

"Perhaps I can be of assistance," Arnaud murmured. "You could stay in my rooms if you wish . . . just until your funds arrive, of course."

"Oh, Monsieur, I couldn't possibly—"

"Well, perhaps we can talk to the hotel management and see if there are other possibilities—extension of credit, perhaps,"

Arnaud said as he started to rise from the table, but Bertie clutched at the older man as if in desperation.

"Oh, Monsieur. I feel so faint. Perhaps we could just sit here for a while more."

"If you feel faint, why don't you come to my room just for a lie down?"

"Well, perhaps."

Once in the room, Arnaud helped Bertie to his bed and stretched him down on his back.

"Air. I could use some more air," Bertie murmured in a breathy voice.

"It's these tight clothes. Here, let me help you." Arnaud unbuttoned Bertie's shirt and exposed a fine young chest. He also loosened Bertie's belt.

"Oh, you are so kind, Monsieur. My heart is still palpitating so. Here lay your hand on my breast, you can feel it beating madly. This is such a nice room. Is this the only bed?"

The rest unfolded as it naturally would, both Arnaud and Bertie willing it to move in that direction, and Bertie proved to be an expert at the fuck—to Arnaud's great delight, although Arnaud hadn't been fooled for long concerning the nature of Bertie's "friendship" with the departed Englishman.

Bertie cried out best in passion when Arnaud laid him sideways on the bed, on his back, and spread the young man's legs and crouched over Bertie's torso with his own and pumped his ass hard and deep at the side angle. And they tried several positions before they arrived at this "favorite."

Now when Henri returned on his brief visits from the diamond fields, he was made to sleep on the floor of Arnaud's room, as there was room in the bed only for Arnaud and Bertie. Still, if Arnaud was feeling especially affectionate, after he'd fucked Bertie to sleep, he'd slip out of bed and pull Henri up on all fours on the oval rug in the center of the room and take him like a dog.

All of this changed when Henri brought his first handful of large, rough diamonds back to Dakar. Then Arnaud booked a separate room for Bertie—and when Henri was in town, he slept with Arnaud and was attended to when Arnaud returned from Bertie's room.

When Henri had collected a small fortune in diamonds, the three of them booked for a return sail to France. Bertie and Henri registered as Arnaud's two sons—for Arnaud's convenience.

Arnaud hadn't been a complete lump while Henri was gathering him a fortune in the diamond fields. He'd spoken enough with the gentlemen at the club—many of them diamond merchants or assessors—to have picked up some knowledge of the diamond trade. He'd learned at least enough to bluff his way in the diamond trade as he—and, indeed, his whole family back through generations—had done in all of the trades and skills they had dabbled in.

Thus fortified, Henri was enlisted to sew the raw diamonds he had collected in the seams of Arnaud's great coat and decided that, along with Henri, who served him, and Bertie, with whom he was now totally sexually besotted, Arnaud would rejoin his family and set up a diamond merchant operation in Paris.

* * * *

"But surely you've seen them, Monsieur . . . with the sheik who came onto the ship in Morocco . . . and his son."

"Nothing of the sort, Henri. Stop speaking of Bertie this way this very instant. You've had nothing good to say about him from the start. You're jealous, that's all. Stop it this instant and go fetch my tea as I asked."

Not only had Henri seen Bertie with the two Arab princes, but he stopped along the deck en route to the kitchen and looked into the porthole of the sheik's cabin now, and he saw them at it still. The sheik's son was reclining on the fainting couch and Bertie's head and shoulders were invisible under that robe-like tunic the Arab was wearing and a globular orb could quite clearly be seen between the young prince's legs were his crotch was, bobbing up and down. The expression on the young Arab's face left no doubt what Bertie was doing under there. And there was even less doubt what the old sheik himself was doing. His pelvis was presented at Bertie's bare behind and he was holding both of Bertie's hips and was thrusting at Bertie with his midsection.

But no matter how often Henri tried to tell Arnaud that Bertie was not being loyal to him, Arnaud just was not willing to listen to that.

Nor did he claim to believe it once they were at the Van Briand chateau outside Paris and Henri espied Arnaud's older brother pumping his meaty pelvis in and out between Bertie's spread legs at the edge of the brother's bed one afternoon while Arnaud was in Antwerp.

That Arnaud was getting wise to this himself, though, could have had something to do with his sudden decision that he wanted to be a diamond merchant in the Americas—in New York City, he hoped—rather than in Paris after a mere four weeks of trying to ply his trade in France.

There were other contributing factors, of course. Arnaud had hoped to enjoy some backing from his family, but as soon as he had stepped foot in France, they had all tried to borrow money from him. The Van Briands hadn't been completely honest—or clever enough in this generation, for that matter—in their own business and financial dealings. And the French had reached the end of their tolerance of these erstwhile nobles.

And beyond that, Arnaud had found the diamond traders of France, Belgium, and Holland to be far more knowledgeable than he had hoped.

"I can get three times that amount for this stone in New York," he had told one merchant in Bruges, having had to search that far afield in short order as he quickly exhausted those who would deal with him.

"No doubt you can," the man had said dryly. "The Americans aren't the brightest stars in the sky concerning the diamond trade yet."

It had been meant as an insult, of course, but Arnaud saw opportunities wherever there was a glimmer of them, and he started planning his move, with his two "sons," to America. Arnaud could not bring himself to part with Bertie and the possibility that Henri was to be his lucky charm someday just could not be shaken out of the back of his mind.

There was another factor that impelled Arnaud to move on from France, but he was so enthralled with Bertie that he hadn't seen the real danger of that factor until he was almost run down on his horse in the Cherbourg forest and murdered by a man he recognized as a relative of Henri's but, too late, saw the hate and murder in the man's eyes.

It had been twenty-three years since Arnaud had hurriedly left France for Central Africa three steps ahead of Henri's father and the suddenly combined ire of the families of the many young men Arnaud had debauched in his early sexual career. And although Arnaud considered himself a new man when he returned to France after an absence of two decades, the young men he had debauched—some mostly because he had then cast them off and deserted them—had not left France or escaped the gossip about what they had let another man do to them.

Thus, there were families and no-longer-young men aplenty ready and willing to take their long-festering revenge on Arnaud Van Briand.

Four weeks after arriving in France, Arnaud and his two "sons" were on the move again, booked on the maiden voyage of the passenger liner "of the century," which departed from Southampton, England, on April 10, 1912, and would pick up passengers later that evening in Cherbourg, France, and push off ultimately for New York from Queenstown, Ireland, on the afternoon of the 11th.

At 10:00 PM on the 10th, after a hectic two hours of boarding at Cherbourg and the bands-playing, confetti-flying steam away of the new passenger ship from the pier at Cherbourg, Arnaud called Henri to him.

"Bertie is in the bar at the lounge, Henri. Kindly fetch him to my side, please."

"Bertie is not in the lounge, Monsieur," Henri patiently replied.

"I left him there myself."

"Bertie departed right after you left. He went with one of the ship's officers to the crew's quarters. I am quite sure that the ship's officer is already fucking Bertie right now—and that Bertie is quite pleased that he is doing it."

"Henri!"

"I'm sorry, Monsieur. I can't take watching you being taken for a fool anymore. You must wake up to the fact that Bertie opens his legs for anyone who he fancies or who can provide him advantage."

Enraged, Arnaud unbuckled his belt and drew it out of his trousers and began beating Henri with it. Henri sank to the floor under the blows and cried out but did nothing to try to stay the hand of the man who had been his master from childhood. In the process Arnaud's trousers fell off his legs and his rage turned into lust and he set upon Henri and fucked him hard and roughly on the floor of the slightly pitching ship.

Finished, Arnaud fell back on one of the ship's bunks and stared expectantly at the door of the cabin as he panted until his breathing became regular and, at length, he slept.

Henri dragged himself up from the floor, moaning, and collapsed on the bunk opposite to Arnaud's and kept vigil on Arnaud through the night. He didn't bother to look at the cabin door, as he knew it wouldn't open—or, if it did, Bertie would be full of spice and unapologetic. Henri also knew that whether or not Arnaud flew into a rage over this, it would be Henri, not Bertie, who would get the beating.

Now, twenty-two years after Arnaud had first debauched him, Henri was ready to accept that nothing would change here. And suddenly he had no desire to go to America whatsoever. In the wee hours of the morning, as the ship docked in Queenstown for its short, last stop in the old world before sailing to the new world, Henri stood, took up his great coat and bag, and left the cabin.

When Arnaud awoke, he was alone in the cabin. He staggered up and went in search of his "sons." Bertie wasn't hard to find. He was breakfasting at the captain's table and was receiving close, jolly attention from more than one of the ship's officers, who had their arms around Bertie's shoulder and hands on his crotch. Bertie waved jauntily at Arnaud when their eyes met, but his eyes immediately slipped off to devour those of yet another hearty blond in pure whites who had a hand possessively on Bertie's thigh.

Arnaud rushed back to the cabin to see if there was any sort of clue where Henri might have gone. Seeing Henri's bag and great coat gone, it dawned on Arnaud that Henri must have left the ship.

"Well, all right, you ungrateful cur," Arnaud muttered to the four walls of the cabin. "After all of these years, you desert me. Just see if I care."

But then he took another look at the two great coats hanging on the hook on the wall, and his eyes opened wide in fear and consternation. There was Bertie's flamboyant one and there . . . there was the one slightly too small for Arnaud.

Henri had taken his great coat by mistake. Or was it a mistake at all? All of those raw diamonds sewn into the seams of Arnaud's great coat—by Henri himself. What were the chances that Henri had taken the wrong coat?

Arnaud's mind was screaming, "Thief!" His fortune was on the run.

Instinctively, without a thought to any consequences, Arnaud ran out of the cabin, along the deck, and to the gangplank leading down to the Queenstown dock. Scrabbling down the gangway, he ran into the streets of Queenstown and started searching high and low through the pubs and hotel lobbies near the docks for Henri—and, more pointedly for his great coat.

At a bit beyond 2:00 in the afternoon, Arnaud found Henri in a pub, drinking his third beer and trying to stitch his circumstances back together again.

"Henri!" Arnaud cried out accusingly.

"Monsieur Arnaud," Henri said in surprise, clutching his coat about him. "Why have you sought me out? You have said I am nothing but bad luck and a nuisance for you. You have your Bertie and your new life in America. You must get back to the docks. Your ship will—"

"My coat. You took my coat, thief," Arnaud cried out. "The diamonds. You took the diamonds!"

"Your coat? This is my . . . oh, Monsieur, you are right this is your coat. In my haste . . . I did not know."

Henri's last statement came in a totally silent drinking room that, until Arnaud had cried out the word "diamonds," had been filled with boisterous talk and raucous laughter.

All eyes were turned to Arnaud and Henri, the interest of all was piqued, lips were wetted.

And above all, floating out over the sounds of the street outside, was the great blast of the horn as the greatest passenger ship in the world, the *Titanic*, cleared the Queenstown harbor for its momentous maiden—and last—voyage to New York.

Elsewhere in the world there was an old gypsy woman who stopped suddenly in the process of threading her needle, inclined her head at the knowledge that her fortune for Arnaud Van Briand had finely come to fruition, and then cackled a happy laugh and returned to her sewing.

Oblivion

"And I don't believe there's any place like Bar Harbor in the late summer. There's a beach just below my family cottage there where some of the hottest men come that time of the year. You'd fit in very well there. So, we really must . . ."

Tim was looking out on the street from where he and Howard were sitting at the sidewalk café on Wisconsin Avenue. There was a man across the busy-traffic street, in front of the Bethesda Residence Inn, who was walking two Cavalier spaniels. Slender figure, but broad shoulders. Straight as a ramrod. Tim bet the man kept his body in great shape and was doing well with the battle against time. Expensive-looking suit. He looked almost European. Gray sideburns but his hair still auburn on top—and every hair in place. He reeked of money—and of exquisite taste, given the choice in dogs. Tim liked pedigreed dogs. He liked pedigreed men too—and older. Not too old to cock well, but a bit past forty at least.

Tim imagined the man stripped down to a Speedo and playing with his dogs in the surf on a beach—somewhere up north, Maine maybe. But while it was still warm enough to swim in the ocean. He liked the cut of the man, slender at the waist, but a well-muscled chest and biceps—at least that's how Tim imagined him. Hair on the chest, but in an intriguing cascade down from underneath both pecs, down a flat belly, and curling into the low-rise waistband of the blue Speedo. Salt and pepper hair. A nice bulge at the basket and good, strong, firm legs. Tim bet the man ran regularly.

The beach was one of those exclusive places that rich residents of weathered wood-shingled, rambling mansions they called their weekend cottages banded together to keep for the use of a small tight community that only appeared from the city three or four times a year. The houses lined a bluff well above the sandy beach, and if you stretched your towel out where Tim envisioned he had, you could be in the sun but away from the prying eyes on the decks of the houses above. It was a place where there was hardly any beach traffic during the week—mainly the servants in the houses above with nothing to do for weeks on end until receiving notice that the masters of the house would be there. Tim only thought of the male servants. The women would be busy actually doing something—too busy to come down to the beach. These were mainly chauffeurs and gardeners and handymen—hot young men who shared the secret of cushy, nondemanding jobs with their fuck buddies. They were mostly what could be seen on this beach during the week. And then young men like Tim who had heard of the hot men on this private beach and sneaked in for some action of their own.

Tim is lying on his towel, his attention split between the elegant older man playing with his Cavalier spaniels in the surf and two young men up the beach, who have laid out one large towel and are already stretched along each other's bodies, facing each other, and kissing and touching. Other than these men, the beach is deserted. And such a beautiful, sunny, warm day. It is a wasted week day—well, for everyone but Tim and these other guys on the beach. No doubt the beautiful weather wouldn't hold into the weekend when at least a few of the "cottages" above would be occupied.

Tim has taken off his own bathing suit, seeking that all-over tan. He's turned toward the ocean, sitting, with legs spread and forearms on raised knees. The older man in the surf turns and looks at him and then up the beach at the couple, where Speedos have already been shucked and the two are turned to each other on their sides, the hands of both of them busy between their bodies, their lips plastered to each other.

The man smiles and starts to walk toward Tim. Tim spreads his legs further and reaches down and cups his balls and cock with a hand, giving the man a sultry smile. The man stops on the beach at the line where the surf reaches its highest, a line changing from the dark tan of wet sand to the dry, white sand of the upper beach, a line demarcated by a band of small, mostly broken up sea shells. There, in that spot, the man slowly strips off his Speedo, and Tim swallows hard and moans at the sight of how beautiful the man's body is and how well-equipped he is. All power and grace, aged extremely well. As the man stands there, Tim goes to half erection, lifting it in his cupped hand as it lengthens and thickens so the man at the tide's edge gets a good view of Tim's arousal. Then he arches his torso back and spreads his legs wider and gives the man a saucy little look.

The Cavalier spaniels are bounding happily around the man as he starts to walk again, slowly, but deliberately, toward Tim. As the man reaches Tim, he kneels on the towel between Tim's spread legs and buries his fists in the sand at each side of Tim's chest. They hold there momentarily, staring into each other's eyes, conveying just what each wants. Then the man dips his face down to Tim's and Tim opens his lips for the kiss and sighs at the sweet taste of the man's mouth.

After a sweet kiss, the man's face moves further down and his mouth closes over Tim's cock. Tim sighs and closes his eyes.

The spaniels lay down at each side of the blanket and start panting happily. Tim hears the panting but takes a few moments to realize that it isn't just the spaniels. He is panting as well. The man's face is back, pressing into Tim's, and his tongue invades Tim's mouth and moves in and out, deeper into the cavity with each renewed invasion. More insistent, more brutal, more possessing. Fucking Tim's mouth cavity with his tongue. Tim gags and is finding it hard to breathe, but he doesn't want the man to stop. He opens his mouth as wide as he can, wanting the man to climb inside and take him completely.

One of the man's hands is wrapped around Tim's cock and is squeezing and stroking it. Tim moans and moves his hands around to the man's back, palming his shoulder blades and pulling the man's torso down to his chest, seeking to merge their bodies, make them one. The man's now fully erect and very proud cock is rubbing up and down on Tim's belly and is dueling with Tim's own cock. He traps both cocks with a hand and strokes them together.

No lover like an experienced lover, Tim thinks as he jerks and ejaculates for the first time. And only an experienced lover knows that there is more to come, if properly coaxed.

The man pulls away from fucking Tim's mouth with his tongue and his mouth moves down to the hollow of Tim's neck, where his tongue traces the throbbing vein there. Tim looks over toward the other men on the beach to see that one is on his belly on the towel and the other has mounted him, straddling his hips between his legs. His hands are on the other man's shoulder blades and his bulbous buttocks are flexing and releasing and moving languidly back and forth between the other man's cheeks.

Tim's own man has moved his lips to Tim's nipples, but his dick is still stroking Tim's belly.

Tim moans and whispers something and the man whispers back. Tim reaches over into the beach bag beside the blanket. One of the spaniels leans his muzzle over to Tim's hand, and he licks the tip of Tim's finger. Tim smiles and pets the spaniel on the muzzle but then he jerks a bit and arches his back and lets out a moan. The spaniel has turned his muzzle away. There is another tongue giving Tim attention, though. The man has moved down and wrapped his strong arms around Tim's thighs and parted and lifted them and his tongue is invading Tim's ass channel.

Tim turns his head to guide his hand into his beach bag in search of the condoms and lubricant he has placed there. The young men down the beach are going at it hot and heavy now, the dominating man having brought the other up on his knees and wrapped his arms around the other's chest. The bottom has arched his back into the chest of the top and reached back and cupped the back of the head of his assaulter. The top is banging the bottom hard in loud, slapping sounds that reach their way to Tim on the sea breeze along with the cries of the young man being deep fucked.

The cries of passion are becoming louder, more distinct, and in stereo. It takes Tim a moment to realize that some of those cries are his, as the man is crouched over his chest again, his cock head has gained entry inside Tim's channel, and his hard tool is beginning to thrust deeper, harder, deeper, harder, deeper . . .

". . . and the yacht's just up in Baltimore. We could take the sea route to Bar Harbor. I've just had the vessel refurbished. I think you'd really like what I've done with the captain's cabin. There are mirrors—even over the bed, and . . ."

"Uh huh, nice," Tim murmured. He could feel the toes of Howard's socked foot nudging up under the hem of his trousers and rubbing against his shin.

Tim had first met Howard at the law firm where Tim, still in law school, was clerking. Howard apparently was some sort of important client—at least everyone had been told to hup to on that day when Howard came in. There were more senior partners sitting at hopeful attention in the conference room that day than Tim had ever seen there before.

They had been at it—all with their coats off and looking like they were in a disaster-relief planning session, all except for Howard Crandal, who sat there in his expensive three-piece suit, cut to his brawny, Zeus-like body, and perfectly groomed gray hair and manicured nails on his beefy, gold-banded fingers, looking all tanned and relaxed. The disaster relief image had come to Tim's mind because that's what he'd heard one senior partner tell another that they would have to do around here if they lost the Crandal account.

Tim had been called from the file room with some files they needed in the conference room. As he walked across the floor to the head of the table, where the managing partner was sitting, Tim felt Howard Crandal's eyes follow him. He thought he recognized that look.

He became sure he had correctly assessed the look Crandal had given him in the law firm's conference room more than a week later when Tim next saw Crandal.

Law school was expensive and Tim had expensive habits. It was a good thing he was a looker and had a great body too, because he was using that in a second job to make ends meet.

Tim was a dancer in the Green Lantern, a gay bar off Wisconsin Avenue, on the outskirts of the town of Bethesda that had been swallowed by the creeping tentacles of the greater Washington, D.C., metropolitan area. Tim danced a pole in a G-string on a small stage there for three sets a night, two nights a week. He also, if everything seemed right, would let a patron fuck him in one of the cubicles behind the stage between sets. He made more money these two nights than he did from his part-time job at the law firm. It all helped to keep him in law school—and, he thought, was better than what most of the other students were doing to stay in school. And he didn't have parents who would subsidize him.

One of the other dancers asked him one night how he could do this, considering what he wanted to do in life and, in particular, how he could let some of the older guys who came to the club fuck him. Tim thought on that for days before tracking the other dancer down and telling him that, first, he liked older guys fucking him. But, beyond that, if they were slobs and for those times he was dancing the pole and guys were wolf whistling and making suggestions and touching him wherever they could reach before a bouncer intervened, Tim just turned his mind off and thought of being someplace else and doing something else. He just drifted off into oblivion. The other dancer just gave Tim a funny look, no doubt having forgotten he even asked. But Tim was studying for the law. He liked to pin things down—when he wasn't daydreaming, of course.

Howard Crandal and he had encountered each other for the second time because Crandal had come into the Green Lantern while Tim was doing one of his stints on the pole. They didn't do more than make eye contact and both do a double take at seeing each other in this venue, but at that instant, Tim remembered the look Crandal had given him while he walked the carpet alongside the conference table back at the law firm, and Tim knew what Crandal was and what he wanted.

So, when Tim went back to the dressing room at the end of his last set, he wasn't at all surprised to see the message sent backstage to him—in pen on a bar napkin—proposing that Tim go have a coffee with Crandal at the outdoor café across the street from the Bethesda Residence Inn the next afternoon at 3:00 PM. Crandal was definitely in Tim's zone of good-looking, well-built, rich old guys, so he'd shown up as scheduled.

It wasn't a real good venue for Tim. He had a hard time focusing when there was a lot going on around him, and Wisconsin Avenue in Bethesda in the midafternoon was one very busy place.

He smiled at Crandal, who smiled back at him and augmented the toe rubbing on Tim's calf with a hand dropped to Tim's thigh.

"The bed I had put into the owner's cabin is king sized and it has a vibrator. Those aren't as popular as they once were. I can't really understand why . . ."

"Um humm," Tim murmured. The man walking his Cavalier spaniels across the street had moved on now, but Tim felt someone watching their table, and when he looked back toward the door into the café's interior space he saw that there was a young, handsome guy about his own age, looking intently at he and Howard from just the next table and taking in everything Crandal was talking about with a funny, intense look on his face.

But there, beyond that guy, Tim's eyes focused on the host at the reservations table just outside the door into the café. He was maybe in his late forties. Tall, well-muscled. Sort of a Greek look about him. And dressed in some sort of uniform.

" . . . has a full crew, so we wouldn't even have to come up for air before we'd passed Long Island," Crandal was saying.

"Yes, interesting," Tim offered.

They had exchanged looks even as Tim was walking up the gangplank onto the cruise ship he was taking out of Baltimore Harbor for a long weekend cruise to Bermuda. The officers of the crew were standing in a long line of pristine-white uniforms on the rail three decks above the gangplank. The one with the most gold braiding on his uniform caught Tim's eye, and they exchanged interested glances in a way that Tim had learned to recognize oh so well.

Even then it was a surprise to Tim when he received the invitation to sit at the Captain's table on the first night out to sea. The captain turned out to be that man who had been wearing the most gold braiding on his uniform that afternoon while the passengers were embarking.

The captain was tall and well-built. He was maybe in his late forties and had the look of a Greek god about him, a mature one, though, a regular Zeus. He certainly was in full command on this ship. The rest of the crew seemed to scuttle around doing his bidding without him even having to give a verbal command.

Tim is sitting beside him at the table, obviously a place of honor, and the other passengers at the table are looking speculatively at Tim, wondering what manufacturing mogul he's the son of. Tim feels the socked toe work itself under the hem of his trousers and move up and rub against his shin. When Tim feels a strong hand squeezing his thigh, he turns his face toward the captain, who is giving him a piercing look.

"After dinner I will show you the captain's cabin and we will fuck." It is whispered in Tim's ear, but it isn't a request. Tim knows it's a command. Two of the captain's officers are standing near the captain's table and giving Tim a look that tells him in no uncertain terms that out here on the open seas the captain will have what he wants.

Tim stops inside the door into the captain's cabin and is caught short, standing there in awe. Facing him is the foot of a gigantic four-poster bed, set in an alcove. What catches his attention, though are the mirrors—on the walls on each side wall of the alcove, on the back wall, and even on the ceiling above the bed.

He shudders and leans back into the captain, who is standing close in behind him, kissing him in the hollow of his neck, his arms wrapped around Tim, and his hands working the buttons on Tim's shirt and then the buckle and zipper of his trousers. And then his cock. Holding Tim there and stroking his cock, both of them watching in the mirrors, until Tim ejaculates.

The captain is standing over Tim, the gold braid once cascading down the front and sides of his pristine-white jacket now binding Tim's wrists to the headboard above Tim's head and his ankles high up on the posters at the bottom of the bed. The captain is naked from the waist down, a gigantic erect phallus curving up from his belly. He's still wearing his jacket, but it is open in front, revealing a deep, strong-muscled chest.

The captain is asking how Tim likes his chest. Has he ever seen such a barrel chest, the captain asks. He says it's because he is a champion swimmer, that it has given him the breath power and stamina to go for hours. He says Tim will like that, and he laughs and Tim cries out as the captain's cock breaches Tim's channel ring, and the captain starts to breath in and out and stroke in and out, in and out, in long, deep, rhythmic strokes, making Tim imagine he is in a scull listening to the rhythmic cadence of the strokeman's call.

The world is in motion, and it takes Tim several moments to realize that they haven't hit rough seas but that the bed itself is vibrating. The captain is grinning down at him and stroking to the rhythm of the vibrating bed, digging deeper and deeper, the cadence picking up. Tim ejaculating again and begging for mercy, but none coming. Stroke, stroke, stroke. Thump, thump, thump.

"Sir, sir, are you all right. Are you having a seizure of some sort? Should we call someone?"

Tim returned to full consciousness, suddenly aware that he was gripping the table top with white-knuckled fists and thumping it up and down on the brick surface of the outdoor café. The waitress also was gripping the table top, trying to hold it steady and to keep the china on top of it from tumbling to the ground.

"Sir, are you OK?" the waitress repeated. When Tim loosened his grip on the table top, so did she, and she handed forth a table check. "Sir, the older gentlemen said you'd take care of the tab for the coffees. Are you OK now?"

Tim turned his head this way and that way, fighting to bring his focus back to the sidewalk café on Wisconsin Avenue. Howard Crandal was gone from the table now—as was the handsome young man who had been so attentive at the neighboring table.

He took the check from the waitress, but he couldn't stand up for several minutes. He found that he had ejaculated in his trousers and was still half hard.

Separate Vacations

"Charlotte wants to do Florence and Venice and take a cruise in the Adriatic."

"Sounds good. I'll take the butter please."

"She doesn't want to go alone, but Andy has no interest in art at all."

"No, he doesn't. That's for sure."

"You'd probably be bored stiff too."

"Yep, I would. Dinner's good—as always."

"Thanks. They were just putting the kale out at the market. I couldn't resist. Anyway, Charlotte wants someone to go with her, and I think a sisters' vacation would be just what we need. Our lives have grown apart and I feel like I hardly know her anymore."

I turned my eye to the back garden through the sliding glass doors out onto the deck. I didn't want her to see the smile on my face. "I think it's a splendid idea. We used to do separate vacations now and then—and I think it did us both a world of good. Tell Charlotte you'd love to go with her. Two, three weeks?"

"Three, I think. The cruise itself is ten days, she says."

"Go for it, hon."

I continued looking at the azaleas at their peak in the soft hours moving into twilight. Indeed it had been far too long since the last separate vacations. I'd supposedly gone to D.C. on a Smithsonian crawl while she went to London with her sorority sisters from college. And I had gone. But just not right away. Tennis with Samir. A hard-fought battle on a sweltering day where we'd both wound up "skins," and I ultimately lost in the third set because I was looking at his brown, well-muscled torso and his dancer's flexibility more than where the ball was being returned. Then we were fucking in the backseat of my Mercedes sedan at the back edge of the club parking lot, me riding his cock hard, him licking the sweat off my chest and chewing on my nipples. The first weekend of the vacation I found myself in my bed—Judy's and my bed—with Samir, young, virile, and hung, teaching me sexual exhaustion. Then I did go to D.C., Samir in tow, and spent more time sheathing his churning cock at the Key Bridge Marriott than visiting the museums on the mall. I was sore and unable to close my legs when Judy flew back from London—but I was purring like a sleek Persian cat. Best vacation ever.

But that was three years ago. Both of us retired now, Judy and I found that there was no reason we couldn't schedule our vacations together.

Another chance now. But a pity that Samir went back to Beirut nearly two years ago. I'll have to think. I've never had to look for it before. But it's been a long time. I'm not the young man I once was, although I've done what I could to hold off time. I think the gray hair suits me even better than the chestnut brown—and I may have thickened a bit, but it's not fat. Judy clearly still finds me sexy. She couldn't be hiding her responses in bed, and I've heard her girlfriends talk of their envy of her. Some of them have even been brazen enough to suggest a side sampling to me—when Judy wasn't listening, of course.

There's Daren out at Edgeworth. We had our fling before Samir strutted into my life, demanding my full attention. Luscious and exotic and so cocky—with every reason to be so. I'd go out and help Daren hay his fields. When we'd worked up a sweat and were having trouble keeping our eyes off each other stripped to the waist and pumping up our muscles with the lifting of the bales, we'd break open the beer in his barn and he'd lay me on my back on a freshly set bale of hay, wishbone my legs, and feed me with his cock. Daren was older than I was and I liked them younger. But what a monster of a cock. When Samir arrived, Daren and I sort of drifted apart, and we haven't spoken for more than a year now. Is he even at Edgeworth? He spends half his year on Long Island. And I think I read in the papers that he has a new wife.

* * * *

Judy and Charlotte left on a Monday morning. I drove them to Dulles and stayed around until I knew the plane had lifted off. Then I drove back home, a two-hour drive, and took a nap. Some way to start an unsupervised vacation, I thought, but I'd had to get up in early dark and I wasn't a morning person. I was bushed, feeling my age. I knew this wasn't a good start and that chances were dim I'd actually do anything. But I needed the sleep. I had Oratorio Society practice that evening, and those sessions were always grueling. It was free going for the next several days, though. There was plenty of time to decide what, if anything, I could do to make the time free of Judy memorable.

"Hi, you're in good voice tonight, Carson. What do you think of the Haydn?"

"Not really my preference, Jean," I answered. "Too many difficult runs that don't have much meaning for me. And thanks for the compliment. Harmonizing with your rich baritone makes me sound better than I'm really capable of alone, I think."

I was sitting on the edge of the tenor section, he at the edge of the basses, and I wasn't lying when I said I liked my singing to blend with his voice. When we were singing next to each other and his part weaving in with mine, I found it sexually arousing—raising images of our bodies entwined and working in harmony. I had almost moved away from him when I'd first had that sensation, but it was too enticing. Now I found myself seeking him out to sit next to in these sessions. And, as often as not, when I returned home after an Oratorio practice, I went straight to my bathroom and masturbated the arousing experience away.

131

We had both returned early from our fifteen-minute break between practice sessions and found ourselves sitting alone while other choristers swirled around us, still enjoying their break. He was French, a graduate student at the university. This was his first year with the oratorio society, and he was a real asset to our blend.

Tall and dark-haired, but alabaster skin. The complexion of a scholar, but he was well muscled. I knew he played soccer— which he called football—for the university team, and was somewhat of a star in doing it. His hair was long and curly—in fact, all that I could see of his body was covered lightly in curly black hair, contrasting starkly with the whiteness of his skin. His fingers were long and sensuous, and, what had disconcerted me the most, were his long toes, with dark curly hair on them and the top of his feet. He always wore sandals, with no socks.

And all of this was what made me want to sit next to him at oratorio society practice—his sexy appearance even more than his voice. His feet in his open sandals were so sexy. I fantasized sucking those toes. Samir had taught me that. I had sucked his toes when I massaged him before we fucked and then he'd suck mine as we were both building up to another fuck.

"Will you be joining us at Lucky's after the practice," Jean asked me. Lucky's was where those who lived and breathed the choir gathered after practice. I didn't live and breathe the choir and had never joined them for socializing afterward.

"No, I don't think I will."

"Have to run home to the wife?"

"No. She's off on a three-week art crawl through Italy— with her sister. I'm batching it."

"And still no incentive to have a drink with us?"

"No. Home to bed. An old man."

"No, that's not true. Age has been very kind to you."

"You don't have a wife to go home to?"

"No. Not even a boyfriend at the moment. I take my chances at the bar after choir practice."

His open expression of a boyfriend struck me dumb without knowing what to say next. I was saved by a familiar sound from the center of the room.

The conductor was tapping his music stand with his baton, insisting on a resumption of the practice session. I had no time to do more than give Jean a curious look, wondering if there was less behind Jean's comments than it seemed—whether I was just keyed up and looking for a connection too hard. He was French, and they were always on the make in words. Not always in action, though. Jean wasn't looking back at me, though. He was opening his music and giving his attention to the conductor.

I spent the rest of the practice looking at his long, hairy toes whenever I could, wondering if the length of his fingers and toes carried on to his other appendages, and also wondering if his chest and legs were as hairy as his arms. I liked a hairy man. Samir had been hirsute. His hair, even darker than Jean's, had been coarse and thick, though. I had enjoyed tonguing him and making swirls of hair on his chest, belly, and in his armpits after we've made vigorous love. Sami had obviously enjoyed that well enough as well to often give me another round of deep-plunging loving.

Another tenor asked me a question about whether we were on the right notes during one of the vocal runs on the Haydn right at the end of the practice. When I turned around after consulting with him on that, Jean was gone.

I was so keyed up now that I couldn't go home and go right to bed. Instead I drove from practice to Water Street, parked in a lot there, and walked the two blocks to Club 216. I hadn't been there often—and not since Judy had retired. When I'd gone before, I went in the afternoons while she was safely tucked away at her office. It's where I met Samir. It's where, tonight, I hoped I'd find some relief to start off my vacation. It didn't have to be someone long term or even for the length of the vacation. I was so keyed up tonight that I'd settle for a quick suck and fuck in one of the club's back rooms with someone I'd never see again. It would be nice if he were just young and had some body hair.

It was a busy night—a lot of movement around the big, dimly lit, smoke-filled room, with the only strong light being from the spot lights on the dance floor, where couples were clutch dancing, man with man, woman with woman. The tables surrounding the floor were similarly segregated, and as far as I could determine, a lot of testing out and shopping was going on. There were some gray hairs, but not many. And once again I felt too old doing this.

I headed straight for the bar and sat on a stool and ordered a beer. My eyes went to the door to the corridor off to the back of the club, where a beaded curtain separated the world of the shoppers from that of those who had settled on a deal. I knew what went on back there. It hadn't been that many years ago that I had gone with men to the cubicles back there and been transported to paradise—if only for twenty minutes.

Just beyond the beaded curtain, I could make out the silhouettes of a long and lean couple—young men—both in black leather. They were embracing, one having the other backed against the wall.

"Hi. Haven't seen you here before."

He was young. Blond, his head hair long and with downy hair on the forearm he had laying on the bar next to my beer bottle. If he had a pattern of hair on his chest too . . .

"I've been here, but not for some time."

"Been out of commission?"

"A long-term relationship." I didn't think he needed to know it was with a woman.

"Ah, so, into long-term relationships?"

I was listening to him but looking at the couple beyond the beaded curtain. The man pushing the other against the wall was dominating. A shirt was unbuttoned and open and a face was buried in a bare chest. A leg of the man against the wall was already raised and hooked on a hip of the other.

"Not necessarily," I answered. "Not tonight, at least."

"Interested in something?"

"Maybe. The night is young, though."

"And so am I. Here," he continued, as he took my hand and brought it to his crotch. "Young and hung . . . and available."

The couple beyond the beaded curtain were doing it now. As they were kissing. Legs were wrapped around hips and hooked at ankle. A butt was thumping against the wall, being pumped in a steady rhythm by the pelvis of the dominator. Fucking.

It's what I wanted to be doing.

I let my hand linger on his crotch, measuring him. He was hard. Hard for me. It was an exhilarating feeling.

The blond leaned his lips to my ear. "Thirty dollars for a suck, either or both, fifty dollars for a fuck. I do the fucking. Seventy-five for the full service."

I dropped my hand from his crotch, in shock. It wasn't that I didn't have the money. It was the shock of the assumption I'd pay for it. I'd never paid for it before in my life. It was deflating. I'd keyed myself up so high, and just like that, I had tumbled down.

"Uh. Thanks, but no thanks," I said. I turned and took a swig of my beer. And when I turned back he was gone. I could see that the couple beyond the beaded curtain were also gone— probably farther back in the bowels of the club, into one of the cubicles, to finish off with more privacy.

In my mind I tried to follow them in what they were doing back there—legs more spread now, cock digging deeper, a steady thumping rhythm established—but that exercise only depressed me. The atmosphere in the club was suddenly ugly and harsh. I felt like everyone was looking at me, staring at my gray head, wondering what the hell I was doing there. I wondered that myself too. I tossed down the money for the beer, not even finishing it. Lowering my head and not making eye contact with anyone around me, I walked briskly out of the club and to my car. When I reached home I stripped and went into the shower and, under a stream of water as hot as I could bear it, beat off to fantasies of what might have been. And then I climbed into bed and slept the sleep of an aging, forgotten man.

* * * *

It took me until Thursday to build up the courage to venture out again in search of the thrill that earlier separate vacations had brought me. The day was glorious, and I drove toward the mountains to one of the wineries that dotted the foothills of the Blue Ridge. The excuse was that I had a quarterly

135

order of wine club bottles to pick up. The real reason was that Edgeworth was just seven miles past the winery, on the same road. I figured that if I got to the winery and chickened out on going farther, I could always tell myself that all along I'd only intended to come out as far as there to pick up my order of wine.

After I had gotten the wine, though, I turned the nose of the Mercedes farther west rather than back east, toward the town.

After pulling into Edgeworth's farm lane and driving several hundred yards, the barn came into view and then, over a rise, the antebellum house with its white columns a football field's distance beyond the barn. There were three cars parked between the two structures. Daren's old Bentley was there, a sign that he was home. He insisted that he drive that to Long Island to have with him even if it needed to take several service garage stops en route. Beside that were a sleek new Jaguar sedan and a BMW roadster. I parked the Mercedes beside those and walked up to the house.

"Yes, Daren is here. But he and my nephew are out riding. Can I tell him who called."

"Carson. Carson Daniels. I'm sorry to have disturbed you."

"Ah, Mr. Daniels. Yes, I've read your books . . . and Daren has spoken of you. He will be sorry he's missed you."

I looked hard at the woman. She was anywhere between her early and late fifties, depending on how much work she'd had done on her. A statuesque blond, no doubt a model at one time. Tall, angular, New York chic. And with an English accent that I couldn't tell was affected or not. Elegantly dressed for not expecting visitors out in this isolated slice of paradise. Pretty much like all of Daren's earlier wives.

Not all of my books, I thought, as I was walking back to my car. I was sure she hadn't read all of my books. Not the early books—the ones that had brought me into the office of Daren DeMourier, the New York publisher, in my very fresh early twenties. The explicit books that told Daren, a good ten years my senior, he could close and lock his door and fuck me on the publisher's version of the casting couch. But he had been good to me then and for the years intervening, as we both aged—he preferred to call it mellowed. I'd aged better than he had, I thought, except for that thick, talented dick of his. He'd seen that I could write mainstream mysteries as well as I could write gay male smut. He'd done me a good turn there. And in watching him at work, I was able to make the transition to publisher myself in my later career, when I started running out of ideas for straight mysteries when what I really wanted to do was write about a New York homicide detective who loved taking cock rough and often.

The top of the barn was in my line of vision as I walked to the cars, and as I walked up to the rise of a hill, no doubt put there by man to block the line of sight between the house and the barn when farming was no longer the central and only reason for living here, I saw the two horses. Sleek thoroughbreds, they were. Standing politely at a hitching post at the side of the barn, their saddles still on. I knew enough about horses to know that if they'd been taken for a ride, their saddles should have been stripped off of them when the ride was over.

I was still looking at them when I arrived at the car park—and I just kept on walking toward the barn.

I could hear them before I saw them, so there was no surprise, really. The young blond man was laying on a hay bale. The legs I could see on either side of Daren's buttocks were, strangely, still booted in shiny black leather. I saw the ruins of a set of tawny-colored jodhpurs thrown to the side on the ground along with evidence of a red thong. These must have been cut off his body with a knife for him to still be wearing his riding boots. One of the booted feet was lodged in a wooden railing next to the hay bale. Daren was holding the other one up and out with his fist.

The youth was slim, the bared and heaving breast arching out of the flaps of his open riding blouse almost that of a boy. He couldn't have been much over legal age—but Daren would have been careful to establish that he was. That was what he'd done with me when he'd fucked me on his publishing house couch. I had been young looking too. That's how Daren liked them then. He made me show evidence that I was old enough. Then he'd fucked my lights out. He hadn't even asked me if I'd been with a man before—and I hadn't been as intensely and totally as he took me that first time.

Obviously Daren still liked them young—and as fresh as possible.

Daren's riding blouse was off, and the sinewy muscles of his back and arms were straining. He was still wearing his jodhpurs and boots, but I could tell that the fly had been undone and flared out so it wouldn't be an encumbrance. The way Daren was straining and the young blond was warbling and writhing under him—and the wild expression on the youth's face—told me that this likely was the young man's first experience with Daren's cock. In time, Daren stretched his young men's channels to fit. But at the beginning it felt like a telephone pole was being rammed up there. My butt twitched at the memory of that staff.

As I watched—just for a few moments, but long enough—I saw Daren reach for the youth's throat and stretch the young man's body up and his other hand ball into a fist that he not so lightly beat on the blond's pectorals briefly before reaching down and fisting the young man's cock and slow pumping him. I knew this was a sign that Daren was fully in—but probably still growing in thickness, stretching the youth's channel to the limit. And then the young man's body went limp and his head lolled to the side and the wildness of his eyes turned to a mixed look of awe, resignation—and want. Daren's buttock muscles began to contract and loosen, contract and loosen in the rhythm of the fuck, and the youth began to groan and moan deeply. These were phases of Daren's mastering that I knew so well.

I wondered briefly if Daren wore a condom now. In the days we'd first fucked, that hadn't been considered necessary. And Daren had a forceful ejaculation that both flooded the channel in ways that really let you know you had been seeded and that went on at great length. I missed those days. When Daren had fucked me, I knew I'd been fucked. When Daren's buttocks tightened and he grunted his completion, it certainly looked to me like the blond nephew knew he'd been fucked as well.

I turned and walked back to the Mercedes. There was no relief for me here. Daren still liked them young. I had probably been lucky that we went about it for so long that he hadn't realized that I had aged out of his preference zone until there was a hiatus in our relationship.

* * * *

"I wondered if you'd ever come home."

"I had a pickup at a winery out toward the Blue Ridge," I said, holding the three-pack carton up for Jean to see—as if I needed to justify my absence from my own house. I had seen him sitting on my front porch by the front door as I drove up the hill of the curved driveway and into the garage I'd opened automatically. Rather than going on into the breakfast room from the garage, I came back out of the open garage door and to the front porch.

"I don't understand," I said, genuinely confused. "How did you know this address?" I'd only seen Jean at the Oratorio Society practices. I had no idea how he knew where I lived. Although then it occurred to me that we all had access to a master Oratorio Society mailing list on the Internet. But I was running up a false lane on that.

"I followed you here. Monday night."

"Monday night? I didn't—"

"No, you said you were coming straight home. But you didn't. I wanted to see you more than I wanted to go to the bar with the choristers after the practice. So I followed you. You went to Club 216."

I stood there, looking into his face. He knew what Club 216 was. And he knew I'd gone there.

"I saw you in the club. And I saw you leave and come here. I find you very attractive. I would like to fuck you if you'll have me. I tried to tell you that the other night."

That was the point that I almost dropped the carton of wine. But he was quicker than I was, rising out of the cushioned garden chair on my front porch and steadying the wine before it crashed to the ground, helping to lower it to the brick walkway and pulling my numb fingers away from the handle. My eyes were downcast, looking at those elegant, sexy, hair-covered toes of his. As always he was wearing leather sandals without socks.

"Shall we go inside?" he asked.

"Yes," I whispered—in that one word telling him all he needed to know, giving all over to whatever he wanted.

"Here, give me the key; I'll do it. I'll do everything," he said, as I botched the job of trying to get the door key in the slot, my hands were shaking so badly.

"Are the French always so straightforward?" I murmured as he worked the key in the door.

"When we see what we want, yes. And the French are inventive in love," he continued. "I hope you don't mind."

We didn't get the door shut behind us, but we pulled far enough into the foyer to not be seen from the street—although there was enough tree cover between the house and street set below the rise the house was on that there wasn't much danger of that happening anyway.

We stood there rocking against each other, deep in a kiss, his hands cupping my chin to hold me too him, and mine ineffectually drooping at my sides. My thoughts went to the couple fucking against the wall on the other side of the beaded curtain at Club 216 and my cock gave a lurch. Jean obviously felt that as he pulled away from the kiss and gave me a smile and low, throaty laugh. He moved his hands to palm my buttocks and pull me tight into his crotch, and I could feel the hardness of him too. He began moving his pelvis against mine in a slow rhythm, and his lips went back to mine and I opened mine to him.

His hardness against mine and his tongue inside my mouth cavity inflamed us both. We were tearing at each other's clothes. We were in a duel, as he unbuttoned my shirt and pulled it off my back while I was busy at the same time trying to pull his T-shirt over his head. My heart raced at, first, the sight, and then the feel on my chest of the profusion of black curly hair on his chest. My hands went to his belt buckle and fumbled with his zipper, while he just took the waistline of my trousers on either side and jerked down hard, making them clear my hips and fall down to my knees. I stepped out of them, while he knelt before me and started sucking my cock through the cotton material of my briefs.

I stood there for several moments luxuriating in the exotic working of his tongue and teeth on me through the material. I was swaying slightly, not sure I'd be able to remain standing, not even sure I wouldn't fire off much too quickly. Then he was pulling on the waistband of the briefs and I was stepping out of them and he was swallowing me deep—and humming—the resonance on my cock making me groan with pleasure. His hands were clutching my butt cheeks—possibly the only thing that was holding me upright.

"Wait. Please," I murmured. "I don't want to come yet. Here. Sit over in this chair. Please."

He pulled his mouth off my staff and looked up quizzically at me. But he smiled. "No, we wouldn't want you to come too quickly, would we?" he said. And then he obediently stood and walked to the chair we kept next to the secretary in the foyer and sat down and looked coyly at me. Upon retrospect, I think that was the last time he let me give a command for the next several days. And I shudder with pleasure at the memory of the commands he gave me.

As he turned and sat, I pulled his trousers and briefs down to his knees to make it easier for me to remove them, which I knelt and did. Looking up and seeing his cock for the first time, I gasped with pleasure. It wasn't thick, but it was impossibly long and curved menacingly up toward his flat belly like a Saracen sword. A perfect match for his long, sensuous toes and fingers. And he was hirsute. He was pelted with black curly hair all over his body.

He looked on in amusement and then with astonishment and interest as I unlaced his sandals, one after the other, and licked up the soles of his feet, again one after the other—and plopped his toes—one after another—in my mouth and gave them suck.

He was breathing heavily and running his hands through the gray hair on my head as I tongued my way up his pelted calf and thigh. He groaned as I took his balls into my mouth, lodging one in each cheek, and began to hum just as he had done with my cock. The suck I gave his cock would have been almost anticlimactic after that if I hadn't also run a hand between his thighs to his hole and snaked a finger in to find and rub on his prostate.

I was working his piss slit with my tongue when he croaked "Enough of that. Now it is I who might come too quickly."

I laughed and said, "Just as you said, we couldn't have that. Come, I will show you what's upstairs."

I offered my hand to him, but he rose on his own, taking his trousers up with him. "Show me."

I started to mount the stairs, Jean behind me. But half way up the stairs, I felt his chest come down over my shoulder blades and he was forcing me down on the stair treads.

"What—?"

"Hush. I can't wait for the top of the stairs. And I'm French. We do it right here." He was encircling my waist with his arms, but he also had his trousers in a hand and was fumbling around in the pocket, coming up with a string of condom packets. He ripped one off the string and heaved the rest of the string up onto the upstairs landing.

I remembered that these had once been called French letters and I laughed nonsensically at the coincidence.

I panted, plastered to the stairs, breathing raggedly in anticipation, as he opened the packet and rolled the condom on his cock. Then he was pulling my hips up with his arms embracing my belly and pulling my knees up onto one of the stair treads.

I felt his bulb at my entrance, and then I closed my eyes and panted and moaned as I felt him enter and enter and enter me. Having gotten the measure of my channel and demonstrating to me how deeply I would be pierced, he pulled back and, with that upcurved cock of his started rubbing, punishing, making love to my prostate as one of his hands went to encircle and squeeze and work my cock.

I came quickly and would have collapsed if he wasn't holding me up with an arm wrapped around my belly. He laughed a low, throaty laugh, whispering something in French. And then I was yowling and writhing under him as he thrust deep inside me again and rode me hard in long and deep strokes to his own ejaculation.

"Can . . . can we . . . go up to the bed now," I whispered through heavy pants.

"No, not the bed. We do it in every room, on every other surface. In positions you've never imagined before—so often you'll be begging for mercy. I will take you to hell and to paradise. But not on the bed. I'm French."

And we did all of that—for most of the remainder of my glorious separate vacation.

It was three days even before I remembered that the front and garage doors were open and a carton of wine bottles was sitting out on the front walk.

Silas Collins's Ecuador Op

Silas rose from his crouch between the young blond's thighs and turned and walked slowly over to the easy chair where Ramiro Garcia had been sitting and watching and slow pumping himself.

As Silas approached, Garcia raised his head and looked at the heavily muscled giant with slitted, half-glazed eyes and a sloppy grin on his face. Silas could see that the man was on the edge of a drug-hazed blackout, and he leaned down and took hold of Garcia's upper arms and pulled him up to an uneasy standing position.

"It's showtime, Mr. Vice President," Silas murmured as he moved behind Garcia and, almost fully supporting the man in his arms, helped Garcia over to replace him by the bed. "Be sure and get this, Mike, he muttered toward the shadows of the room." Another burly man—the only one in the room with clothes on—stepped forward and lifted a video camera to his shoulder.

"Isn't he nice, Ramiro?" Silas whispered. "Don't you want him?"

"So nice. Nice and blond. Beautiful body," Ramiro murmured as Silas helped Ramiro position himself between young Christope Jourey's thighs. The young blond licked his lips and looked up at Garcia from below long, fluttering eyelashes and smiled a sensuous smile. He reached up and lightly grasped Garcia's hard, upward-curved dick in his hands and, raising his hips, guided the cock to and inside his hole.

"Oh, Daddy. Be good to me. Be so good to me," Christophe groaned in a low voice. And then as Garcia's cock sank into him, he gasped and cried out, "You're a bull! I feel you stretching me. Oh, Daddy, fuck me hard!"

Garcia was gasping and moaning too. Silas was standing close behind him, his cock running up the small of Garcia's back. Once Garcia had sunk completely into Christophe, the small blond arched his back and started muttering how manly Garcia was and that he was almost more than Christophe could endure. The blond started to roll his hips slowly, and Silas grasped Garcia's hips from behind and started to roll them in a countermotion to Christophe's movement as Garcia babbled incoherently and groaned and moaned and sighed.

Garcia cried out as Silas entered his channel with his own dick from behind and grasped both of Garcia's pecs with the palms of his hands and arched his torso back into Silas's bulging chest.

For several minutes Garcia was just along for the ride, with Christophe working him from the front and Silas from the back—and Mike McGrath moving around taking video coverage from various angles, although never within Garcia's view.

Christophe put an end to Garcia's semen buildup by snaking a hand between their legs and grasping Garcia's ball sac and squeezing the spurting of cum out of him, but the other two kept working him until he had come, weakly, a second time and had finally succumbed to the call of slumber that the drugs he had taken sank him to.

Silas pulled out of the Ecuadoran vice president's ass and turned and told Mike he could stop the video. "It's just insurance anyway," Silas muttered. "This dude is coming back with us to join Noriega in Florida."

He leaned over and pulled Garcia's dormant body off Christophe and moved the sleeping politician, drug kingpin, and errant CIA agent up to the center of the bed, laying the man's head on the pillows.

"Stay with him, Christophe, until he awakes and then give him the fuck of his life when he isn't all drugged out. Then get him to take you with him to the resort in Arashá this weekend when he goes. We can roll him up better there than here in the vice presidential palace. He won't have as many bodyguards around him there." Of the four of them, only Garcia and Christophe were known by the vice president's bodyguards to be in this room. Silas had made sure the lock to the door was thrown, but there always was the danger that someone from the guard force would intrude somehow and discover that the vice president had more guests than they thought he had.

"Jack Steele and the others will back you up in Arashá," Silas was saying to Christophe, "and Mike and I will meet you there after we've arranged for air transport in Guayaquil." Silas was putting his clothes—all black-colored commando gear—back on while he gave this instruction. And when he was finished, he and Mike McGrath, who were similarly dressed, silently departed the way they had come—via the French windows that Christophe had unlocked for them while the vice president was in the bathroom shooting up and otherwise preparing for what he thought would be just him enjoying the body of the small, blond cabaret singer who had enchanted him so much down at the Purple Parrott lounge in the red-light district of Quito.

If Christophe took good care of him when the drugs had released him, chances would be good that he wouldn't realize that the big stud of a piano player in the lounge had been here as well in the evening. And if he remembered Silas and his fucking at all, chances were good Garcia would just write it off as wishful thinking while he was pleasantly drugged up.

* * * *

147

Ramiro Garcia, the recently "elected"—election being a bit misleading in the country's political process at the time—vice president of Ecuador, was being special Oped because he was becoming just the type of thorn in Washington's intelligence community side as Manuel Noriega had once been—and for the same reasons. A success story that the U.S. intelligence community really didn't covet was when one of their foreign assets—invariably in Central or South American—rose to high political power in their country and then began to run U.S. intelligence as hard as intelligence had been running him.

This was the case of Ramiro Garcia, and the CIA's answer to him was to do the same to him that they'd previously done to Panama's Manuel Noriega: bundle him up in his own country, sovereignty be damned, and kidnap him to the States and throw him in a Florida prison where he couldn't talk to anyone about his past associations with U.S. intelligence.

Garcia had been recruited as an agent in place for U.S. intelligence when he was a young army general and his brother was governor of a southwest Ecuadoran province where both gold and copper were mined. The sights of CIA headquarters in Langley, Virginia, were on the brother and Garcia was merely a pawn to get to him. But a year later the brother had mysteriously died and Garcia had just as mysteriously taken his place in the province. In subsequent years, Ramiro Garcia's name had increasingly come up in reports of Colombian drug smuggling, and it became apparent that he was no small player there. He also was increasingly taking over the mining operations in his province. All of this made Langley a bit skittish, but not much. It took a trip he made to Cuba and his recent rise to the Ecuador vice presidency to set the CIA in motion to neutralize him.

Silas Collins received the assignment to do so because of Garcia's other well-rumored interest. He liked young, blond men. Collins, a former Marine who specialized in both martial and dirty arts and had been recruited straight into the Agency when his sexual interests became too well known in the Marines, was channeled into spy candy Ops in the Agency and was one of Sam Winterberry's original recruits into a unit that used sex to gain information and to suborn foreign assets. Some elements of

Winterberry's section took a soft approach to this; when a hard punch was required, though, Silas Collins was often the choice.

When Collins put together a team for an Op such as this one, extracting an unwilling national leader from his own country, he went to a small handful of other men very much like himself: ex-Marines, gay, having ripped bodies, and ready for dirty action. Collins was a leader above such men because he was much more than the sum of the rest of them. He not only had a first-rate brain and impeccable survival instincts but he was also a Renaissance man. He was a fine artist and a highly skilled musician and, despite his bulk, he looked splendid in a tuxedo and had the breeding and manners, when necessary, that would not make him stand out at a royal dining table. Or, at least, he would not stand out if he wasn't such a massive, muscle-bound, handsome brute.

The Garcia Op might have gone just fine if Collins had been able to have the team he wanted, but, unfortunately, Ramiro Garcia wasn't drawn to hulking ex-Marine studs; he liked lithe, androgynous blond young men. Collins put together the men he needed to do the extraction—first and foremost the man he always wanted at his side, Mike McGrath. And after that, Ollie Blandford, Jack Steele, Larry Cane, and Clifford Yates, all ex-Marines, all fit and ready to fight. He was still missing the bait of the operation, though, which, to his later regret, he let Larry Cane provide.

Larry's main punch at the moment was a young Agency code clerk named Christophe Jourey, who was on the cusp of being drummed out of the Agency because of his sexual preferences. Being gay was quite all right in Sam Winterberry's unit—indeed, it was the centerpiece of one aspect of the work he supervised—but it was not permitted in the general Agency population. To save his lover's position, Larry Cane offered Christophe up for the Ecuador Op. He fit the need and both he and Larry Cane saw this as an opportunity for Christophe to survive in the Agency.

Almost against Collins's better judgment even at the time, he had agreed to Jourey's transfer to Sam Winterberry's unit and then his assignment to Collins's team. Collins was to regret this. The subsequent Op was deemed a success, because it had obtained at least the backup goal. But it never was seen as a success by Collins, and the breakup of his team because of Christophe Jourey was always seen by Collins as his worst failure in those years heading "wet" team operations in South and Central America.

The worst of the situation came at the camp the team had set up outside Quito, when all were together after months of preparation and, for the first time since they'd come in from the States, Christophe was set loose with both Larry and Jack. Collins's plan—a double tradeoff scheme that, itself, worked a charm—had divided the team in two parts. Mike, Larry, Jack, and Clifford were posing as mining engineers and had been inserted into an intelligence-friendly U.S. company to advise Garcia's mining companies on small-mine extractions. Their real purpose, though, was to get chummy with Garcia and to bring him to a club in Quito's red-light district when both the rising vice president and his American engineer buddies "fortuitously" were in Quito at the same time.

Christophe was an accomplished and sultry singer, and during the months the rest of the team, under Mike's supervision, were becoming friends with Garcia in his home province, Collins, as a pianist, and Christophe, as a cabaret singer, were becoming settled as the talent at the Purple Parrot gay bar in Quito.

At last Garcia was coming to Quito to take up his vice presidential duties. And by happy happenstance, his new American friends and drinking buddies were granted R&R in Ecuador's capital as well. The team left the mines in Zaruma several days ahead of Garcia, just so as not to be too obvious. And in this time, the long-developing double tradeoff scheme almost shattered.

Christophe literally fell into Larry Cane's arms when the team arrived in camp and Larry bundled the young blond up and took him into his room—a room he was to share with Jack Steele—and he fucked Christophe continuously for two days. Steele found someplace else to sleep, but he also found plenty of time to visit his old room and watch Larry and Christophe fucking.

During the time the lovers came up for air and a meal, Christophe pranced around in his briefs and gave all of the other men the come-thither eye. It was a game he liked to play, and it was a game that only worked on Larry—and on Jack. Christophe tried hardest on Collins, but to no avail.

One evening when Christophe had gone to the shower, which was just an open-to-the sky enclosure with a water pipe on a jungle path from the hideout building, Jack followed him. Christophe's squeals were heard in camp and all of the men picked up their rifles and headed for the direction of the screams. Jack had Christophe belly over a bench and his arm pulled up tight behind his back, and he had mounted the young blond from the rear and was giving him a hard, rough cocking.

Collins jerked the rifle out of Cane's hands, or Steele would have died right there and then—and possibly Jourey too, as the two bodies were too closely entwined for a shot in Cane's body not to go through Jourey's as well. But as Collins took the rifle, Cane launched himself at Steele and there was a hell of a fight, which Collins allowed to proceed until he saw a danger that one might really harm the other badly. He pulled the two men apart and sent them separate ways. And then when he turned to Christophe to see if he had been harmed, what he saw was a self-satisfied little bastard with a small smile on his face looking coquettishly up at Collins as if to say that Collins could have a ride too.

After that the strain in the camp was almost to the breaking point and Collins was still deciding who to send back to the States to bring the team back into equilibrium, when the plan fell into place and was moving along too quickly for him to take other action.

Collins and Jourey were doing their act at the Purple Parrot, when a raucous group of men came in, quite evidently near the end of a whiskey train evening across the nightspots of the district. It was Collins's team of fake mining engineers and in the middle of the group was a half-looped Vice President Ramiro Garcia. A few members of Garcia's bodyguard contingent strung themselves out around the periphery of the room and held their Uzis loosely in their arms.

The group sat there, listening to Silas play and Christophe breathily sing, and the American engineers did what they could to build up Garcia's arousal for the small blond singer. Their job wasn't too difficult and was made much easier when Silas and Christophe went on break not long before Mike told the group he needed to take a piss and asked if anyone else did. Luckily Garcia said he did, and the two, Mike only apparently half-drunk, and Garcia genuinely half-drunk and already dipping into the drugs, went into the corridor at the back of the club.

Mike, with a snicker, pointed out figures in the shadows at the end of the corridor, beyond the door of the men's room, and Garcia adjusted his eyes to gaze, arousingly, on the figure of Silas fucking Christophe up against the wall and Christophe moaning at the taking.

It was the first and only time that Silas fucked Christophe—and he was only doing it to arouse Garcia—but Christophe enjoyed it so much that he begged Silas to take him on to one of the back rooms and fuck him fully and to make him cum. But Silas only laughed and told Christophe to concentrate on the mission.

Back in the bar, with Silas and Christophe beginning another set of music, the American engineers continued egging Garcia on until Garcia called over one of his bodyguards who was directed to approach Silas to set a price on Christophe's services.

Silas set a high price, and very soon thereafter Garcia and his bodyguards were escorting Christophe to the vice presidential limousine and Silas and Mike were in the back of the club changing into their black clothes of the night.

* * * *

Years later, Collins decided that he should have taken Jack Steele with him to arrange for the plane in Guyaquil and left Mike McGrath in charge of extracting Garcia and Jourey from Garcia's private compound in the Arashá spa resort a two-and-a-half-hour drive southwest of Quito. But Mike was the one with the contacts in Guyaquil and Collins was the one with the access to the line of credit to pay for the air services.

In the event, Silas and Mike had no inkling that the mission had gone sour until they arrived at the rendezvous point southwest of the spa and didn't find the team there. After three hours, they decided to backtrack toward Arashá and see what the holdup was. They couldn't wait longer for fear that the team was trapped in or outside Garcia's compound and needed reinforcements.

They found the jeep not more than ten miles, albeit grueling miles in this jungle environment in the foothills of the Andes, from Arashá. Garcia was propped up in the backseat of the jeep, looking stoically at them as they approached the vehicle—with unseeing eyes. He had several bullet holes in his chest. Stopping only long enough for Mike to fire off some photos and to collect Garcia's military jacket with its medals and barely dried blood—needed for DNA matches—Collins and McGrath retraced their steps and moved to the backup rendezvous area on the road to Guayaquil. There was no sign of any other bodies or blood from wounds in the area of the jeep, which gave the two both pause for consideration and hope that the members of the team had all escaped alive.

No one was at the second rendezvous point, either, and after two days, Collins and McGrath gave up the wait and flew out of Guyaquil.

Most of the rest of the team got back to Langley before they did. Only Jack Steele was missing.

"Where's Jack?" Silas turned on Clifford Yates and asked. "And what happened with Garcia and why didn't you show at either of the rendezvous points." He was addressing Yates with the intuitive knowledge that whatever happened had the hand of Yates behind it.

"Jack didn't make it," Yates answered.

"What do you mean Jack didn't make it?"

"We were caught in an ambush, and Jack was killed trying to cover Garcia. It looked very much like Garcia was the target rather than someone they wanted to rescue. Who knows about these southern dictatorships, though? Maybe the analysts can figure that out."

"We were there," Mike McGrath said in a quiet voice. "There was no evidence anyone but Garcia got shot."

"Well, what can I say, we all saw him dead," Yates said. "Didn't you three see him dead?"

Ollie Blandford, Larry Cane, and Christophe Jourey wagged their heads vigorously. Christophe's eyes were wide open and glassy and Silas had an urge to take him aside and grill him. He knew there was more to what happened then that. But the chief of the division had interceded and it didn't look like Silas was going to get to do much questioning at all.

"And you didn't make it to either one of the rendezvous points because—?"

"We were tracked by the ambushers for two days," Yates said. "When we could get our bearings, the closest place we knew how to get to was Zaruma."

"All the way back to Zaruma, Garcia's provincial headquarters? His mine area? And how the hell did you get out of Ecuador from there?"

"We hiked."

"Over the Andes?"

"Yes. Into Peru."

"I think that's enough questions, gentlemen," the chief of the South America Division interjected. He was wearing a smile. So were Yates, Cane, Blandford, and Jourey. Only McGrath was scowling—and Collins was looking thoughtful. "Garcia was neutralized. In some ways that was better than our original goal," the division chief continued. Silas didn't particularly like the way he was rubbing his hands like he was washing away the mission, though. "I think we can just leave it like that. We can mark it up as a success—a well done by everyone around."

Collins never was quite able to mark it up as a successfully completed mission, though. When reports came in of the Ecuadorans being outraged that the fortune that Garcia was reputed to have salted away somewhere seemed to have evaporated and these were added to the rumors coming out of Ecuador of four gringos hauling sacks of something out of Garcia's Zaruma palace, Collins tried to take these to the South American division chief, but he wasn't able to get an appointment with the man until months later, when Silas's services were needed for another mission. And then, the division chief would only talk of the coming mission.

Collins couldn't let the issue be, though. He found the time to find an Ecuadoran airplane pilot who claimed to have flown the team out of Zaruma and into Peru. Collins also enlisted foreign assets of his to search the area and they found the body of someone who quite possibly was Jack Steele in an abandoned mine near Zaruma—a mine where Garcia was rumored to keep hordes of his money and gold bullion. Collins went back to the South America Division chief and presented this evidence, but, once again, he only got a smile and an invitation to come see the division chief's new mansion he was building on the Potomac palisades.

Yates stayed with the Agency—even longer than Collins did, and then when he took early retirement, he just moved over to work internationally with counterterrorism and was murdered on the Orient Express train between Bucharest and Varna while carrying classified material from Paris to Istanbul. Cane, Blandford, and Jourey all left the Agency soon after this operation. All lived lives beyond their means until, one by one, they ended up dead under suspicious circumstances.

Mike McGrath, the only one of his old team that Collins truly trusted, bit his gun when he was told his only option was early retirement with reduced pay. The day he did so, Collins began preparing his own exit strategy.

As for Jack Steele, although Silas liked him the least of all members of the Ecuador Op, Steele had been a member of his team; Collins felt the responsibility to account for him and to take care of any family he'd left behind. He remembered that when Steele had left the Marines, he'd been serving in Okinawa and that he stayed on there until the Agency picked him up. By careful research, Collins found the woman he'd been living there with and her child and had ensured that, even though they hadn't been married, the Agency sent a small stipend to both until the woman died and the child became an adult.

Collins himself stuck with the Agency until, being considered part of an embarrassing obsolete era, he was offered the position of station chief in Beirut, a surefire suicide mission, and then he quietly disappeared one day and started a whole new career in personal intelligence work while moving around the globe just one or two steps ahead of his former employer.

The Duchess's Brother

Young Robert came to with a start. The pain and sense of tightness and fullness in his ass channel were excruciating. His breeches, hose, and boots were off; he could see them tossed in a bundle in the ferns by the rocks cascading down to the stream where his horse—and that of the duke—were nuzzling their noses into the gently rolling water. He felt pain elsewhere too— at his temple, where he'd landed and blacked out when his horse threw him; at the side of his face, where the duke had backhanded him back into unconsciousness when he was coming to; in his shoulder, which he'd bruised in the fall; and in his arms, pinned uncomfortably under him on the rough-surfaced ground beneath the fern bed he'd landed in. All of his weight was on his arms, and his wrists were bound underneath him.

"Sire. Your grace!" he exclaimed in pain and shock, as he looked into the face of the Duke of Farnstead, his father's liege lord. The imposingly figured man was crouched over Robert, his body wedged between the young man's thighs, his hands holding Robert's now-bare legs out and up from his body, and his cock digging ever deeper into the center of the young squire.

"Shut up and take it, boy. I will have my pleasure."

"Oh, please, mercy. You are hurting me unto death."

"It's your own fault. Those saucy looks and golden ringlets. I swear, of all of your father's offspring and by-blows, you are the prettiest by far. I've wanted to put you to my sword for two days now. It is done now, the gates are breached—and, believe me, that was no easy storming—so take it."

"Sire! Ohhhhh. I've never!"

"What, you've never been put to the sword before?" This claim only made the duke laugh and push in deeper and begin to stroke slowly and deliberately in a rhythm that had Robert groaning and panting. "Not even by your father? I've heard of his ways. Must have been saving you. Don't be so tense and it will go better with you. Relax and open to me. You are undone now; you might as well enjoy it. I'm told I do it very, very well." And again that laugh.

Robert found that it did help when he relaxed his body. And, indeed, there was little he could do about this now. The duke was liege over his own family's land. By the right of the laws, he had access to the cunts of any of the women in his dukedom—and in this day and age dukes and kings tended to call upon the right liberally. Surely that held for the ass channel of any man in thrall to him as well, if it was the duke's pleasure.

"There, that's better, isn't it?"

And indeed it was. Robert started to moan now and his hips began involuntarily to roll with the rhythm of the taking. It mortified him that he was becoming increasingly willing to accommodate the duke. The more his channel opened to the duke's cocking, the more his own pleasure and arousal stole in to mix with the shock and pain and sense of violation. He couldn't call it violation, of course. The duke had his rights. And the duke wasn't old and fat. He was young and virile and in prime condition. And his cock had a way of making Robert's channel walls grab and release and shudder—something Robert had no idea they could do.

158

The duke's bulb had found Robert's prostate and was sending waves of electricity through his body. He moaned and trembled and murmured his wonder, which heighted the duke's arousal. The duke laughed lustily again and, with one hand, tore open the front of Robert's doublet, exposing pert little nipples to his lips and teeth. Robert groaned in reply and began moving his hips more vigorously against the thrustings of the ducal rapier.

"Why, you little vixen," the duke muttered. "You can't get enough of it now, can you?"

"Oh, sire," Robert whimpered. "Oh, my liege."

"This staff I have between your legs is your liege," the duke crowed. "And you are its mistress."

"Oh, ohhh, ohhh," Robert cried as he tensed, arched his back, and let loose his seed.

"This is the only thing you can do before me," the duke said wickedly, "In all else except coming for me, you must walk behind." He laughed at his own joke and then continued, taking Robert's jaw roughly in his hand and bringing the young man's face close to his own. "Like this. I want to see your expression when I paint your insides with royal seed." Then at belabored, exhausting length. "Yes, yes . . . ugh . . . very pretty. Very pretty indeed."

"Here, cinch up that doublet better. Not all of the buttons are broken," the duke said after he was finished, had risen and adjusted his breeches, and had freed the lashes of the riding whip he'd used to tie the young man's wrists. "All can be explained by your unfortunate fall. But do walk around a bit and lose that bow-legged stumble—or the rest of the hunting party will gossip when they've come upon us. Which should be soon. I told my lieutenant to hold them back on one excuse or another for a good half hour—and you have such a sweet ass, I almost overlived my time. But you rejuvenate me. I should have made the command an hour. I could have well done with a second— and you could have used that for your education, as well."

"Oh, sire."

"And don't snivel. You were sure to lose your virginity sooner rather than later with those eye lashes and willowy figure of yours. You told me true? I am the first dip of the wick?"

"Yes, my lord," Robert said in a soft, subdued voice. He couldn't look at the duke now. At some point in the taking, it had overwhelmed him and had become near paradise to him. But before and after . . .

"Well, you are honored then. The sword of a duke was first. You'll get no better unless you manage to make your way to the king's bed."

"Yes, my lord," Robert whispered with a near whimper. They both turned their heads at the sound of hoofbeats.

"Ah, the rest of the hunting party. Your father will be beside himself that we have become lost from the main hunt. Retrieve the horses and stand beyond them. You still have a wildness about your eyes. Do something about that while I tell them of your unfortunate tumble off your horse."

"Yes, sire."

That evening, Lord Charles, Robert's father, stood at the lord's table, raised his goblet, and hushed those gathered. Robert was sitting almost in the shadows at the end of a side table. The lord's table was taken up with the duke and the principals of his retinue, Robert's parents and three sisters, and his elder brother—the heir to the family holdings and minor title.

"This is a momentous occasion," Lord Charles spoke loudly, slurring his words a bit, not quite in control of his wine flagon. "The great Duke of Farnstead not only honors this humble house with his presence, but he also has honored us for all time by asking for the hand of our precious daughter, Caroline, to become his duchess."

There were cheers all around, while the duke and Caroline stood and the duke leaned over Caroline's hand and gave it a noble peck. His lieutenant, a tall, well-muscled strapping young man, was standing behind him, looking intently into Caroline's face. Sensing the attention, Caroline lifted her gaze to his. And she blushed and gave a shy little smile.

"And extending the honor he does our estate," Lord Charles continued, "The duke has given permission for our entire family to join his at the Castle Hamstead."

There were oohs and ahhs all around, especially from those fretful parents who would be all the more comfortable to know that Lord Charles was off in Hamstead and their sons and daughters weren't.

Not long afterward, the duke leaned over to Lord Charles and told him that he was tired from the hunt and perhaps they could bring the festivities to a close so he could withdraw.

"And I have found that I have come some away from Hamstead with an insufficient number of squires to attend my chamber. Would it be possible for your young Robert to attend me?—and I may have need for him in the service in Hamstead as well after the wedding and when your family joins me there."

"But certainly, I would be honored," Lord Charles murmured. And although he had, indeed, had his own eyes of lust on his youngest son as the youth had grown into manhood, it was the greatest of honors for a son of his to be on bedchamber attendance to the duke. And it would solve the age-old problem of what an English nobleman could do with a second son as long as the first one was robust. This would be like money in the strongbox—his second son at someone else's table until and unless he was needed at home by some misfortune to the estate's heir—and no need for messy scheming when Lord Charles went on to his ultimate rest.

He looked up to catch the eye of his son, Robert, but the young man was nowhere to be seen. In fact, he could not be found anywhere on the estate that night or before the duke's party left for Hamstead.

* * * *

"Come to me, squire."

Robert moved a bit farther into the duke's bed chamber. He had been escorted straight here from the wedding banquet hall. And during the entire church ceremony and the wedding banquet, he had been flanked by two of the duke's sturdy house guardsmen.

The duke and his lieutenant, stripped of their formal doublets, were sitting in front of a draped window on either side of a small table. They were playing chess. They were both bare-chested and their physiques told of many hours of exercise for combat readiness. The younger lieutenant was somewhat broader of chest and narrower of waist than the duke was, but the duke was in his prime as well.

Robert's sister, Caroline, had departed the wedding banquet more than two hours previously to prepare for her nuptial night, which apparently was going to take place in the duchess's chamber adjacent through a sturdy wooden double door directly from the duke's bed chamber.

"That was unkind of you to avoid me that last night at your father's house," the duke said. Robert knew the man was addressing him, although both the duke and his lieutenant were bent attentively over the chessboard, and the duke was holding a pawn in his hand.

Robert felt very much like a pawn in the duke's hand at that moment. "I'm sorry, sire. I—"

Much to Robert's relief—at least momentarily—because Robert really had no idea what he could say beyond what he had said, the duke overrode his murmured apology.

"No matter in the end. The absence has served to whet my appetite. That was a pain yesterday, but at this moment it is quite beneficial to my mood. And here you are. Ready to begin your service to me in the bed chamber."

"Yes, my lord."

"As this is your first night in this service, I wish to see how well you do before you come in touch with me. Come over and undress my lieutenant."

"Sire?"

"The first lesson is not to question but just to do," the duke barked. The tone of his voice sent Robert stumbling forward. And while he did so, the lieutenant stood, and, with a wicked smile, took a wide stance with his legs.

Robert approached him, bent at the waist, and unclasped the lieutenant's hose and rolled them off his meaty legs, taking the slippers off his feet at the same time. Then he pulled the man's breeches off his legs, and the lieutenant stood there before him, as he was born, his prodigious manhood and balls hanging down between his thighs. He was still smiling as if he shared in a secret that Robert did not.

Which, as it happened, he did.

"Now kneel before him and use your mouth to make him ready for my duchess."

Robert's face snapped up to look at the duke in shock and confusion, but at the duke's barked "Do it!" the lieutenant's foot snaked around to the back of Robert's knee and jabbed at the tender tissue there, sending Robert crashing down to the floor. And, the soldier brutally grasping the back of his head by the hair, bringing him back up to his knees, and, ultimately, controlling him, Robert's lips were being breached by the lieutenant's engorging, monstrous staff. Robert gasped between moments of gagging as the lieutenant set his pelvis in motion, cruelly using Robert's mouth cavity for his growing pleasure, pushing to the back of his throat, hauling him from the floor by his long, golden ringlets, and shaking his body like he was rag doll. While this transpired, the duke continued speaking in soft tones.

"As you might suppose, I do not waste time and seed on women. They are only good for begetting sons, and I have none of the pretentions of most on having a son who looks like me. The lieutenant is going to serve that duty for your sister, the duchess. I trust she will enjoy it—although, as you can sense, he does like to be a little rough in his taking. I understand many women enjoy that—and many young men too. We'll see what you enjoy. And even if she doesn't enjoy him, I trust she is a smart enough lass to not care where the seed comes from that gives her sons as long as I acknowledge them as mine. As a squire of my bed chamber, you will learn that whatever secrets I have are your sworn secrets too. And if you can't hold them . . . well, my castle moat is wide and deep."

After a bit, while Robert learned the rhythm and touch that was expected of him in this act and the lieutenant settled down to more interest in rhythm and touch than brutality, silence reigned in the chamber except for the heavy breathing from the lieutenant, who was being brought to full arousal; the murmurings of the duke, who was enjoying the entertainment and anticipating what followed; and Robert's gasps, gurgles, and repressed gagging. The duke had his own cock out of his codpiece and, though it was not as long and thick as the lieutenant's, it was manly enough and showing great interest.

Robert could see the strong upcurve of it that had given his prostate so much direct-bulb attention by the stream during the hunt.

"There, that is enough. Although he might need some more help ere he removes himself to the bridal chamber. Now, do the same for me. But be better at it and more willing for it than you were with my lieutenant. I will help; I like it slower and with more loving attention."

After Robert had undressed the duke and serviced him in the same way as he had the lieutenant—being expected now to make love to the cock rather than just serving as a vessel for it—the duke gave direction again.

"Now the preparation. Strip down yourself, Robert, and make a play of it. Then go and lie belly down at the foot of the bed. Jason, prepare him for me, if you please."

Without a word, after Robert had slowly disrobed, the lieutenant nudged him over the bed and pushed him down on his belly. Robert moaned, but he didn't struggle—how, under the circumstances could he have?—as the lieutenant stretched his arms out at either side and tied off his wrists to fastenings on the bed boards at the side. Robert was to find out that there were such fastenings all over the frame of the duke's bed.

Coming behind him, the lieutenant pulled Robert's legs out to either side and tied off his ankles to hooks on the bedposts at the end of bed as he had done with Robert's wrists.

Then he knelt behind Robert, and the young squire felt fingers and a tongue at his channel opening and a fist grab and pull his cock through his thighs and to start milking him like he was a beast of the pasture.

Robert moaned and writhed under the attention and his eyes latched onto those of the duke, who stood beside the bed and watched and stroked his own cock. The duke was naked except for the signet ring of his nobility and the riding crop he was holding in his hand. Robert moaned and opened his mouth to speak when he saw the riding crop, but then, knowing it would do him more harm than good to object, he shut his mouth and continued to roll his hips in answer to what the lieutenant was doing in his ass with his tongue and to his cock and balls with his fist.

The duke gave him a slight look of disappointment, leaving little doubt that he would have enjoyed a little more resistance and begging for mercy.

"Enough. My bride awaits. Leave the door open. One wants to know if his wife is a screamer."

Robert watched the lieutenant move, naked, through the door, his manhood standing straight and tall and long and thick from his body. He heard the cry of shock and the scuffle and screams of distress and objection and violation from the other room immediately after the lieutenant had entered the duchess's chamber. His sister, Caroline, seemed to be under the misapprehension that the lieutenant was taking liberties and all she need do is call the guards outside her door. Although the guards undoubtedly would have preferred coming into the chamber to enjoy the entertainment, they didn't.

As it was, the duchess was putting up a struggle for her new husband's rights. She ran from her bed and made it to the open door between the chambers before the lieutenant caught up with her. Standing behind her, he held her there, his arm around her waist, her body half bent over, his massive, heaving chest looming over her back, her body still enshrouded in her billowing, white wedding nightgown, for both the duke and Robert to see the tableau of the two of them together as well as the shock in her eyes as she saw the duke bent over her brother's spread-eagled and bound back, both duke and squire naked.

The duke and Robert, suspending their own action, watched as the lieutenant bunched Caroline's gown above her waist and his free hand went under it and brutally grabbed and squeezed one of her breasts. And duke and squire watched as she screamed when his cock found her cunt and pushed to work its way into her. And then she was wrenched away from the doorway and back toward her bed.

The duke seemed to be enjoying this. He had begun flicking Robert's bare rump and his balls with the riding crop as a gurgling cry from the other room marked the instant his sister, Caroline, became a matron, and then Robert's own whimpers and yelps and silent screams took over his senses until after his own moment of piercing came—a somewhat anticlimactic one, for certain, as the duke had visited his channel before. Still, Robert cried out and arched his back and strained at his bounds as the duke thrust inside him. The pain of abrupt stretching and plunging overtook the stinging of Robert's red-raw buttocks gradually until, at last, Robert was able to handle and tolerate—and then, embarrassingly enough, enjoy and, finally, want—beg for—the stroking inside him.

As he got his own emotions into check, Robert became aware that the sounds from the other bedchamber had changed too. His sister, Caroline, always a quick study and obviously having figured out the lay of the land—and, she'd have to admit, getting a very able man out of the deal—indeed was vocal in the fuck and now clearly couldn't get enough of the lieutenant's master cocking.

The duke had won. This arrangement was going to work for him.

The duke leaned over and whispered in Robert's ear, "I foresee a long and enjoyable life of service for you, my pretty one. If my duchess will let him out of her bed, I'll give you a taste of the lieutenant's cocking on the morrow. I like to watch almost as much as I like to fuck—and as you have seen, the lieutenant can ream you a wider channel."

"Yes, sire," Robert murmured with a sigh of resignation—and, increasingly, of want.

The Giver

"Oh shit . . . Oh SHITTT!"

"Am I hurting you? Tell me, if so. I don't want to—"

"Oh, god, no. Faster, deeper. You are so big—so beautiful. Oh, god, no, don't stop. I haven't . . . in so long. Ohhhh, SHIT Yes!"

"I'm not hurting your legs? This position's OK?"

Guy's legs were running up Craig's naked torso to his shoulders on either side of his head as Craig held Guy's butt cheeks in a firm grip with his hands, squeezing and separating them. Guy was laying sideways on his small studio couch, his head almost pounding against the wall, a rolled-up pillow under the small of his back. His pelvis was elevated to the angle of Craig's cock, although the bed was low enough that Craig had to stoop a bit for the right position to work it all inside the other man's throbbing channel.

He'd been leery about feeding it all in, he was so big and thick, but Guy wanted it all—and Craig knew this was so unlikely to happen often for Guy that he wanted to give Guy what he wanted.

"You can't hurt my legs; they're dead. But my ass is alive, keep feeding it . . . oh, god, oh, god. Yes like that! Oh, Shit! Why, why are you doing this? I shouldn't be—"

"Shush. I'm doing this because I want you. You're a sexy hunk, and you turn me on."

"Oh, god . . . I'm not . . . anymore. You couldn't . . . OH CHRIST ALMIGHTY! There, right there. Like that. I'm gonna commmmmm!"

"That's the idea," Craig said, with a low laugh.

Guy had been stroking his cock hard, his back arched. His legs were paralyzed and withering, but that only added to the strength of his torso and arm muscles. He hadn't given into it. He was still fighting and exercised hard to keep whatever parts of his body that functioned in tip-top condition.

Craig quickly withdrew from him and went down on his knees on the floor in time to push Guy's hand away with his lips and cover Guy's cock with his mouth as the paraplegic spouted off a month's accumulation of cum.

"God . . . you didn't have to do that. You're so good," Guy moaned weakly in release. "What are you doing? Oh, god!"

Craig had risen and stopped Guy's speaking by taking his lips in his, transferring the cum from mouth to mouth and pushing his tongue into Guy's mouth. Then his cock was at Guy's door again, pushing in, and the former soldier shuddered and trembled and started to writhe in earnest as Craig took up the rhythm of the fuck again.

With strong hands, Guy grabbed the globes of Craig's butt and squeezed hard and held Craig's pelvis close into his crotch, trying to get every centimeter of Craig into his channel.

Craig released Guy's mouth and rose up over his torso again and smiled down at him.

"What? Why? You don't have to—" Guy murmured in awe. "Oh, Christ, that is sooo hot," he moaned.

"I'm going to try to hold mine until you come again," Craig said. "OK with you?"

"Shit, yes. Shit, yes, ohhhh shit!"

Craig had lowered his teeth to Guy's nipples to chew lightly on them in turn.

It had all started some two hours earlier—in a gay movie theater. Guy had been sitting in his wheel chair beside a row of theater seats near the back of the dark room. He had a raincoat over his lap and was working his cock under it while watching the action on the screen.

It was dark enough that he didn't realize right away that a man had come and sat beside him in the last seat in the row he was next to. Men never did that in the theater. He hadn't had a man come near him since he'd returned from Iraq. He didn't expect ever again to get anything like he got out in the isolated checkpoints in Iraq, where the men were bored, scared, and willing to do just about anything to forget where they were and to feel a moment of pleasure and release. And where there were only other American soldiers they could trust to let down their guard with. Out where Guy had been stationed, they didn't send the women soldiers.

"Can I do that for you?"

It had been a whisper and was so unexpected that Guy didn't react at all until the second time he'd heard it. He thought maybe it had carried to him from some other row, where there was an occasional couple together, although most men in the theater were at least three seats from anyone else. They were still connecting, though—looking furtively around. Sometimes making eye contact. Sometimes negotiating just with the eyes and the slight signaling of nods and their hands. And getting up and moving—not together, but in circuitous routes to the curtained door beside the movie screen that led to the private booths at the back of the building.

"I said, can I do that for you?"

Guy turned his head, his disbelief only increasing as he did so. The man was gorgeous—movie star looks, with wavy hair and perfectly straight teeth that picked up the light reflected from the screen and sparkled through his engaging smile. And what Guy could see of his torso was well worked.

Guy's hands came up from under the raincoat, and he had them on the guiding wheels of his chair, ready to turn and wheel away, not knowing what sort of assault this was, but knowing that it couldn't be sex with him that this hunk was after. This couldn't be happening. The man was way out of his

169

league . . . now. He was whole and a genuine hunk. There was no reason for him to be in this theater at all. He surely could have his pick in his office and at any high-class bar he went into. This must be some sort of joke.

Guy looked around to see if this guy had some friends pointing and giggling at them. It was too dark in the theater, though, to be sure. All the men—at least all of them who didn't have their faces plastered together, seemed to be looking at the screen.

"Please, don't be afraid," the other young man murmured. "I can do that for you. You'll enjoy it more if I do it."

Guy was trapped. The man's hand had already gone up his thigh—Guy couldn't feel that, but as dark as it was, he could see it—and under the raincoat and was encasing Guy's cock.

Guy moaned at the feel of a man's hand wrapped around his cock after all of these months of being denied that.

He started to speak, but the man spoke first. "Shush. Don't say anything. Please. Just enjoy it, as I will enjoy it."

The raincoat fell off Guy's lap and he looked down and moaned again at the sight of the hand encasing the cock.

"It's a nice cock; it deserves attention," the man said. Still with that generous smile on his achingly handsome face. "Relax," he continued. "Close your eyes and enjoy it fully."

Guy did close his eyes. And he did enjoy it fully. But the experience was ever so short. It had been so long and it was so unexpected.

"Sorry," he whimpered when he had come all over the man's hand.

"Don't be. I enjoyed it," the man whispered back. And Guy turned and moaned again when he saw that the man had taken the cum-streamed hand to his mouth and was tasting him.

"Is there anything else I can do for you?" the man murmured. "Do you want to taste me too?"

"I couldn't. Really. That was wonderful. No one . . . not for so long . . . but—"

"Do you enjoy sucking?"

Guy didn't respond. He was completely flustered and at a loss for words.

170

"If you do. I think you'd enjoy mine. And I'd enjoy it too."

He'd enjoy it. Of course Guy would like to do it. And the man had said he'd enjoy it too.

The man correctly interpreted Guy's feelings about that, and he stood, facing Guy, and unzipped his pants and took out the most magnificent cock Guy had ever seen. He had a brief flash of envy and resentment. No one that beautiful and hunky deserved to have a cock like that too.

Guy groaned as the man pulled the wheel chair up so that the side was level with the leg room in the row and give him space to place his leg and then straddled the wheelchair over Guy's lap and took his chin in one hand and the cock in the other and laid it on Guy's lower lip. Another moan and Guy opened his mouth to it and slid his lips down the shaft as the man gently pushed it inside his mouth cavity.

Closing his eyes, Guy did what he'd never forgotten to do out there in the Iraq wasteland when another soldier offered him his cock.

After the man had come, he lowered his mouth to Guy's, and they exchanged a lingering, cum-filled kiss.

The man rose up but remained standing over Guy's lap. He looked down into Guy's eyes and murmured. "Is that all? Or is there more you have done and long to do again? I am an exclusive top, but I could—"

"Oh, God. I couldn't possibly ask you to—"

"Would you be comfortable going behind the draped door . . . to the back?"

"I live only a block away. But I don't understand why you would—"

"Would you like me to wheel you, or would you prefer doing that on your own?"

After they had fucked on the narrow bed in Guy's studio apartment, they sat at his table separating the kitchen from the bed-living room and drank a beer together. Guy was still incredulous.

"It was a land mine. We were on patrol. I was the lucky one—or maybe Larry was. He died instantly, his body shielding mine except for the legs."

171

"Sorry to hear that. Doesn't decrease your hunkiness a bit, though. You've got some talented channel muscles. I'm hard again just thinking about where my cock's been and how well you welcomed it. And look at those biceps and pecs—and the washboard belly. God, I've got to have more of that."

"Now? You can't be serious."

"I'll show you serious—unless you don't want me to do it again. If you don't want it or you think you don't deserve it, don't believe you have the most talented channel in the city, just say so. But, as for me, I'd like to have more of that."

Guy stared at him, full of awe and wanting it again so much he couldn't refuse, although he knew he should—that something about this just wasn't right. Guys like this didn't bother with guys like Guy.

"I didn't think so. See, I'm not lying about what my cock wants."

He pushed his chair away from the table. Neither of them had put on any clothes since they had fucked on the bed.

"And see. You're ready to go again too."

With that, Craig sank to his knees on the floor in front of Guy's wheelchair and the fingers on one hand sank under Guy's balls and an index and middle finger went up into his channel in search of his still-very-much-alive prostate. The other hand wrapped around Guy's revealingly hard cock, and Craig's tongue went to Guy's ball sack.

"Oh, god, oh god," Guy moaned as he collapsed into the chair and his hips started an involuntary roll. He clasped his hands behind Craig's head, holding it close into his crotch.

When Craig sat back in his chair, he brought Guy's body out of the chair and onto his lap, positioning the bulb of his cock for Guy's channel just to slide down it, as Guy groaned and arched his back, and one of Craig's hands went to the small of Guy's back to hold him steady on the lap. Craig's mouth went to his nipples.

Guy's legs dangled uselessly at the sides of Craig's bent legs, but Craig was busy showing him that they weren't needed for this pleasurable activity at all.

* * * *

172

The man was giving Craig furtive looks as both moved around the adult book store shelves, looking at titles and picking up video boxes and DVD cases and reading the blurbs.

The man was dying to see what sort of material Craig was picking up, and audibly drew in breath when he saw that it was gay male material. This was arousing to the man, and he let his hand glide furtively down the fly of his trousers.

This was, in fact, pretty much the extent of the man's activities in places like this—or, at least, had been for nearly twenty-five years. At one time he was as active as any other hyper-sexed guy. He had been a sailor and had been built well and took care of himself. He'd never been a looker, but, on the ships where he'd served, they were out at sea for months or years. No women were in the navy then, and most of the sucking and fucking went on in the dark, so no one really cared about a pretty face. His body had been good, his cock had been good enough—and his technique had been considered to be superb.

That was then, though. And this was now. Now he was over sixty, what little hair he had had gone stringy gray, he had a bit of a paunch as well as a stoop, and he carried a cane and wore a hearing aid. He didn't see too well, his arms were flabby rather than muscled, which made the tattoos he'd gotten in the navy look sad indeed. Everything about him drooped. And he hadn't gotten a bit less ugly in the face. Unfortunately, he still had a cock that could stand at attention at the slightest arousal.

And the greatest arousal he could look forward to these days was watching achingly pretty young men like the one who was waltzing around the store with him, like this—undoubtedly knowing that he was being watched and appreciated and dreamed about.

And maybe he was getting a bit of arousal out of being ogled and ached for too before he went to his gentlemen's club and took the pick of the men there back to the sauna and fucked their lights out to their delight.

This had put Nelson into such a reverie that he didn't even know the young man was behind him until he smelled the tangy aftershave lotion. He'd gotten whiffs of it before as he had moved into spaces the young man with the wavy hair, movie-star face and build, and the sparkling white, straight teeth had recently vacated in front of the shelves to vicariously play off the covers that enticed the young man to take them off the shelf and read them.

This alone made Nelson hard. After this, he'd go back to his small two-bedroom bungalow and sit in his Laz-Y-Boy and slowly jack off while one of these videos in here was running on his TV. He hadn't gotten around to getting a DVD player yet.

Right after he sensed the aftershave lotion, he took his breath in sharply in shock. The man was right behind him—and he meant right behind him—and he had moved a hand around Nelson's waist and was covering and feeling Nelson's hard on through the material of his trousers.

"Oh, god," Nelson muttered, as all of the air came out of him and he almost keeled over.

The man moved his other arm around his waist to hold him up. The first hand was pulling down his zipper and getting skin-on-skin intimate with his cock.

Nelson could feel the other man's cock at the small of his back as well, and he almost hyperventilated to find that it was hard—and enormous.

"Don't speak," the man hissed. "Just nod yes or no. If I'm wrong I apologize, and I'll stop and leave the store. But you've been following me around. I think you want me. And I want you too. I won't bottom, but I'll suck and be sucked, and I'll top—with pleasure . . . for both. If that interests you, they have rooms in the back we can use."

Nelson moaned and didn't say anything. But he'd involuntarily moved a hand down to his crotch to cover the hand that was on his cock—and he was making no move to push the hand away. The hand was slow pumping his cock. It was driving him wild—beyond his wildest imagination of what could be happening now. Or could have happened any time in the last twenty years.

"Nod yes or no," the man persisted.

Craig sat on a table in the back room, trousers and briefs off and smiled down at Nelson as he sat on a chair between Craig's thighs and made love to Craig's cock.

Old as he was, he hadn't forgotten how to make masterful love to a cock, which Craig had assumed might be the case, and he quite happily and easily engorged and throbbed for Nelson's mouth and bathed Nelson's throat deep down with his cum.

Nelson looked up at him then, tears in his eyes.

"Can I. Can I see your chest as well?"

"Certainly," Craig answered with a warm laugh and he started to unbutton his shirt.

"May I . . . May I do that."

"Yes, of course."

Nelson reverently unbuttoned the shirt and took it off Craig's back—and moaned, as Craig reached down and encased his cock in both of his hands and worked it.

Nelson's hips started rolling in an old, familiar, but long unused rhythm, moving inside Craig's loose hold on his cock, as his tongue worked on Craig's nipples and up into his pits and then started working down his chest to where he planned to give Craig suck again.

But Craig laughed and lifted Nelson up with hands on his arms. "It's time to give you the cock, if you are interested in that."

"You would? Why? I don't understand. I'm just an old man . . . and you are a god."

"If you want it, I'll give it to you—and I'll tell you why. There need be no explanation for letting you suck me. You are a master of that. And age doesn't take that talent away. But do you want the cock or not?"

"It's so enormous. I don't—"

"Your throat took it. It remembered. Is there any reason why your channel doesn't remember—or doesn't want it?"

Nelson groaned and moaned and quietly wept in appreciation as he was bent over, belly on table, and Craig gently split and filled and worked inside him.

Nelson's ejaculations were weak, but there were two of them before Craig gave him his seed.

Then Craig sat on the table again, with Nelson on the chair between his thighs, cleaning Craig's cock with his tongue and licking his balls and, although he didn't intend to, helping Craig engorge again.

"You asked why," Craig murmured. "I haven't always been like this. I once was ugly and skinny as a rail. I knew I wanted men, but men didn't want me. What you see is a manufactured body. I've had work done to change nearly everything, including intensive work to tone up my body. I remember how it was to not be the center of the attention, to wonder if any man would ever take me. And, so, when I tire of men who know they are beautiful and preen themselves, I want a man, who like I once did, knows how to fully appreciate the fuck—who doesn't get as much as they need and who I know will make the most of what they now have."

"And now," he continued, "As you can see, my cock wants more of you. If you'll rise from the chair, please, I'll take your place and we'll see if you remember to lap fuck another man."

* * * *

Craig had had his eye on the young man for some time. That's why he'd come to this gym, known as a gay pickup venue. He knew he'd find someone like this here, because when he was young and before his body had undergone all of the work it had, he was this gawking youth himself. He had come to gyms just like this and gazed longingly at the hunks working out just like that guy over there was doing.

As Craig moved around the gym floor, working the various apparatuses, it became increasingly obvious that the young man, bumbling, barely legal, tall and gangly with a pimply horse face, was zeroing in on Craig as his object of worship.

It was late in the evening, just as Craig had planned it to be. Dex, the gym's night manager was a friend of his—someone he'd helped develop an indifferent body into a terrific one and to transform a complex about sexual relations with men into confidence and an ability to seduce and dominate.

So, Craig went over and talked with Dex briefly at the reception desk when he saw the gangly youth follow another of the guys with a great body off the floor and to the showers, no doubt hoping to get a look at the guy in the altogether and have a foundation on which to build a fantasy of a great sexual experience. In his absence—temporary, Craig was sure, as it was oh so evident the youth was most interested in following Craig to the shower room—Craig made a request of Dex and received a key.

As the crowd on the floor thinned out, Craig kept exercising, slowly and deliberately, giving the young guy all of the eye candy the youth could wish for.

At length it was just Craig and the pimple-faced, frustratingly shy young guy. Even Dex had packed it in.

Craig went over and locked the door of the gym from the inside, while the young guy, confused and only now realizing he was alone with Craig, shrank back into the shadows of a line of hulking treadmills with all the bells and whistles attachments.

Craig circled around and came up beside the youth and encircled him with one arm, while his other hand palmed the surprised young man's belly and continued under the hem of his gym shorts until Craig could take full possession of the half hard on he found.

"Uhhhgh," The young man sputtered in surprise. But now he was riveted to the spot, all of his attention going to the sensation of another man—not just another man, but a veritable god—fisting his cock.

"Don't talk," Craig said in a low voice. "We're all alone, locked in. I know you're scared and don't know how to start and probably have no one to start with."

"Oh, god," the youth whimpered. He was trembling and Craig had to hold him up to keep him from collapsing.

"Go to the showers and clean yourself real well—including the ass canal. Get that good and clean. Then go into the sauna. I'll follow. I'm going to make your first time something really special, an experience you'll never forget. We're going to have a ball, you and I."

The Mural

It arrested my attention as soon as I walked into the room. Bigger than life it was. A mural of four hunky American Indian warriors, three standing on a prairie and the fourth astride one of three saddleless pinto ponies. All of them were decked out in war point, wearing just loincloths and animal-skin boots and with beaded necklaces fashioned like chest armor. They were all looking at the door to the room with belligerent expressions on their faces as if daring anyone to enter.

Since it said on the door that this was the Apache suite, my guess is that they were Apaches. They were rendered in full, vibrant color on a white wall.

I was duly awed and intimidated. It was an unusual touch in the rooms of the Casa de Coronado that I certainly hadn't expected. I hadn't expected to be in this room at all, in a boutique hotel at the corner of Albuquerque's Old Town. It was quite a find—sections of white-painted adobe guest rooms set haphazardly in a lush garden. I might easily have passed it by and ended up in a nondescript chain hotel.

I had come to Albuquerque in search of something special, though. Although what I'd come to find was something entirely different from the Casa de Coronado and its lush setting and huge murals on the guest room walls.

This had been Pete's idea. We had been living together for nearly six months now, starting off as a casual setup of sharing the same studio apartment in Dallas that each of us used only part time, as both of us were in jobs that put us in Dallas less than a third of our time. We had met through a mutual friend who had thought we would hit it off, but both of us had gone into the arrangement purely from a cost-efficient expectation and with the hope that we'd never actually overlap in our need to use the apartment.

But we did overlap and it was a small place with just one, double bed. I was to find that Pete was gay and aggressively so. I hadn't even thought of this as a possibility of a choice. I guess I was more taken with myself—narcissistic—than with anyone else, male or female. I'd slept with women before, but more because it was expected of a rising young advertising executive than because I particularly enjoyed the encounters. Relieving sexual stress was OK, but the woman all seemed to expect something from me that I had no inclination to give.

This bothered me, of course, and I grew to believe there was something cold as ice inside me, something that held me back and made it impossible for me to completely let loose, something that made sex unfulfilling for me and my partner both.

The same thing—the cold as ice thing—happened with Pete.

The first night we both found ourselves at the studio apartment with just the one double bed after a full day's work in the separate jobs that brought us to Dallas—Pete was an urban architect—Pete seduced me. Pete never seemed to find this difficult to do. He certainly had me compromised before I fully realized what was happening to me. He was a gorgeous hunk with a healthy ego and an overpowering libido. And I was as naïve as they come—my weakness helped by a good wine buzz and a highly successful day in the workplace.

Pete had me naked and on the bed, with him stretched alongside me, his mouth on mine, and his hand stroking my dick in a progression of seemingly innocent and innocuous stages of seduction that raised no flags of doubt and resistance—well, few. I did rather think it was getting out of hand, but he was so charming and we were trying to adjust to being roommates, and I didn't want to be impolite—until he had my dick in his fist. And then he was giving me so much pleasure that I didn't want it to stop. I didn't want it to stop when he was also swabbing the inside of my mouth with his tongue. And I didn't want him to stop when his lips descended my torso, giving special attention to my nipples and arm pits and navel—and cock and balls. And I didn't want him to stop when he was showing me what his tongue and fingers could do in my asshole.

I did freeze up and want him to stop, though, when he had his knees between my thighs and was rolling a condom on his cock.

I froze solid then. I didn't try to throw him out of bed—we slept in each other's arms in the single double bed that night and every subsequent night we found ourselves in Dallas together. I even soon learned to give him suck to ejaculation too. But each time he tried to mount me, I froze and cut off the progression of the coupling.

It wasn't that I didn't want it—I most certainly did. I just froze. I couldn't take that next step.

Pete was good about it and patient with me, but I could tell that it wasn't satisfactory for him, that he wanted and needed to go all the way.

I told him I didn't mind if this was as far as we went and that he got his fulfillment in other ways—and even brought them back to the studio apartment while I was there to fuck them. And he did bring a nice young man to the apartment one night—a yielding, dark-haired handsome youth who was quite willing to do a threesome with Pete and me. We lay in triple embrace on the bed and I kissed the youth as Pete fucked him. And I was aroused by this and Pete had his bulb pressing on my opening before I clutched up and just couldn't go through with it. The youth volunteered to hold me in an arm lock for Pete to force me beyond the threshold, but Pete wouldn't do it. I don't know what I would have done if he had forced me. It might have been enough to rid me of my inhibitions, but I'm glad Pete didn't chance it. I have a feeling it would have ended the relationship right there.

I'm not sure why my failure to do it all didn't end the relationship. But Pete told me that he had fallen in love with me—that he was willing to take me the way I was and for us to go no farther than we did. I believed he meant what he said—intellectually. But I was equally sure that he could never accept a limited relationship like that emotionally.

I told him I was willing to adjust my life to his—but only if and when we got over that hurdle.

That's when Pete suggested Gentleman Jim's ranch outside of Albuquerque.

"It's essentially a male brothel," Pete said. "I can arrange for you to go there and be conditioned, if you like. If it doesn't work, it would not be me that you had the bad experience with and we could at least continue on the same level we now have."

"I want to be with you fully, I really do," I had assured him.

"I know you do. But I obviously can't take you that extra step. When you have been initiated, I'm sure we can fuck like rabbits and both enjoy it immensely. But I am not going to force you."

"You say conditioned."

"Yes. If you go there and we pay ahead and you sign a contract, they will take you over the threshold one way or the other."

"One way or the other?"

"Yes. If necessary, they will force you—not roughly but inescapably—and then they follow up. If after the third or fourth time, you aren't conditioned to it—don't want to do it—they will stop. You will have signed a contract to absolve them of all guilt and responsibility, though."

I shuddered at the thought. But I agreed to it. I truly did want to be able to go all of the way with Pete. If this didn't work, we'd be no worse off than we were. Or so I told myself.

Arrangements were made and on the Tuesday in a week I'd taken off for vacation time, I drove from Dallas to Albuquerque, arriving early on Wednesday. I drove straight to Gentleman Jim's ranch.

I was quaking in my boots when the jovial fatherly man met me at the ranch house door and guided me into a central, two-story room with a log-beam ceiling and set up like a Wild West saloon bar.

"Here are your gentlemen of the afternoon," he said. "Zack and Mex." Zack was a big-boned, strikingly handsome cowpoke type with great muscle tone, sandy hair, and a warm smile. Mex was an even bigger and hunkier Mexican of swarthy, slightly mean-looking demeanor.

"Two?" I said in a decidedly choked-up voice.

"Yes. Your contract calls for completion of the service, regardless of the wishes you express in the bedroom, and then conditioning. You are booked for two nights here. Zack and Mex will accommodate you until tomorrow morning and then you will be assigned to another two for tomorrow afternoon and night. We service such contracts with two of our gentlemen at once to assure that the contract will be fulfilled. Only one will be servicing you at a time, of course."

Well, thanks for that "of course," I thought. I swallowed hard on that. I had no doubts that either of these hulks could have me if they wanted—that I wasn't strong enough to hold off either one of them.

"Once you walk through that door with Zack and Mex, you are going to be provided what is in the contract. If you cannot agree to that, don't walk through that door." The man was still smiling affably and he had spoken softly, but I could feel the panic rising inside me.

"Uh. Thanks. But not today, I don't think. I need to think about this longer. Can I reschedule?"

"Yes, of course—for a 10 percent penalty, because you have taken a time slot that cannot be filled by another. You've already paid and if you wish to reschedule we can charge that card for the balance. But you really needn't come back this far again unless you are prepared to go through with the contract. We don't really have time to keep making and putting off appointments. Of course what you've paid is nonrefundable."

"I understand," I said. But I didn't really understand. It wasn't the arrangement I didn't understand. What I couldn't understand was what kept me on the edge, not being able to go in one direction or the other. It would have been different if I had rejected the notion of having Pete's churning cock in my channel—but, intellectually, I didn't reject it. I welcomed it and ached for it. I was even ready emotionally for it, I thought. But I . . . just . . . couldn't go over that edge.

I retreated as far as Albuquerque to think this through. I needed a night or two in solitary to either build up to it or prepare myself to say good-bye to Pete and go looking for some other apartment arrangements in Dallas. It wouldn't be fair to Pete if I couldn't make this work.

This is what led me to stopping at the Casa de Coronado almost by whim. I had decided to drive all of the way to the Rio Grande beyond the Old Town, eyeing the possible motels on the way, and then coming back to the one that had seemed the most attractive. The most attractive, though, had been at the end of my run—just a golf course separated the hotel grounds from the banks of the Rio Grande. I was sure they wouldn't have a room available. But they did. They said they had a signature suite unoccupied, the Apache Suite. And I said I'd take it.

The room was more than adequate. It was large, although the overpowering mural—especially the menacingly expressions on the hulking Apache warriors—made it look smaller. There was a sofa and tub chair under the window wall beside the entry door and an enormous bureau in the corner of the other side. It must have been eight feet tall. The insets of the doors of the armoire were lined with white cowhide with brown splotches—matching the coloring of the pinto ponies in the mural. The base of the bureau held drawers and the top a large TV. The bed was a high king-sized one with sturdy logs as the frame. The mural was on the wall at the left of the door, with the bureau holding down the end nearest to the door, a desk at the base of the mural, and an adobe Southwestern-style fireplace in the far corner.

The room was more than adequate for the one night I would stay here.

At twilight I walked into the Old Town. They were having some sort of concert and Mexican dancing on the square, which had caused crowds to gather, but I walked beyond that and turned right into an alley of shops leading toward the art museum, which was already closed at this hour. I found a small French restaurant tucked back into a corner.

The waiter was very attentive—and quite cute. He guided me through the menu at leisure like I was the only patron in the place, which wasn't true. It obviously was a popular eating place. It had been one of the ones the attendant at the front desk of the hotel had recommended me to. There weren't too many recommendations once you got past Mexican food, which didn't often appeal to me.

The waiter, who said his name was Emile, and who could really have been French for all I knew—his accent sounded authentic enough in my limited knowledge of the language; I'd taken German in college—was impressed at my wine choice. Frenchmen I knew little of; French wines I was conversant in. I should have had a companion for dinner or thought less of the wine. My head was fairly spinning when I left the restaurant.

The waiter had asked about whether I had a companion and clearly was making suggestions that I could have one if I wanted, but if I wasn't going to open my legs for Pete, I didn't see doing it for a French waiter in Albuquerque.

The entertainment was still going full blast when I walked by the plaza en route to the Casa de Coronado. And it made me feel sad and isolated. And mad at myself for not loosening up. I had wasted a perfectly good French waiter with my barriers and my unwanted prudishness.

When I opened the door of the Apache Suite and entered my room, I scowled back at the Apache warriors and fished a book out of my bag to read. I started a fire in the fireplace—it was there so I might as well use it—and settled in the tub chair.

The fire from the fireplace, though, cast dancing light onto the mural and made the Apache warriors look even more menacing and determined to be doing something more than just being plastered in place on the wall.

I couldn't concentrate on the book and I was in a haze of good wine. So, I stripped my clothes off, took a shower, turned off the light, and nestled under the covers of the king-sized bed. As far as I could determine, I went immediately into a deep sleep.

I woke to the sensation of a body lowering itself next to mine. Imagining myself back in the studio apartment with Pete, I sighed and turned on my back, awaiting his overture into a lovemaking that would go no further than a sixty-nine suck but that would be sufficient for me if not for Pete.

I did, indeed, feel a hand on my cock, and I moaned and began to move my hips in slow motion to the grip on the cock. But this didn't feel like the type of approach Pete made.

I opened my eyes to shock. The first thing I saw was that now there were only three Apache warriors on the wall mural, which was highlighted in a eerie, uneven light coming from the dying fire in the fireplace. All three of the Apaches had their faces turned to me now. And their facial expressions were filled with lust.

I started to cry out when I turned my head to see that the fourth warrior's body was stretched along mine. A strong hand covered my mouth, though, muffling my cry, and the other two warriors not sitting on a pony in the mural came off the wall and on the bed, joining the first in manhandling me. A scarf that had been hanging on the loincloth belt of one of the warriors— no doubt a souvenir of some raid on a wagon train—was being used as a gag to stifle my cries.

Two of the warriors held me down, while another one worked my body over with his lips and teeth, concluding the journey at my asshole, where he opened my channel with his tongue and teeth, while I panted heavily and bit into the scarf. Then I was carried by the three of them, squirming but without effect, back to the wall. They carried me through the wall and out onto the prairie.

The warrior on the pinto pony was scooting back onto the rump of the horse, taking off his loincloth, and smiling lasciviously at me, while the three other warriors lifted me onto the horse's back, in front of the seated warrior, with my back running up the horse's neck. The horse snorted and set its legs, but it held fast. The seated warrior's cock was in full erection.

The three standing warriors held me in place, imprisoning my arms and spreading my legs, while, as I

186

screamed through the scarf and tensed up and arched my back in fear and pain, the seated warrior put the bulb of his cock to my opening, revolved it around at the rim, and then literally screwed it into me. He stopped a few inches inside me for me to adjust to him. Free hands stroked my body and lips went to my nipples and cock.

Pete's words when he came close to taking me flowed into my mind. "Relax, just relax, and let the tension flow out of your body. It will be easier. The pleasure will enter sooner. You'll be able to take the cock. You'll see."

I closed my eyes and willed my body to relax, which, slowly it did. And as I relaxed, my channel yielded to the warrior's cock and he slowly filled me with his warm, throbbing shaft, moving ever farther up into me. The pain subsided and I felt filled, possessed. And then the cock began to slow pump me and all of my senses focused on my channel. I was moaning and my hips began involuntarily to roll with the fuck. My own hard cock was inside a warm, moist, sucking mouth and I could feel my juices rising. And I gave in completely to the experience, not thinking of the strange, exotic circumstances, but going with the fuck, enjoying it, not wanting it to stop.

This couldn't be a dream, I reasoned. I felt every sensation of the experience—the pain followed by the ecstasy of pleasure. I ejaculated, but the pumping inside me continued and the warm mouth held my cock as it softened.

I felt the ejaculation of the warrior inside me and heard his war cry of release. And then I was being pulled off him by the three warriors. They didn't release me, though.

One warrior, the tallest and most muscular of those who had been standing by the ponies, stood behind me, wrapped an arm around my belly and bent me over in half. My feet didn't touch the ground. Then his cock was pushing inside me and he fucked me by swinging me forward and back on his cock until he, too, came.

Exhausted, my eyes swimming in cum, I was carried to the bed then and the other two warriors, one after the other, fucked me as well. Or, rather, I fucked the fourth warrior, pushing him onto his back and straddling his hips, positioning his cock bulb at my hole myself, and impaling myself on his shaft and doing all of the pumping to his first and my second ejaculation.

I woke in the morning, woozy from the wine, feeling like I had slept little, and will a strange pain in my loins. But I was purring. I was laying on my side and when my eyes focused they saw the beads of an elaborate Indian necklace on the nightstand. I couldn't remember that having been there last night. I turned my eyes to the mural. All was in order there—or so I initially thought. One of the standing warriors wasn't wearing a beaded necklace and all of the others were. I could have sworn that they all were painted wearing the chest decorations.

And now that I looked harder, their expressions were no longer scowling and menacing. Now they all had a slight smile on their faces.

I took up the beads and dropped them into my suitcase en route to hobbling to the bathroom. I was hobbling because there was a pain in my ass—and I briefly thought I might as well have eaten at a Mexican restaurant last night if my ass was going to be on fire in the morning anyway.

I showered and then when I came out of the bathroom, I made a call to Gentleman Jim's ranch. It may have all been my imagination—it probably was. But I felt I was across the barrier now. To make sure, I'd keep that date at Gentleman Jim's before I returned to Pete. I felt no inhibitions now about being topped. Now I couldn't wait for the next time. And besides, Pete and I had already paid a big sum for the contract.

Zack had a piston for a cock, fucking me forever until I had come twice. And Mex had a cock that stretched me to the limit and reached for my tonsils. I thoroughly enjoyed them both—and the two guys from the next day almost as much. None of the four could imagine why I'd come to them with any inhibitions about being cocked at all. But I paid them all well, so none of them got into the particulars on what had loosened me up between the afternoon I'd withdrawn from them, a shaking mess, and the day Zack and I fucked on the floor because I couldn't wait for it to get to the bed.

It was late afternoon when I left Gentleman Jim's ranch, so I decided to stop in Albuquerque overnight again before driving back to Dallas. I didn't intend on checking back into the

Casa de Coronado. I didn't need that anymore. I planned to just find one of the chain hotels. But I stopped first at the little French restaurant I had eaten in before. The waiter was still there, but it turned out he wasn't just a waiter. He also owned the French bistro and his rooms were just upstairs. So, I didn't need a hotel room that night and I proved to myself once again that I had no trouble with having my ass pinned to a mattress by a man's churning cock.

All the way home to Dallas in the car the following day, I was wondering if the Indian beads would still be in my bag when I opened it.

The Songbird and the Philanthropist

As a child, Monsignor Rainero had always been considered a clever boy, if perhaps a bit more clever than for his own good. He was known to have very inventive and attractive ideas, but he sometimes was known to overembelish them to the point where the scheme collapsed around him. Having seen this played out time and time again, after Rainero had started out in his father's tourist resort business in Umbria and suggested that the visitors at the resort might enjoy the offering of outings to the region's principle economic ventures—which were pig farming and salami production—Rainero's father steered Rainero to a vocation in the church instead.

The newly minted priest, lifted rather high rather fast because of his family's position in the region, became somewhat of a celebrity for his inventive ideas. The latest of these schemes—a populist radio address from Perugia three times a week in which listeners would be enticed to tune in one way or the other and would, in the context of the program, receive a homily from Monsignor Rainero—was thus what brought Monsignor Rainero to the Albergo La Torre café in Castiglione del Lago on the banks of the scenic Lake Trasimeno on this sunny May morning.

He was sitting at the open-air tables just outside the café's wide doors with the patron he wished to reel in to provide financial backing for his radio program, the Count de la Giovani Montefeltro. Both had just immensely enjoyed the singing of Pepo, a young tenor with pure, haunting tones, who had performed for them as he did hourly at this café in the high tourist season. They were a good distance from Perugia, the largest town in the Umbia region, where the parish that Monsignor Rainero now served existed, but Rainero was from the Trasimeno lake region himself and often came down to the small villa he had inherited on the banks of the lake near where Castiglione del Lago, once the fourth island of the lake, now joined the mainland. For his part, Giovani Montefeltro, who Rainero was now trying to cultivate, was from an ancient noble family of the region.

"This is a pleasant café, is it not?" the monsignor murmured to the patrician nobleman. He had been watching his companion carefully and was gratified that the man's attention had been straying to the corner of the café where Pepo had been singing. Although Rainero lived in Perugia and the count lived in the lake region, Montefeltro habitually came to Rainero in Perugia to give confession. There were a couple of very good reasons for this. The Montefeltros and Rainero's family had been intertwined for centuries, and also what Montefeltro had to confess—which very much had to do with the looks he was giving the young, blond singer at the Albergo La Torre café—was not something the count, married to the daughter of an industrialist who paid the bills for the maintenance of the Montefeltro ancestral estate, wanted to confess to priests in his own parish.

"Yes, quite pleasant indeed," Montefeltro whispered back, without taking his eyes off the young singer, who had finished singing and was chatting with the man at the piano and also with the owner of the café, a big bruiser of a northern Italian named Saladino. The use Saladino was making of his hands at the waist and on the arm of the young singer left little doubt of the nature or extent of his proprietary rights in that quarter.

Herein had been the dilemma that had been set for Monsignor Rainero. The monsignor had first heard the hauntingly beautiful voice of the young tenor the previous month when Rainero had been visiting his family villa, having received permission to air his Perugia entertainment-mixed-with-religion broadcasts but only then realizing all of his plans were just that so far—plans written in a prospectus. He had retreated to Castiglione del Lago to think upon how he could put reality to these plans. He needed money and he needed entertainments that would attract listeners to tune in to his radio program.

Sitting at the Albergo La Torre café one day in deep thought, Rainero's musings had evaporated as soon as Pepo had started to sing. Here, surely, Rainero thought, was one answer to his entertainment needs. He would ask the young Pepo to move to Perugia and sing for him on the radio. The church would pay, of course—or at least some patron would when Rainero solved that piece of the puzzle—but Pepo could also sing just as well—and probably more profitably—in the cafes of the larger city of Perugia as he could here at the lakeside.

As excited as he was about this divinely inspired plan, Rainero rose from his chair in the open-air area of the café and sought out the young singer after he had finished a set. Rainero's progress was arrested, however, at the entrance of the corridor leading from the café's interior dining area to the back of the facility. Just as he was about to enter the shadowed corridor, he sensed motion at the farther end, at an open door at the end of the corridor, into which the sunlight of the day was being filtered.

Two figures were leaning against the wall of the corridor, the larger one encasing the body of the smaller one between him and the wall. Both were men, the singer, Pepo, and the café owner, Saladino. Both were naked from the waist down. Pepo's back was against the rough, white-washed stone of the corridor wall, and his legs were raised and hooked on the thighs of the big brute of a northern Italian, Saladino, whose chest was pushing Pepo's back against the corridor wall and moving it up and down on the rough, white-washed stone, while Saladino's dick thrust up in long strokes inside the young singer's channel.

The café owner must have been nearly fifty, if not beyond. His body was brawny and big boned and his countenance that of a prize fighter past his prime. And yet Pepo was moaning for him and clutching the older man's buttocks closely into him with the digging claws of his hands.

Monsignor Rainero withdrew to plan his line of reasoning with this young man. He could surely do better than the rough and cruel northern Italian café owner in Perugia.

But when Rainero took Pepo aside on his next visit to the café and nudged into his proposition that Pepo come to Perugia to sing on the radio, an offer that surely would be honey to the taste buds of any young man moldering away in the Umbria countryside, he was surprised that Pepo declined, saying that he had a place here that suited him fine. Rainero did what he could to hint that there were better options than the brutish Saladino, but Pepo would not listen to any of this, whether from fear or from fetish for an older, rough lover.

Rainero was amazed at the resistance of the young singer, and this became a conundrum at the back of his mind for the next several weeks. It was even there when next Count Giovani Montefeltro came to Perugia to give confession, and, to Rainero's mind, to place himself in position to be asked to underwrite the costs of Rainero's radio broadcasts. And it was during Giovani's confession that bells started to ring in the back of Rainero's mind.

Giovani was a handsome, refined, older man. He was tall and one might call him thin, but he also was well formed—surely refined and elegant were the best words to describe him. And from his confessions, Rainero couldn't help but discern that the count enjoyed fucking young men. They invariably were stable hands and chauffeurs, though, and just as the monsignor was musing that a noble, refined man like Giovani really deserved a more suitable lover, the thought of Pepo returned to the surface of his mind.

And Monsignor Rainero's mind began to weave an elaborate plan of working his broadcast needs in consort. Thus today and the planned meeting between Rainero and Giovani at the Albergo La Torre café.

"I see you are taken with the café's young singer," Rainero said to Giovani across the café table as he set his coffee cup down and smiled a knowing smile.

Giovani gave the monsignor a shocked look.

"Please," Rainero said in a dismissive tone. "You have brought your confessions to me. Have I ever judged?"

"Yes, yes, I confess I am," the count answered. Then he was caught up short by the repetition of the confession word and its connection to his attraction to the young singer and gave a half distressed look at the monsignor, his confessor. But Rainero just smiled back, clearly signaling that there was no judgment to be seen in his countenance.

"I confess myself," the monsignor whispered, "that I am trying to convince the singer—his name is Pepo—to come to Perugia to sing on the radio program I am trying to interest you in. And you've said you were planning on spending more time at your Perugia residence, did you not?"

Rainero let that linger in the air between them across the café table for several moments, as Giovani gave him a searching look.

Having discerned there was an understanding between them and any shock of what Rainero was working toward had been weathered, the monsignor continued. "I really would like to talk to you more about support for my radio broadcasts, but for now, do you think you and Pepo would like to see my family's small villa here in Castiglione del Lago? It's really quite charming—and very private—and it is nearby."

Giovani looked slightly agitated and then perplexed. "Why are you—?"

"I wish help in convincing the singer to come to Perugia for me. He seems to be under the sway of that brute of a café owner over there. See him? I think young Pepo needs to break from that influence—for his own good. I think he should have more refined friends. Sometimes the priesthood has to work in strange ways to achieve what is best."

Giovani still looked a bit agitated, but Rainero could tell from his change in demeanor that lust and want—and his wish to believe the convenient reasoning he was being given—were winning out.

The count simply curtly nodded his head and looked away toward the lake.

When Rainero sought out Pepo and turned the young singer's attention to the outside table where the count sat, trembling a bit and dreaming of possibilities, the monsignor wasn't altogether unarmed. Other men in Castiglione del Lago had had confessions to make—and although not to Rainero, the brotherhood of priests weren't all pristinely closed mouthed in their discussions with each other. Rainero knew that Pepo would go with a man for a price—that he would more than sing for his supper.

"He won't know there is a price," Rainero whispered to the young singer, as he pressed banknotes in the young man's hand. "He will be more pleased to think of it as a seduction—and you can trust me when I tell you that I have every reason to believe he is good at that."

"Why are you doing this?" Pepo asked. But he had his eyes on Giovani, and Rainero could tell from the slitting of his eyes and the way his tongue was playing on his lips that Pepo needed little convincing to go with Giovani.

"I wish him to be a patron for that radio program I have discussed with you. I only wish for you to help me convince him to invest in that."

Rainero found the seduction of Pepo by Giovani on the balcony of his villa overlooking Lake Trasimeno both touching, and, despite his vocation, arousing.

At first Rainero joined the other two on the balcony, bringing two bottles of wine and three glasses. He stayed with them until all were comfortable and had stripped down to their waists to soak in the sun while watching the boats bob on the waters of the lake. When the second bottle of vino was opened, Rainero faded away into the interior of the villa. The other two didn't even seem to notice he was gone as taken as they were with each other in chit chat and ever-more suggestive looks and exploratory touching.

Giovani had his arm around the back of Pepo's chair, and when he cupped Pepo's bicep in a hand, the younger man leaned into him and sighed.

Rainero saw that the second bottle of wine was empty and he went into the kitchen to get another one. But when he came back, he saw that no more wine was needed—at least on the balcony—as the two men were kissing, and from what the monsignor could see, Giovani's free hand was in Pepo's lap. So, Rainero returned to the kitchen for another wine glass, pulled the cork on the bottle, and sat in a sofa with a full view of the balcony and slowly drank down the third bottle himself.

Pepo disappeared for a while, the view of his kneeling body being blocked by Giovani's back and spread legs. And then a naked Pepo was straddling Giovani's thighs and the two were kissing, with Pepo's hands laced in the well-groomed gray-streaked black hair at the back of Giovani's head. Giovani was gripping Pepo's waist on both sides and moving the youth's body in rhythm to the rocking of the balcony chair they both now occupied and the grunts and groans of the fuck.

When, with a harmonizing tenor and baritone cry of release, the sounds of coupling and the rhythmic movement had ceased and Pepo was sighing and collapsed onto Giovani's body in satisfied exhaustion, the monsignor tiptoed out to the door sill onto the balcony and whispered in Giovani's ear that he had been called away to priestly duties in the village and that the two were free to use the small villa's main bedroom. And then Rainero left. When he returned two hours later, the moans led him to the bedroom, where Pepo was stretched out on his belly on the bed and Giovani was riding his hips like a camel on the desert, crouched over the body of the younger man, his hands covering those of Pepo, their fingers laced together. So intent were they in the pleasure they were giving each other that they had no idea the monsignor had come and then gone.

It was almost morning before the monsignor returned again to find that the villa, at last, was deserted. He barely had time to gather his clothes and motor back to Perugia to be there for the next mass he had promised to give.

Days and then a week and more went by before the monsignor was able to give Pepo and Giovani a thought. Indeed, he didn't think he had to think much about them. He was very pleased with himself and was content in the belief that they both, each working the agenda that Rainero had set for them in exchange for bringing them together, would now come through for his plans for the radio program. It was the radio program that was consuming his time and attention—making all of the preparations for going on air.

At the point where he had to actually provide funds to the radio station, Monsignor Rainero decided it was time for another visit to Castiglione del Lago to settle his two-pronged arrangement with Pepo and Giovani.

At the Albergo La Torre café, the monsignor was met with a sour-faced Saladino, who towered over him, beefy arms crossed, and obviously keyed up and angry.

"Pepo? That worm? He left me, more than a week ago. No notice, no nothing. Not even time to find a replacement, and it's high season."

Backing away from there, and without giving it much thought, Monsignor Rainero drove out to the Count de la Giovani Montefeltro's nearby country estate, where a somewhat surly servant answering the door told him the count wasn't there, and a disheveled countess, appearing at the door as Rainero was opening the door to his car, screamed in distraught tones that the count indeed was gone and a curse on him and all men.

It dawned on Rainero that it was possibly natural that Pepo and Giovani wouldn't be at the Montefeltro villa. Perhaps he should have checked the count's town home in Perugia before he came here. Perhaps they were already set up there. But then, again, perhaps they were at his own small villa here in Castiglione del Lago.

A check there indicated that, no they weren't there—that no one had been there since he had hurriedly left himself. The bed was still unmade and there were two empty wine bottles on the balcony and another one on the floor at the base of the sofa.

As he was leaving the villa, a village priest was walking up the road.

"The count?" the village priest responded to Rainero's query. "You mean Giovani Montefeltro, who fucks young men

198

and thinks others don't all know he does just because he goes to you in Perugia to give his confession? Why, he and that young singer at the Albergo La Torre café ran off to Florence more than a week ago. The word is that neither one is coming back, either."

Monsignor Rainero withdrew back into his villa and sat heavily down onto the sofa. His foot hit the empty wine bottle and he watched it roll away from him.

A radio program to pay for and format within a week and so far he had nothing. Less than nothing, he thought bitterly. He had paid for the first fuck of Montefeltro's from Pepo and he was out three perfectly good bottles of wine. Well, two, he admitted. He'd drunk this one all by himself.

He sat there and thought and thought and thought. Maybe he shouldn't make such elaborate plans all the time. Maybe he should make simpler plans and let them build on their own if that happened naturally. And then he looked at the wine bottle again. It was from the winery of Landolfo Ordelaffi, who lived just outside Perugia and who brought Rainero a bottle of wine from his vineyard each time he came to confession. Funny that he should think of Ordelaffi, the monsignor was thinking. That man's latest confession was that he had taken the young opera mezzo-soprano Melina Doria for his mistress. "Hmm," Rainero thought. "Ordelaffi has plenty of money to burn and Melina Doria's voice would be simply divine on my radio program."

The Whisper Man

"So, you think you might be OK, now? A different perspective, I hope?"

"Yes, yes, thank you, . . . You know I haven't gotten your name. I feel so . . ."

"No need to, son. You can just call me Dingle. And I won't be seeing you up here again, I do hope."

"Umm. I kinda hoped that—"

"Oh, I didn't mean it that way. Of course you can come visit me whenever you have a hankering to. I meant I hoped I wouldn't see you climbing around on the cliff top again. It's mighty dangerous over there."

"No . . . no, sir, I don't think you'll see me . . . walking around there anymore."

They looked at each other, both knowing what was meant but not said.

They were standing, awkwardly, at the door to the lighthouse in the evening mist so heavy now that, although the structure stood at the edge of a precipice over the entrance to the harbor and they could hear the surf pounding on the rocks at the base below, they couldn't see the water.

Dingle watched the young man as he, mercifully, took the path leading down to the shore rather than the one that ran precariously out along the top of the cliff. Then Dingle sighed a satisfied sigh and withdrew into the base of the lighthouse, which was also his living quarters—his bedroom the next level up and then the bath and a small laundry. Two smaller floors of storage rooms rose above that in the narrowing tower, with his "operations" room at the top, capped only by a strobing light chamber bulbing out over the whole, erect structure.

You had to be in great shape to manage the stairs in a lighthouse, and Dingle was, even though he was well into his fifties. He was in great shape. Working out was his second favorite activity. There wasn't much else he could bide his time with on this isolated promontory jutting out to sea over the entrance into the harbor. It was a solitary life, and the requirements of the lighthouse weren't onerous. The harbor town, such as it was, was a good twenty miles inland, the harbor being long and narrow, and the shipping and fishing industry hereabouts not being what it used to be.

There were moments when Dingle was afraid they might close down this lighthouse. But the passage through the straits here was treacherous and there was a more modern, bustling, and heavily populated harbor city beyond here just up the coast requiring an assurance of safe passage through this patch of difficulty.

Dingle didn't know what he'd do if they closed him down. This had been his life for nearly fifteen years now.

There were no working family farms or sheepherding ranches out this way anymore. A large conglomerate had bought just about everyone out with the stated intention of putting a power plant out here and also going into cattle raising for the market down at the big city in a big way. But the downturn in the economy had put that on hold.

"Thank the gods for that," Dingle mused as he puttered around the semicircle of kitchen cabinetry that followed the curve of the wall on the first level. He hadn't had time to put the tea things away before they'd gone up the ladder. He thanked the gods for the delay in settlement around here, because it would surely put this good thing—his whole life—in peril.

It was only Dingle and this lighthouse for miles about—with the exception of the young men's military school on the shore just inside the entrance to the harbor.

An isolated, foreboding chunk of fearsome concrete, it was. Placed there to intimidate the young men sent there—of college age and great athletic program material, most of them. But recalcitrant, lazy, slow learning, or, worse, criminal young men. Some of them young men who just didn't fit—who had chosen what was not acceptable. It was an institution of last resort for most of them—shape up and meet the specifications for getting on that football team on a scholarship at Big U or shape up and take one last chance to stay out of prison or a life of unacceptance. Or else.

They weren't coddled at that school, no sir. And, being young men coming in with chips on their shoulders or fears in their hearts into a regimented institution that naturally formed its survival cliques and pecking orders, it was a stressful environment for any young man who couldn't fit the mold—or couldn't convince others he did. The only difference between the Hansen Military Academy and a prison for hardened criminals was that more of the inmates at Hansen were not hardened—in fact were quite vulnerable—young men, and that the students at Hansen had periods in which they could leave the school grounds. Of course, not many left very often, because there wasn't much of anyplace to go.

There was, though, a path leading up to the high cliffs overlooking the perilous entrance to the harbor—and there was the lighthouse.

* * * *

Young Daniel wasn't headed in any particular direction when he left the barracks. He'd just known he had to get out of there. They'd been teasing him again. Left that DVD on his nightstand so that any of the other guys who passed by—and a lot did—could see the photo on it, would know instantly what it was. And would assume he put it there—like he was advertising or something.

203

Why had that Jack Tangier from his neighborhood been sent here too? In truth, it was Jack who came here first—and he, Daniel, was only here because his parents had found out about the place from Jack's parents.

But for the same reason Daniel's parents had sent him here, they shouldn't have sent him where another guy from the neighborhood was sent. Jack's issue was that he and some others had stolen a car one night and gone for a joy ride. He'd been slated to start his second year down at Florida State this year, with a guaranteed spot on the basketball team. But the drunken escapade with the car had scotched all of that. Still, he was good enough on the basketball court, that all of that had been hushed up and the worst he got was a year here at Hansen to straighten himself—and his faltering grades—out.

Daniel had been sent here for another reason. And Jack Tangier had known what that reason was. And even before Daniel had arrived at Hansen, so did nearly every other young man in the school.

And they teased and harassed him mercilessly. And he couldn't take any more. The DVD and the comments and threats and demands that came after that had sent Daniel stumbling out of the barracks and away from the school grounds at dusk.

He had no idea where he was going. He only knew what he wanted to do. What he was determined to do. The only thing he thought there was left to do.

He found his feet leading him to the path that went up to the cliffs at the entrance of the harbor. He'd been up there a few times in the daylight. And it had scared him. The footing was treacherous. The slightest misstep from the path—obviously made for goats—and you'd be tumbling down onto the rocks and into the surging surf thirty feet below. The cliff-side path had been posted, of course. They didn't keep the guys from Hansen from going out there, though. And it was one of the rites of passages at the academy—to make it all the way from one end of the path to the other.

Daniel had only been there the once. It had scared the shit out of him. He hadn't made it down the path. It had been an easy way to die, he'd thought. And that thought now propelled him up the cliff—to the path leading along its top.

He had been standing there, for some time, on the edge. Crying quietly and going over all of the events of his life—all of the reasons why he'd do this, why there was no other choice. Trying to build up the courage to actually do it.

"It's becoming a cold evening. Fancy a cup of coffee, son? I know I'm ready for one."

The voice was soft, almost a whisper—coming from the edge of Daniel's vision in the misty gloom.

Now that he'd heard it, he felt like it was at least the second time he'd been addressed. It was so easy for words to be snatched away and wafted out over the sea here on an evening like this.

"What?" His response wasn't brilliant. But it was a response. He was engaging. And it drew him back a step from the edge.

"I said that I'd just put the pot on when I saw you walking up the path from down at the shore. I bet you're from Hansen's. You wouldn't have guessed, but I get a lot of the lads visiting me up here from Hansen's. I'd like to think it's the conversation. But I think it's probably the coffee and cookies. Don't get much of them down at Hansen's, I wouldn't imagine. It can be a bit too strict down there—and not understanding enough. Don't you think?"

He was rambling, certainly, and Daniel had to strain to hear him. He was still doing barely more than whispering. Daniel had to step back a few more steps to hear him, even though the whisperer was drawing closer to him.

"My name is Dingle, what's yours?" he was asking as he drew near. Daniel almost tripped on a projecting rock as he stepped closer another step—to hear the man better—and Dingle extended a hand to help keep him from falling. When Daniel had steadied himself, Dingle left his hand on Daniel's elbow.

"My name is Dingle, what's yours?" he repeated. Still the soft, reassuring, neutral whisper.

"Daniel. Thanks. I think I'd better . . . though."

"You're shivering son. How about a nice cup of coffee before you go down. Ever seen a lighthouse?"

"No. I haven't." Daniel looked up at the lighthouse, looking from here like it was rising out of a cloud at its base. From here, like this, the phallic aspect of it didn't escape him, and he moaned softly.

"Coffee and cookies? What do you say to that?"

* * * *

"So, what you're saying is that you fancy going with other boys—men? Well, if so, there's nothing wrong with that. It's just a thing of nature. The only shame is feeling the shame and letting others make you feel it."

Dingle was talking about it—his voice still not that much above a whisper—like there was nothing to it. That all Daniel had to do was recognize and accept it. This was something Daniel had never heard before. Everyone else either wanted it on the sly or wanted to lecture him about it being a sickness, a sin, a weakness that he had to "cure" or hide or run away from.

"I can't go back. They all—"

"Do you know the look of a man when he wants you, Daniel?"

"Yes. Yes, I guess I do." Daniel hadn't thought about it before—he certainly hadn't been able to talk to anyone about it. Dingle was the first one he could be open to about it. But he'd answered right out. Without thinking about it, he guessed, he did know that look.

"Go back and look around at the senior-most students there, Daniel. The biggest, most popular athletes. Pay attention to them looking at you. You are someone they would look at. Don't downgrade yourself there."

"Yes, but—"

"And when you get that look from one of them—and you will, I can guarantee it; I can give you a few names even, if you want—when one of them looks at you like that, give him what he wants. He'll protect you. You won't have trouble from any of the other guys after that."

Daniel was silent for a moment, thinking.

206

"And it will be freeing. It won't be just the protection you're getting from him. Trust me on that."

After a pause, Daniel looked up and spoke. "No one has talked to me about it like this—like it's just normal for some guys. Not something to fight—or to fight about. Thanks. I don't know how to thank—"

But then he looked up at Dingle and into his eyes. The look. The look was there, and Daniel knew how he could thank Dingle.

Looking at Dingle before they had climbed the ladder to the second level, leaving the half-finished coffee things where they were on the small wooden table, Daniel saw a weather-beaten, graying man more than twice his age. But seeing Dingle upstairs, unclothed, and then lying under Dingle as he deeply plowed him over the next hour, Daniel saw and felt a tower of strength and power—an experienced man with a lighthouse of a phallus who could work his body as no one else ever had in his earlier furtive couplings.

And it wasn't just the fucking. Dingle laid Daniel on his back on the small cot of a bed in the center of the circular chamber and knelt between his trembling thighs and sucked and stroked with his hand and worked Daniel's rim with his lips and tongue and teeth until, writhing under him, Daniel came in a profusion of release. No one, in all of his brief, secret fumblings, had made love to Daniel's cock and rim like this—centering on Daniel, concentrating on giving him the ultimate pleasure. Before, it had always been furtive and almost comically inexpert.

Dingle was a masterful lover.

And, oh, the fucking. After Daniel's release, Dingle rising up on his feet between Daniel's thighs, telling Daniel what he was going to do and showing him the massive staff he was going to do it with—and then doing it—slowly, drawing out every sensation of the taking. Slow slide in, slow, slow, deep, deeper. Daniel crying out, the pace quickening and Dingle moving the positions, seeking ever deeper access, ever more intimate embraces and fervent kisses. Showing Daniel ways of taking he'd never dreamed of before. Daniel ejaculating again—and then again. Dingle taking his time, no one to worry about seeing or hearing them. An hour and more of the most glorious taking Daniel had ever had.

Being shown, in the clearest way possible, how good life could be.

Still holding hands at the door, Dingle whispered—as he had done with other young men before and before that, "No need to walk on the cliffs now, Daniel? A bit different perspective on life now? Not so bleak?"

"Yes. Oh, yes, Dingle. Can I—?"

"Come back to see me? Yes, lad. Anytime you have the notion. Anytime you need reminding that it can be something special—and is worth living for." Said in a whisper. But now, fully in tune with the master, Daniel clearly heard every word, felt deeply its meaning and salvation.

* * * *

"I have a secret, Dingle," spoken in belabored tones, his back arched against Dingle's chest, a leg raised over Dingle's thigh, Dingle's hand palmed on his breasts, thumbing his nipples, while Dingle was still moving his cock deep inside his channel.

"We all have secrets, Sean," Dingle whispering in Sean's ear, teething an earlobe and enjoying the gasp at the magic his cock was playing out in Sean's channel.

"Yes, but mine is about you. I should not tell."

"Then don't."

"I didn't come up here to jump. Others haven't either. I'm sure some have, but most haven't."

"Ah."

"I came up here for your cock—your fucking. It's legendary."

"That's perhaps no secret to me—the part of why some of you come up here. My young men, ones who come back—and come back for years after Hansen. Some have confessed. But it doesn't matter, Sean. Some do come up here to jump. That is why I am still here when a young man comes struggling up the path."

All told in a soft, melodious whisper.

unfathomable

I had sat there at Joey's beachside bar for more than an hour, watching the young man playing in the surf. When I'd first arrived at the bar, both bored and out of sorts, I'd seen him on his surfboard, riding the waves and doing quite well at it. At length, however, I saw him tire of that and come up on the beach and bury the tip of the board into the wet sand, with a strong force that, in itself, would have arrested my attention.

He was probably not over twenty and had a natural sensuality that made me catch my breath. He was tall, but not overly so, and on the lithe side, but even there, it was not at the expense of natural body tone, hard muscle, and a perfect balance of symmetry and beauty. His hair was dark, as were his eyes when he came close enough for me to see them. The hair was long and silky, and I was to learn it came down to below his shoulders, although when I first saw him it was tied back in a ponytail. The sun had tanned him deeply—he might even have been of Hispanic ancestry. His legs were strongly muscled without being heavy, and much of his body was covered—but again not overly much—in tightly curled black hair. His chin had that five-o'clock shadowing that so many young men prefer these days, and the body hair was more prominent on his forearms and legs and undergirded his pectorals, with a line running down his sternum and pronounced six pack and into the waistband of his low-rise, almost thong, navy-blue swimsuit. His nipples were pronounced, the aureoles large, and peeked out of his curly chest hair enticingly. A silver ring in one nipple only heightened the sensuality and mystery of him.

It was easy for me to be smitten. I had sent Scott packing earlier that day. It wasn't just that he had become grasping and was taking for granted that I would give him anything he wanted just to be in my bed when I wanted him there. I had become bored with him. His only conversation was about some electronic toy or clothing item he wanted. And he'd become untrustworthy, hanging out with other men his age, whispering to them knowingly—I'm sure talking to them about me and what I did for him—what he did to me. And his eyes had been roving, like he was looking for his next sugar daddy rather than concentrating on the one he had.

He hadn't been pleased when I'd had Thomas pack his bags and put them by the front door in the foyer and laid just enough cash out on the top of a suitcase for him to fly back to New York. But I had no commitment to him. I was bored.

Unfortunately, I also was horny and I hadn't thought ahead too well. I wanted what Scott gave me. I just didn't want it to be Scott who gave it to me. Always before when I'd come down here to the beach, I'd had someone in tow. I hadn't had to go to bars alone or hadn't had to try to cruise. I was a little too old for cruising, I had to admit. And I hadn't had to do it for years. I always brought my young men down from New York— where they sought me out. Where they wanted to be close to me, to be seen with Peter Cordell, to appear perhaps in photos in the society pages, where they would be lurking behind me and whatever beautiful super model I had on my arm for public appearance sake.

When Scott was gone, I walked the streets of the resort town, thinking that I would enjoy doing so when I was free and when no young man was cajoling me to look in this shop or that and to buy him this or that. But I quickly found that I didn't want to be alone. I just didn't want to be constantly wheedled to give, give, give.

I'd found myself at the patio bar off the back of Joey's—really just a vine-covered trellis over a deck out on the sand behind a rather seedy beach bar—and watching the activity on the beach. There wasn't much of it.

But my eyes would have picked out the dark, young man even if the beach had been crowded. He moved like a dancer. Fluid motion. As he moved, I could see his burnt-gold skin stretching over hard muscle. This was accentuated when he stretched out as he drove the front edge of the surfboard into the sand. In what was almost a connected, extended motion, he'd stripped off the tight black Lycra leggings he'd been wearing to surf—and I almost became breathless at seeing him just in a skimpy swimming suit. What were surely heavy balls and a thick cock were pulling the front of the thong-type suit down to where I could see a good inch of curly black pubic hair. I found that the beer glass I was holding was trembling. I wanted to palm his belly and move my hand down under that waistband.

After he had planted the surfboard in the sand, he walked slowly up the beach toward where I sat. His eyes were cast off to the side of me, though, and his feet were carrying him on a veering path off toward my left. For the first time I looked along the beach at the verge between sand and vegetation and saw that there was a line of red- and white-striped cabanas, the door flaps of some closed and of others lifted on stakes to make a sort of entrance porch.

The young man was moving toward the first of these, his smiling eyes latched onto an older man sitting on a beach chair in the shade of the open and raised flap of the first cabana to my left. The man looked like he was in his late fifties. A banker perhaps. He too was deeply tanned. His hair was gray, including a thick patch on his chest. I wouldn't say he was heavy, but he had the look of a man who once had been well-toned but was beginning to be defeated by time. Distinguished looking, though, at least from the side angle I got. And his eyes were plastered on the movement of the young man as he approached.

And whose wouldn't be? I know mine were.

The two only had eyes for each other, though, and as the young man drew closer, I saw that he had a gorgeous, almost mischievous smile that melted hearts and launched propositions.

The young man stood there in front the older man for a brief moment, as they conversed. The older man had been reading a hardback book, which he turned over in his lap without closing it.

I watched, almost in shock, as the older man put a hand on one of the younger man's thighs and the younger man leaned forward and took the older man's lips with his, while one of his hands slipped underneath the book on the older man's lap. The older man responded, the two of them still lost in the kiss, by raising his hand from the other man's thigh and cupping his basket through the barely covering material.

They came out of the kiss and the older man rose and turned and walked into the cabana. The younger man looked around—I looked away just in time for him not to think that I had been watching—and then entered the cabana as well, pulling the flap closed.

I sat there, trembling, for several minutes, not realizing that I was holding my breath until I almost passed out from the lack of oxygen.

I couldn't help myself. I was drawn to the cabana like a moth to the light. Standing and looking around to see if anyone was watching me, I sauntered—or tried to make it appear like I was aimlessly sauntering—off the deck and onto the sand. I'd already paid for my drinks. I walked off to my left, down the beach and parallel to the water's edge until I'd passed four cabanas. When I reached the fourth one, I walked around to the rear of that cabana and started working my way back toward Joey's, all the time looking around as casually as I could muster to see if anyone was watching me. There was almost no one there. It was late in the season and a weekday. The resort coast was nearly deserted.

I had already seen that the cabanas were constructed like panel flaps, so that the material didn't bend around the corners and the panels of the tents would lay flat when the cabanas were taken down. The material was slit there and the corners were held together by a series of ties from ground to roof. Standing at one of the back corners of the cabana, I could easily part the panels between ties enough to spy what was going on inside.

I almost gasped as I saw the older man, chest down on a beach lounger, and up on his knees, his buttocks in the air, with the younger man, crouched athletically over his hips, hands clutching the older man's waist, and slow fucking the older man, using the leverage of his feet on the lounger next to the older man's thighs for control in the rhythm of the fuck. The young man's black, silky hair had been let loose and it did, indeed, cascade to below his shoulders. It shimmered in the rhythm of the fuck. The sounds and murmurings both made indicated that they were taken with each other and thoroughly comfortable in the fuck. They weren't hurrying; there was nothing furtive in their coupling. This wasn't a chance encounter, I knew.

They were displayed at an angle from me, their butts toward where I was positioned. The older man's buttocks were milky white, but there were almost indistinct tan marks on the younger man's undulating buttocks. I watched, mesmerized, at the beautiful butt cheeks of the younger man clinching and expanding as he fucked the older man. And I gasped again when I saw the younger man's cock withdraw a good half foot from the ass of the older man without losing purchase and then sliding in again. And again, and again, and again.

My hand went to my zipper. In time, the younger man moved the older one to his back and crouched between his thighs, lifting his legs up and out, and continued fucking him in long, steady strokes. The younger man lowered his face to the older one's periodically and they kissed like longtime lovers.

The older man was moaning and clearly was in seventh heaven. Who wouldn't be?

When I had come, I zipped myself back up and withdrew. I couldn't bear anymore. I wanted the young man to do me too.

I left the beach then and went cruising. I knew all of the bars to go to, but it was low season already and the pickings were slim. I regretted having thrown Scott out now rather than when we got back to New York. But that didn't matter much. I wouldn't have wanted Scott for the same reason that I didn't find anyone in the bars that night who I wanted. I wanted the young man on the beach.

I spent a restless night, dreaming of me and the young, burnt-gold man with the long, silky black hair. I got up in the morning, went to the gym, and ate a humongous breakfast at a pancake house on the main boulevard. I was fagged out when I got home and fell onto the bed and slept for two hours. At three, I got up from the bed, already knowing where I was going.

I was the only one that early in the day on the back deck at Joey's on the Beach. The beach was deserted and the flap was down on my angel's cabana. That's how I was thinking of him—my own dark angel. And mine. After one beer, which I nursed for a half an hour, I started thinking of leaving the bar. But just as I was about to rise from the bar table, the flap came up on the cabana, and the young man jogged out into the sunlight. He was wearing a black bikini swimsuit this afternoon, the sides of which were held together by large metal rings. He had a large, multicolored beach towel under his arm, which he dropped on the beach a few yards above the high-water mark, and he was holding a pair of sunglasses in one hand, which he leaned over and put down on the towel after he had spread it out.

I took my breath in and held as I watched the muscles stretch in his lithe body as he leaned over the towel. He only lingered there a minute, though, before he turned and ran into the surf. When the water was above his knees he dove into an incoming wave and I lost sight of him. I didn't let my breath out until I had.

He was out of sight now, swimming out into the water, although I fancied I could see his head and the curve of his churning arms from time to time out beyond where the surf was breaking.

I turned my attention to the cabana. The older man emerged, raised the flap on the poles and stood there, his eyes shielded by a hand, obviously searching for his lover out in the ocean.

I couldn't help myself. As he stood there, I compared him to myself. He was older than I was, and not in as good a shape—certainly heavier than I was—and, although he'd been well-muscled at some point in his life, there was a sag of skin under his upper arm as he held a hand over his eyes. There were other signs that he was losing his muscle tone, and his tanned skin looked just that way—tanned to a leathery brown. I fancied from what I could see that he wasn't as handsome as I was. I know, from my observations of the previous day, that he wasn't as well-endowed as I was. He could be richer than I was, although most certainly not as accustomed to fame—in New York and internationally, at least. I didn't recognize him as anyone of import. Of course, perhaps my dark angel wouldn't be as impressed by the nature of my fame as some others would. Still, there was the possibility that my dark angel was a dancer; he certainly moved like one.

What did this old man have that would make the dark angel choose him over me? Nothing, I optimistically told myself. So, it was mostly a matter of getting the young man's attention.

While I had been assessing the older man who now was sitting in the beach chair under the cabana flap and had opened his book, the younger man had returned from the ocean and now was lying on his belly on the towel.

I gasped and my hand involuntarily went to my crotch when I saw it—it was lying there beside him on the sand, next to the towel. The black bikini. He must be naked, taking the sun in totally, I now realized. I ached to go out onto the sand and see him this way. It didn't matter that I'd seen him naked and fucking the older man the previous day. There was something so much more sensual about seeing him naked on a towel on the beach—where anyone else passing by could see him too.

I kept my eyes riveted to him, fantasizing going out there and straddling his hips, holding his cock erect as I descended on it, and leaning over and taking that nipple with the ring in my mouth and teething him until he groaned and lifted my face to his in a long, lingering kiss. When he turned over, I had looked away momentarily, and I castigated myself for not remaining alert and on watch, as if just a brief glance of him would make my day.

And it obviously would, because there, while I was watching him, he stood in all of his glory, facing my direction, his glorious cock and balls hanging free in a patch of black, curly hair between his thighs, as he reached down and picked up the bikini and put it back on, reattaching the rings somehow at his hips. That's when I saw that he had a ring in his cock head too, and I felt my sphincter muscle clutch, already feeling it rub against my inner channel.

And then he was walking. Not toward the cabana, but toward Joey's. I tore my eyes away from him, looking down into my almost-empty beer glass, as he climbed the three wooden steps to the deck. As I was looking down, I could see his feet and I wanted to groan. The feet were slim, but long, the toes also slender and long. And there was a patch of black hair on the top of each one. I was feeling very hot.

I heard him ask for a drink and then say, sorry, that he didn't have money with him and that he'd have go to his nearby cabana and . . .

I built up the courage to intervene at that point. I think my voice sounded strained and squeaky. Nonetheless I couldn't let the opportunity pass me by so I stood and offered to buy his drink for him—"and I need another beer too, bartender"—so that he could quench his thirst before having to traipse over to the cabana and back.

"Yes, thank you . . . if I can join you for the drink."

Could he join me? I was doing all I could do not to hyperventilate.

"Have you been swimming in the ocean yet?" I asked. "Is it too late in the season to do that? The temperature too cold?" I felt like an idiot for not coming up with anything better to say than this. And then he proceeded to confirm my idiocy.

"Surely you know I've been swimming in the ocean, Mr. Cordell. You've watched me do it, haven't you? Yesterday as well as today."

I was shocked, but then I felt all sorts of posturing and foreplay was being brushed aside. He obviously was in the game. And I knew this game so well. He was approachable.

"You know who I am, do you?" I didn't have to sound surprised. I was. Not necessarily that he'd know who I was, given what he obviously was. But that he would be so straightforward in getting to the bottom line. It was almost refreshing.

"Yes, of course. You're the Peter Cordell who produces for the Metropolitan Opera, aren't you? I read the New York papers."

"Yes, you have me there. And you are?"

"Raul. You can just call me Raul."

Ah, yes, Hispanic. I very much liked the passion of a Latin lover. Scott was West coast, sun, beaches, muscle shirts, and all about himself.

"Ah, the newspapers."

"And we have a few mutual friends too."

"Oh?"

"Yes. For instance, I know one of the members of the Met's permanent dance troupe. Jason Deavers. You might remember him."

"Yes, of course." Certainly I remembered Jason. I opened my legs for him nightly for a month two years ago. Raul most certainly was direct. Well, I could be direct too.

"I would like to see you. Away from the beach," I said. I turned my face to him and looked directly in his eyes.

"I'm rather attached," he responded.

"Yes, I have seen that. But you may be interested in reassessing your situation."

"I rather doubt that," he answered. I looked away then. This obviously was going to be expensive. He wanted to haggle. But then he surprised me.

"Did you know that they give performances in the old opera house in Charleston?" He asked. "The local troupe is quite good, I think. I have an extra ticket for a performance of Mozart's *Idomeneo* for tonight. It's a powerful work—Greeks and fated lovers and tragic promises and all. Very melodramatic, but not much performed anymore. If you wouldn't be too averse to a busman's holiday . . ."

"He certainly is resourceful," was my thought as I clothed myself in a tuxedo that evening, after having already been to the barbers and then having a long shower and primping and making myself the best I could be. He was going to great lengths with me. This then, I knew, was going to be very, very expensive. But I had seen him fucking the older man, and I was assured that he would be very, very worth it.

The ticket he left for me was for one of the private boxes high up above and at the corner of the stage. It was angled, so that no one from the audience could look into the

217

box, and only singers positioned well up into the height of the set could see much of anything in the shadows.

I was the only one in the box until shortly after the first interval. In the interval, I had craned my head out around the edge of the box and scanned the audience and seen that, yes, both Raul and the older man were seated in the orchestra section. Raul looked magnificent in his tuxedo. That must have cost the older man a fortune. And the older man was probably paying for all of these empty seats in this box as well—and perhaps didn't even like opera. Raul had his hooks into that man really good. He should be grateful that I intended to take Raul away from him.

After the lights went down following the interval, I felt more than heard that someone had entered the box. I turned my face and saw that it, indeed, was Raul.

There were practically no preliminaries. I heard the zipper of his tux trousers being lowered after he'd sat in the chair beside me and felt the hand on the back of my neck, coaxing my face down into his lap. And to the glorious live, opera music of Mozart, sung rather well for the provinces, I gave Raul the best blow job performance I could muster up—luxuriating in my tongue's play with his cock ring.

He stopped me short of making him come, though, and I watched in fascination as he took a condom packet and a tube of lubricant out of his jacket pocket. He leaned over and whispered in my ear, "Strip off your trousers and briefs, please, and sit on my cock. Oh, and you look quite handsome tonight."

I sat, skewered by his cock, holding myself slightly off his lap at his request, bearing my weight on the balls of my feet, while I watched and listened to a Mozart opera on stage and he rhythmically fucked up into my channel. I made a little yipping noise each time that cock ring dragged across my prostate. He had his hands snaked up under my shirt and worried my nipples while I stroked my cock to completion. At his suggestion I had my linen handkerchief draped over my lap to catch as much of the cum I spouted as possible—to keep both of our tuxes clean. At the point of my ejaculation, his mouth went to the hollow of my neck and he lightly teethed my throbbing artery as I sighed my release. Timing was everything, and I knew I would remember that moment forever—the ejaculation came at the height of a love duet on stage.

He left me just before the second interval, after standing close beside me in the shadows and holding my face to his crotch as I cleaned his cock with my mouth and then helped to readjust his tux. As he was leaving, I gave him my card and hissed that I had to see him again—that he could come to my beach home any time he could get away. The sooner the better.

It had been the best of all setups for Raul to be moving to a new sugar daddy. Not only was he a hunk to view and a stud in cock play, but he was brilliant in his choice of claiming me. I—a veteran of the New York Metropolitan Opera—had never had such an uplifting sexual experience as being fucked to a live staging of a Mozart opera. I was bowled over. I was dangerously close to being in love. I certainly was in deep want and lustful need.

It was three maddening days before he appeared at my door. He was driving a BMW sports car that, I thought, must have set his older daddy back nearly a hundred-thousand. I had gone to the beach every day, spending the entire morning and afternoon at Joey's. But neither Raul nor his sugar daddy appeared the first day, and a family took up residence in the cabana the following two days.

He was all smiles and not the least bit apologetic for leaving me hanging. "I had business meetings," was all he said.

Yeah, right. He had business meetings. He was out spending daddy's money. That's what he was doing.

"It doesn't matter," I said. "I want you again." I took him by the hand. I planned to lead him right back to my bedroom, but Raul's Latin temperament was clicking in. We stopped in the middle of the living room and rocked back and forth against each other's bodies, kissing and feeling and unbuttoning and unsnapping and stepping out of clothes. And then, naked, we were kissing and feeling again.

He had extracted a condom and lubricant before his trousers hit the floor, and he simply pushed me back into the center of one of my deep couches and knelt between my legs. He worked my cock briefly with his mouth and then rolled my hips up and was going after my entrance with his lips and then lubricated fingers, as I groaned and stroked my cock and floated on the clouds of heaven.

He fucked me there, crouched between my thighs, my ankles resting on his shoulders, and his hands working my cock and nipples. Bringing me to the brink again and again and then holding and then renewing the plowing until I couldn't take it anymore and ejaculated in a cry of ecstasy. Virile young man that he was, though, he continued stroking and I was ready to come again before he did.

We held there for several minutes, as I felt him ebbing away from inside me.

"That was nice," he said. "I do like a bit of variety now and then. If you are coming down next year, we should arrange to do this again."

"Next year?" I exploded in surprise. "I want you in the next ten minutes again. I want you every night. I want you in my bed."

"Sorry, old chap. I have a live in." Raul was almost jovial, as if he wasn't angling for anything at all here.

"A live in? That old man I saw you with at the beach?"

"Well, yes, actually. Teddy's my permanent. He indulges me with a side blow from time to time. I have rather a fetish for interesting older men. But we've been together for three years now—and I plan for that to last forever."

"Who is he? A Rockefeller?" I asked, becoming frustrated and a bit angry now. Raul hadn't even pulled his dick out of me yet. But he'd gone flaccid, and although I was trying to arouse him again, it didn't look like we were going to manage that. "God, I want you again now," I growled, giving up all of my pride.

"Sorry, Teddy and I fucked before I came over here and he'll want it again when I return. He's insatiable."

"Again who is he? Think of him and think of me. What does he have that I don't."

"My love, actually. I'm sorry. But it's a permanent thing with us I'm afraid."

"What is he paying you? I'll double it. Whatever it is."

He gave me a funny look then and pulled out of me and walked over to the center of the room and started separating his clothes from mine.

"You don't know who I am, do you?" he suddenly asked, turning and looking at me hard.

"You're Raul. That's all you told me."

"Ah, well. We'd mentioned New York papers. I rather thought you had seen my photo in the society pages at least as often as I've seen yours. I didn't think I'd need to give you my last name. I'm Raul Delaplane. Of the Argentine Delaplanes."

Delaplane. The Argentine Delaplanes. Richer than anyone not from the Persian Gulf. Oh, shit.

Then he gave me the funniest look. "Oh, you thought I was some sort of gigolo and Teddy was my sugar daddy, didn't you?" As he was pulling his briefs on, still looking like a luscious dark angel, he reared his head back and laughed. "It's rather the opposite, I'm afraid," he said through attempts to cease chortling. "Teddy's penniless other than what I give him. He was my tutor, and my first love. And, I hope, my last love."

After Raul had gone, I lay there, my legs still open, mourning the loss of his cock, and contemplating how unfathomable this scenario of Raul and his old lover was. What was this fickle thing called love? I wondered. And would I ever find it for myself?

Who's Jeff?

The cook had fed us with steak and cleaned up and left, leaving the two of us alone. My host put some soft music on and lit the fire. The wine had been excellent and I was feeling it in my head. The white bear-skin rug in front of the fire looked so inviting, and I wanted my head to stop spinning, so I laid down on that on my belly, facing the fire, staring into it and becoming quite mellow. My host left me there for a short time, letting the fire and the music and the soft rug and the buzz from the wine float me away.

He was back, in a short cotton robe. He must have been at least in his late forties or early fifties, but he'd aged well. His leg muscles were firm and I thought that he must have been an athlete at one time—and probably still worked out. As he leaned down to me, the front of the cotton robe opened and I saw a well-developed chest with a matting of salt-and-pepper curly hair running from his chest down in a thin line to where the lapels of the robe met.

"Some port or Cognac?" he asked in a rich baritone. His face was distinguished. A lawyer or a banker or corporate CEO. Even after two weeks, I didn't know. He spoke little about himself, showing more concern for me. So kind. If he hadn't found me at the side of the desert highway, brought me to this big house on the ridge above Santa Fe, and had a doctor in to look at me after what the beating and the hours on the sand by the highway had done to me . . .

The steel gray hair was expertly cut, a perfect-teeth smile. A slight scar under his left eye—his eyes were hazel and so alive—only served to emphasize how handsome his chiseled features were. Model handsome. A healthy Santa Fe tan smoothed out the laugh-line wrinkles.

"No thanks, Mr. Grimes. Another drop of alcohol and I'd go right to sleep."

"We couldn't have that, now, could we?" he answered, the low laugh conveying his mood. "And I've told you, it's Bill."

"I have trouble with that . . . Bill. You've been so kind, and there's such a divide between us."

"We must see what we can do about that too. Here, take a look at these. I work with photography. I'd like to know what you think."

He was handing a folder to me. I opened the cover to find a set of loose photographs. The ones on top were art shots—nudes—of a young, handsome youth. A bit younger than me. About nineteen, I'd guess. The photos were expertly done, although it wasn't the artistry of them that took my attention. Toward the bottom of the pile, the photographs were more explicit—much more explicit, I saw, as I leafed through to the bottom of the stack. And the youth wasn't alone. Grimes too was in these photos. I turned my head toward the sofa to see the cotton robe fall onto it in folds.

I shuddered and stiffened as his body came down on top of me, covering me full length. My torso was raised on my elbows, as I was fanning through the photographs. His hands laced in underneath me and he was unbuttoning my shirt and then pulling it off my arms.

"Relax," he whispered in my ears. "Just concentrate on the photos and let your body drift with me."

I did what I could to let the tension in my body flow away. "Mr. Grimes. Bill," I whispered.

"Sure you don't want to try the Cognac? I still have the taste of it in my mouth," he whispered back at me. He cupped my chin and turned my face toward his, and I tasted the rich, full-bodied nectar of the wine in his kiss.

His hips were moving against my butt, and I felt the hardness of him through the material of my jeans and briefs.

I felt the palm of a hand on my belly and fingers working at the buttons of my jeans. Instinctively, without conscious control, I lifted my butt into his crotch as the zipper of my jeans was being pulled down. I wanted him to know there would be no struggle, no indecision, no holding back for whatever he wanted. He had paid for this in full. All of the hardness went out of my jaw and I opened my mouth totally to him.

The moaning I heard was almost detached, but I recognized it as mine.

He wouldn't release the hold of his lips on mine and in the wake of the taste of the Cognac, his tongue had invaded my mouth cavity. I could hardly breathe. But I didn't care if I couldn't. He was still possessing my mouth as he was pulling my jeans and briefs below my hips.

Skin on skin now below the belly. A hard dick inside my butt crack, stroking up and down on the rim of my hole. I shuddered and groaned and he released my mouth and gave a low, comfortable laugh.

"The photos. Concentrate on the photos," he said.

I returned my attention to the photographs, pushing through the ones of the handsome youth solo, down to the ones of the youth with Grimes. He was moving down the line of my back now. Kissing and licking my shoulder blades, while one hand pulled my jeans and briefs down and off my legs and the other one worked my nipples and then came down to palm my belly as his lips reached the mounds of my butt cheeks.

His teeth nipped at the sensitive skin of my rump and I groaned as I heard the low, appreciative laugh again. I felt a light slap on each cheek and they were being squeezed and nipped again. A hand went between my thighs and pulled my cock and balls through. I tried to widen my stance, but he moved his forearms to trap my thighs close together, tightly against my dick. A hand possessed my cock and slowly stroked down.

"Bill, Bill," I whispered.

"Ah the divide narrows, doesn't it? Surely there will be no trouble with first names now," he answered back. And then that arousing laugh again. He clearly was enjoying this.

"Do you like the photos?" he asked. "Don't the two of us make the smashing pair?"

"Yes." It was a whisper.

"Does the lad look happy? Am I fucking him well?"

"Yes." It was a whimper, followed with a moan.

He had taken both hands and was spreading and squeezing my butt cheeks with them. When he blew across my hole, I shivered and groaned.

"So nice. Such a rosy bud. And already opening."

"Bill," I whispered. "Bill." And then "Bill!" as he kissed the hole and his tongue started working into me. I writhed under him for countless minutes as he tongued my hole and worked my cock with his hand. Intermittently he moved his mouth down to my cock and balls and gave suck, and during these intervals his fingers invaded my channel and found my prostate.

"Bill, Bill! I'm gonna come. You're gonna make me—"

"Oh, I hope so, Rick, he muttered. I certainly hope so." And then he laughed again.

And I came.

He covered my back fully with his body again and his cock was rubbing inside my cheeks once more. I raised my pelvis to him. Presenting to him. Wanting him. Wanting him to know I wanted him. "Bill," I whined.

"Ah, are you ready? Do you want me inside you? Permission to fuck, my young lad? Jeff wants his daddy?"

"Yes," I whimpered, all of my senses focused on the shaft rubbing across my hole, not even fully catching the reference to a Jeff.

He went up on his knees, reaching over to the sofa. I heard the slight rustle of the condom packet as he opened it, and then I felt the coldness of the lubricant he poured liberally between my cheeks and worked into my opening with probing fingers. My chest was flat on the floor, my cheek against the photos of Grimes fucking the young man, my arms splayed out at my side. I was up on my knees, though, with my quivering butt raised to him, my legs spread.

Fuck me, fuck me now, was what I was trying to convey.

He crouched over me, pulling my chest up, me now on all fours. The cock was rubbing inside my crack again, sending electric impulses as it stroked again and again against my hole.

"Please. Bill, Please!" I begged.

He laughed. And then I felt the bulb presented at my hole and he was slowly pushing into me. I gasped and my eyes started to water and both my elbows and my knees began to quiver and to give way. But Bill, crouched over my midsection and continuing to enter me, held me up with strong arms wrapped under my rib cage. I felt his lips at my cheeks, and I turned my face to him, letting him possess my mouth again—masking my groans and moans.

Who would have known he was so thick and hard—and that it would take so much length of my channel for him to bottom?

Coming out of the kiss, my face was suspended over the photographs. The one on top was of Grimes crouched over the hips of the young man, who was on all fours—on a white bearskin rug in front of a fireplace; this fireplace. The expression on the young man's face was one of ecstasy. Bill was looking into the camera with an expression that almost conveyed, "At last; in at last."

Only half hidden below that was a photo of the young man on his back on the same furry rug and Grimes kneeling between his thighs, knees under and raising the young man's buttocks, Grimes fisting the youth's slim ankles and holding his legs up and out, wide. I could see a good two inches of the root of a thick cock at the young man's channel opening. And again, that "gone to paradise" expression on the young man's face.

A third photo was of Grimes completely sheathed, the youth's legs running up Grimes's torso now, his hands reaching around Grime's thick waist and clutching the older man's thin butt cheeks close to him with fingers digging into the flesh, obviously trying to take in every centimeter of the cock. Eyes wild, mouth gaping open, and tongue hanging out. I trembled in anticipation.

He stroked me so long and hard that my elbows and knees did give out and, with a laugh, he rode me to the rug and

227

kept on riding. He was babbling as he fucked me, and I occasionally heard the name "Jeff" spoken. But never the name "Rick."

Fucking me at such depth, and so filling. My channel walls undulating across the shaft as it mastered me. Throbbing, hot, relentless. Strong hands pulling my thighs in tight. Oh, god, the tightness. The almost despair as he pulls back. Oh, no, don't leave me! Oh, shit, yes! at the long hard plunge back to the depths. Yes! Again. Oh, yes! And again. Oh Shit! And AGAIN. Paradise. Faster now—stroke, stroke, hold, stroke—making me pant and writhe against his strong hands and moan—and beg for it to go on and on.

I felt him tighten and take in a long breath and then—with my channel trying, unsuccessfully, to close on his cock and keep him inside me—he pulled out of me, and I groaned at the loss of him and heard the condom being ripped away and then felt the flow of him on the small of my back.

He covered my back with his torso again and continued moving on top of me, stroking the small of my back with his cock through his cum. He hands glided along my arms and took my wrists. I turned my lips to him again. His prisoner for as long as he wanted.

"I'm sorry if you weren't expecting that this evening," he whispered in my ear when he once more let loose of my lips.

"I don't know what took you so long," I answered, with a sigh.

"I thought perhaps I assumed so much. But you are so beautiful and sexy. I couldn't help myself. Hardly a good host."

"You saved my life," I whispered back. "And . . . and the perfect host. Almost too polite, I was beginning to think."

He turned me on my back, my head resting in the pile of his photographs. He covered my body with his, his cock lying against my own between our still-heaving bellies. I looked down the line of his body. His barrel chest with the matting of salt-and-pepper gray standing out in moist curls and below that a still-flat, hard belly—even at his age. I wanted to run my hands through the matting on his chest, to search out the taut nipples I saw hiding there between the curls of the hair. But he had his fists wrapped around my wrists and they were trapped on either side of my shoulders. So, instead, I dipped and raised my face into his chest. I found a nipple almost immediately and sucked it in hard as he gasped and then I nipped at it, which produced a yelp from his mouth and an engorging surge in his cock.

Releasing one of my wrists, his hand grabbed my head under the chin and forced it back into the pile of photographs and his mouth was hungrily attacking mine, his tongue invading, every bit as filling and probing as his cock had been. I gasped and nearly gagged.

I wrapped my legs around his, my heels rubbing up and down his hard calves. His free hand snaked between our bellies before I could completely push in as close as I could to every inch of him. The hand wrapped our two cocks together. And he stroked our shafts and worked my mouth with his until, with a lurch and a shudder, I came again.

He released my mouth and cock then. I could feel he was fully hard again. Amazing for his age. Not so much, though, considering the strength and power of his fuck. He raised his torso off mine a bit and looked down into my eyes. He was smiling that melting smile of his—the one I saw in the photographs when it was clear that he had mastered the young man to exhaustion.

"That's not fair," he said in a tone of false pout. "You've gone twice and I only once. Would you mind terribly if—?"

"I hoped you would," I whispered breathlessly, my mind possessed by what I'd seen in the photographs, as he knelt between my legs, pulled my buttocks up on top of his thighs, and reached over on the sofa for another condom packet. I lifted one of my legs up his torso to hook an ankle on his right shoulder while I watched him roll the condom on his cock and prepared to raise the other to his left shoulder when he was crowned, positioning myself to roll up my rump to receive the deepest thrusts I could eke out of him. I spied three more condom packets on the sofa and shivered in anticipation. I had seen other photos of other fuck positions the young man obviously had enjoyed.

But who, I was wondering, who the fuck was Jeff?

About the Author

Habu is one of the pen names of a former supersonic spy jet pilot, intelligence agent, male model, movie actor, and diplomat. A wild youth in South East Asia was spent enjoying whatever sexual opportunities came his way, and much of his gay male writing is about recalling incidents from those days and inventing ones he'd perhaps have liked to experience. He now leads a very quiet and ordinary happily married family life.

An American, he is a published mainstream novelist and short story writer under another name and in another dimension of his life. He has written or cowritten (with Sabb) over 500 published short stories and nearly 100 published erotica e-books, primarily of gay fiction but also memoir, straight fiction and ménage fiction. His hand and creative writing can be seen in stories and books by habu, sr71plt, Dirk Hessian, Shabbu, and Stephen Kessel—among unrevealed others that might surprise readers. The fictionalized GM memoir *Flying High, Diving Deep* is loosely based on his life experiences. He can be found at the adults only gay male site www.BarbarianSpy.com, which he shares with Sabb and Dirk Hessian.

Our authors always like to receive feedback, and appreciate it when readers post reviews at Goodreads, and other sites.

BarbarianSpy
FOR LITERARY HEAT

Not all books listed below may currently be on release.

BOOKS BY DIRK HESSIAN

Xtreme Erotica

The King's Men
Shores of Tripoli
Prophecy of Noto
Pretender's Fate

General Erotica/Romance

Constantinople
The Beautiful Way
Blue and Gray
Colonel's Treasure
Beginning of Time
Labyrinth

BOOKS BY HABU

Gay Erotica

Memoir Faction

Flying High, Diving Deep

Xtreme Erotica

Second Coming
Vortex: Sacrificed by Curiosity
Dark Angel Sounding

General Erotica

Romance

Gotta Keep Trying
Finding Amnad
Platres Conclave

Other

Beyond the Beaded Curtain
Hard Knocks U
Habu's Christmas Balls
My Neighbour's Spa

Man's Man
Trip Money
Clint Folsom Mysteries Compendium Volume 1
Death to Blonds - Stolen Judgement (Clint Folsom Mystery)
Clint Folsom Mysteries Compendium Volume 2
Grab Bag 1
Grab Bag 2
Grab Bag 3
The Indian Doctor
Sailorboy
Home to Fire Island
The Sporting Life
Brambleton
Fetish Galore!
Choke Hold
Literary Gay Erotica
Cairo Surrender
The Handyman
Homeward Bound
Journey to Mirage
Menage Erotica
13 Ways for Halloween
Luther
The Indian Prince
BOOKS BY SHABBU
Finding Jason
Dirty Pool
Operation Black Jade
Cigars!
Angel in the Barn
Gayly Complicated
Despoiling David
The Tree of Idleness
I Met a Man
The Interview
Rough Road to Happiness
BOOKS BY SABB

The Legend of Holleystone Grange
Surprise Encounters
She is He
Wrong Man
Loyal to his King
Barbarian Tales - Book One - Traveler's Tales
Barbarian Tales - Book Two - Journeys Begin
Barbarian Tales - Book Three - The Inheritance
Barbarian Tales - Book Four - Road to Persepolis
~

www.ingramcontent.com/pod-product-compliance
Lightning Source LLC
Chambersburg PA
CBHW021240260626

47155CB00004BA/1244